LIPSTICK AND LIES AND DEADLY GOODBYES

THE VAMPIRE HOUSEWIFE SERIES

JODI VAUGHN

For everyone who has ever been betrayed, hurt, let down, or disappointed. Don't let that one moment in time define who you are as a person. You are stronger than you know. Grow, travel, learn. And don't ever settle for anyone or anything.

Xoxo
Jodi Vaughn

CHAPTER 1

"It looks like a penis," I blurted out to the landscaper through my cell phone while standing in my front yard staring in horror at my illuminated flowerbed. Normally, I'd feel bad about calling someone at midnight, but this was an emergency. Tonight, I had a giant dick in my front yard.

My hands clutched my stomach, trying to still the nausea rolling around in my gut like a bowling ball. I was oblivious to my expensive heels sinking into the wet ground, and the snowflakes melting against my bare flesh.

I didn't need a second opinion to tell me that this was bad. This was really, really bad.

"Mrs. Jones, I assure you, it's the Ole Miss Landshark. Just as promised." Mr. McIntyre, the premier landscaper of our town, drawled through the phone.

It rarely snowed in Mississippi, and certainly never in March. I should have known it was a sign of something terrible on the horizon, but I was too humiliated by the obscene flowerbed to sense the evil headed my way.

In the South, college sports is a religion, and my husband worshipped at the altar of Ole Miss. Loving wife that I am, I decided to have the flowerbed turned into the college mascot for his birthday. Instead of the Ole Miss Landshark, I was looking at a red dick with blue balls.

"You told me you've done this type of thing before. The Blue Devil for Duke, The Bulldog for Georgia, and the Gator for Florida. This is supposed to be the Ole Miss Landshark." I glanced around my quiet neighborhood. How many of my neighbors had seen the flower penis in my front yard before they went to sleep?

No doubt by tomorrow morning, my phone would be flooded with calls from the neighborhood gossipmongers explaining the rules of the Homeowner's Association. I wondered if there was something in the bylaws about pornographic displays in one's yard.

"Did Fred McDougal put you up to this? I know you two play poker every Saturday night." I also knew they were thick as thieves sharing the same jail cell.

Fred McDougal was the biggest Alabama fan in our small town. While he and my husband were friendly, when it came to college football, there was a deep-seated rivalry. McDougal had started the competition by putting up statues on his lawn with the elephant mascot and decorative flags that said *Roll Tide*, guaranteed to irritate my husband, Miles.

"No, ma am. Fred didn't put me up to anything. No rivalry is worth losing a customer. Once this snow starts melting in the morning, you'll see it looks like your Ole Miss Landshark."

Maybe he was right. Perhaps I wouldn't have an X-rated yard.

The rumble of a souped-up sports car thundered down the street. I turned, terrified it would be someone I knew.

"Nice cock, Mrs. Jones!" Ricky Spencer yelled out the window, laughed, and sped towards his house.

I glared at the foul-mouthed juvenile, wishing his parents would ship his entitled ass off to military school.

"If you want, I can run out there tomorrow and see for myself." Mr. McIntyre sounded as concerned as a cat lying in the sun.

"Perfect, I'll see you tomorrow." I ended the call.

Standing on my tiptoes so my heels wouldn't sink farther into the snow, I made my way through the front yard to the garage. My husband had two long surgeries today and wouldn't be home until after midnight. I knew he wouldn't notice the landscape project until tomorrow. To make sure, I would turn off the exterior lighting of the house when I opened the garage.

I had told Miles that I was going on an overnight trip to Memphis with some girlfriends to see a play and stay at the Peabody Hotel while our two daughters were at a weekend sleepover. The landscaper had worked all day while I had been at the spa getting a massage and a pedicure, as well as getting my hair and makeup done—all part of the surprise I had cooked up for him.

It was hard to buy a birthday present for a man who had everything. I had to get creative.

I climbed into my Volvo and started the engine. I'd been so shocked when I saw the landscaping that I hadn't bothered to pull my car inside the garage.

I pressed the button and tapped my fingers impatiently on the steering wheel. The garage door slowly went up. My heart lurched when I saw Miles' Tesla already parked inside.

He must've gotten out of surgery early tonight.

I pulled in and closed the garage behind me. I turned off the exterior lighting, hoping to camouflage my flowerbed from the neighbors. I eased open the door to the kitchen and peeked inside.

The lights were off.

Music spilled out from the bedroom. Miles always played music when he took a shower after work to relax. But tonight, I had other ways to make him relax.

I took off my heels and padded to the closet in the hall. I pulled out the large red bow hidden in the back. Miles always bought me lingerie, so for his birthday, I thought I'd wear something different, something to spice things up.

I'd gone to the craft store and paid the lady who makes the bows for door wreaths to make me a bow outfit. I figured she'd ask questions, but to my astonishment, she didn't. She made a bow large enough to fit around my breasts. There was a slender red strip that ran from my breasts to loop down between my legs and up my back to tie around my neck like a collar.

I quietly hurried to the bathroom off the kitchen and quickly took off all my clothes. I shimmied into the bow, fiddled with the ribbon, and looked in the mirror.

I turned side to side and then fluffed the bow. I noted the fine lines around my eyes and how my once pert boobs were starting to sag. I was thirty-five. Despite the years and having two kids, I still looked hot.

Miles had loved the golf clubs I had gotten him last year. But tonight, he would lust after this birthday present.

I smiled at my reflection in the mirror.

I was dressed like a sex present.

Hooking my red high heels onto my fingers, I tiptoed towards the bedroom. I stopped when I heard voices. He must have turned on the TV.

The bedroom door was closed.

Weird. Why would he bother to close the door when he was home alone?

4

I shoved my feet into my black Jimmy Choo's and reached for the door handle, slowly turning the knob.

The door swung open, and I stepped in, propping my hands on my hips in a sexy centerfold pose.

I froze.

Blinked.

Forgot to breathe.

My stomach hardened, and my throat tightened. Vomit crawled up my esophagus and threatened to spew across the hardwood floor.

Miles. On the bed. Naked.

A woman straddling him.

Riding him like a stripper pole.

That woman. Nikki.

My best friend.

Screwing my husband.

Having sex in my bed.

No, no, no!

The air left my lungs. I couldn't breathe. My heart kicked in my chest. I thought for a second it had literally stopped beating.

My world crumbled and dissolved like old, burning paper.

I had to leave. I had to get away. I turned without a word, without a sound, and ran for the door.

I thought I'd hear footsteps behind me, or Miles calling out after me.

I didn't.

The only sounds were the click-click of my heels and the pounding in my ears.

The image of my husband having sex with Nikki in our bed burned its way into every cell of my brain. Panic and pain pushed into my throat. I needed to *leave*. I needed to *run*.

I grabbed my keys and flung open the door. I scrambled inside my Volvo. I pressed the garage button and started the engine.

I squealed down the driveway, barely missing the neighbor's mailbox. Tears burned my eyes and streamed down my face.

After all I'd done: raising the kids, keeping the house, being the perfect wife that supported her husband's career...

Hell, I'd even encouraged him to buy the Tesla because I thought he deserved it.

Because I thought he was such a wonderful husband.

My lights bobbed and landed on the face of my neighbor, Cal, loading a large plastic bin into the trunk of his car. He caught my gaze. Both of us stared for a split-second of eternity until I sped away.

Cal had seen me crying and half-naked, speeding out of my driveway. He'd probably tell the whole neighborhood before noon tomorrow.

But I didn't care. Not anymore. Not after what I'd just seen.

I started shivering and couldn't stop. My marriage. Over. In a matter of seconds, my marriage had ended. My life had ended. Hurt and betrayal stabbed my heart, over and over until I was convinced I would die of a broken heart.

Tears splattered my red ribbon. I heard myself make a strangled noise like a wild animal. *Whimpering.* Like roadkill that was injured but wasn't dead.

I accelerated out of my gated community. The snow started coming down hard, and I could barely see the road. I should have slowed down. Should have been cautious while driving on the icy street.

But I just wanted to outdrive my unfaithful, lying, asshat-loser of a husband.

An animal darted out in the road right in front of me. I stomped the brakes and jerked my wheel.

My car lost traction on the ice, and my pain turned to terror. The vehicle slid off the road and down into a deep ditch.

My head whipped back and forth. The seatbelt pulled tight, knocking the wind out of me. My entire body felt as if I'd crashed head-on into a semi-truck.

I sat there, not moving. I took a painful breath. I was still alive.

And my husband was still an ass.

I shoved open my door, sending a sharp pain through my neck. I winced and stepped out into the snow. I crawled up the steep bank, and the wet-cold bit into my bare legs as snowflakes melted on my bare ass.

Why hadn't I grabbed any real clothes? Or my purse? Or even my phone? At least it was after midnight. There wouldn't be many people out this late to see me dressed in nothing but a big, ridiculous bow for my fucking cheating husband.

I made it to the road and stood shivering, the cold seeping into my skin. I wrapped my arms around my body and squinted into the falling snow, looking for help.

In the distance, there was the outline of a small, dark shape near the side of the road. Unmoving.

Over the years, many animals had darted out in front of my car: birds, squirrels, cats, dogs. Every time, I braked then prayed I hadn't hit them.

I made my way over to the animal and squatted on the ground. It was a raccoon. Bits of snow clung to its body, but I didn't see any blood. I brushed my fingers across its fur and stared at its dark, circled eyes.

A loud rumble roared through the dark night.

"Get away from him," a deep voice yelled at me from the

darkness. I screamed and tried to scramble to my feet, only to stumble and fall back, my head hitting the icy road. Pain exploded behind my eyes, and I couldn't see to stand. I heard a loud engine, saw blinding lights.

Then, everything in my world went dark.

CHAPTER 2

"I'm dying," I moaned and clutched my throat. White, hot, stabbing pain seared through my neck and chest. My eyes shot open, and I blinked. I was in a dark room, a place I'd never been in before.

"You're already dead. Or will be soon," a sinister male voice echoed in the darkness.

That voice was vaguely familiar, yet I couldn't place where I'd heard it. I struggled to sit up, but the pain was too great. I gave up and laid back down. The bow gaped, revealing a nipple. I cringed as I remembered that I was wearing nothing but that dumbass red bow. I quickly covered myself up with my hand. "Dead?"

"Yes, dead. I didn't stutter, did I?" he said.

Fear licked through my veins like flames ignited gasoline. I needed to get away, but my body was weak and wouldn't obey my brain.

I wrapped my arms around my chest. He was the guy on the road.

"Why are you doing this?" My neck spasmed in pain. Dear God. Had he cut my throat? I reached up and gently touched my neck, expecting to feel slashed flesh and blood. Instead, I touched soft material wrapped tightly around my throat.

"You should be thanking me." The deadly, deep voice seemed a little closer in the dark.

Beads of cold sweat popped up across my lip, and I struggled to get up. My mind raced with images of how he would take my life, and my heart nearly leaped out of my chest.

"Please, don't hurt me. I have kids. I'm a mother and a wife. I…" The memories of the night flooded into my mind, crisp and clear.

"Finish."

"What?" I jerked my head toward his voice. Intense pain tore through my neck. Surely, he had cut my throat. I struggled to get my hand to my neck, needing to hold the mutilated flesh together to stop from bleeding out and dying. People didn't survive their throats being cut, but I damn well was going to try.

I couldn't die. Not today. I had unfinished business.

WHY WOULD a killer cut my throat and then put a scarf around my neck? I didn't have time to think about his sadistic reasoning. My survival instinct had kicked in. I knew I had to get away from him.

"Leave the scarf alone and finish what you were saying." His voice was thick with impatience.

"I have kids." My crippled voice tripped. A stray tear rolled down my face.

"Most people do. Doesn't make you special." He grunted.

"I have money. If you let me go, I'll pay you." My voice held an unfamiliar urgency. My life had been safe and comfortable, normal. I didn't realize that everything could be taken away in a matter of seconds, and I would be plunged into danger.

"I have no use for money." Heavy footsteps echoed on the hard floor. The faint click of a lamp. A soft, eerie light illuminated the corner of a large room.

I turned my head and gasped at the pain. But I caught a glimpse of his large back as he stepped away from me and back into the darkness.

As if sensing my eyes on him, he turned and looked directly at me. It scared me because his eyes weren't normal. They were red. They were demon's eyes.

Fear wrapped a hand around my windpipe and squeezed. My heart beat so fast, I thought it might go into a lethal arrhythmia, and I would die right there.

No one knew where I was. No one knew I was missing. No one would ever find my body.

"What do you want from me? Why are you hurting me?" The words slipped from my frozen lips and hung in the air.

His red eyes drew to slits. His lips were pressed together —hard, flat, and angry. Like his gaze. He looked like a monster hell-bent on hurting someone just because he could.

"You're asking the wrong questions."

"What should I be asking?" My voice quivered, and I felt cold all over. Like my life was being sucked out of my body, and hopelessness was being shoved back in to fill the void.

"You should be asking why you want to hurt yourself. More importantly, why would you put your life at risk?"

His words made no sense.

"I don't want to hurt myself. You're the one who brought me here. You're the one who stabbed me."

"I didn't stab you," he denied. "Here, see for yourself."

He walked over to the table by the lamp and picked up an antique silver mirror. I looked at him.

He was large, broad as a football player, and I was willing to bet he was all muscle under his ragged wool trench coat and black pants. His hair was long and black, and it appeared he hadn't washed it in a while. He had a scraggly black beard that might be housing a family of mice. His red eyes were glued to me as he stepped closer and handed me the mirror. His overwhelming odor hit me.

I gagged and pressed my hand over my nose and tried to breathe through my mouth. It was as if his stench were coating my taste buds.

He smelled ungodly, like skunk and urine. It was then that I realized I was about to be murdered by a homeless psycho who had a penchant for stabbing helpless housewives.

"Look." He held out the mirror, his eyes and the tone of his voice demanding.

I took the mirror, careful not to touch his fingers.

"Snotty bitch," he murmured.

I started to tell him that I was as far from a snotty bitch as one could get, but I didn't want to make him angrier.

I raised the mirror up over my body and angled it to look down at myself.

I started with my feet. I know it sounds weird, but I wasn't ready to see my bloodied neck. I needed to start with something that told me that part of myself was okay. That a part of me was unhurt. I needed some form of hope to fight against the desperation clawing at my soul.

If I had hope, then I could escape and survive. I had to. I had my children to live for.

The mirror reflected back my heels and bare legs. I quickly tried to cover myself with my bare hands.

"Now you're being modest?" He snorted and walked to the corner of the room. When he walked back over to me, he tossed a small quilt my way.

"I don't even want to know why you were out at midnight wearing nothing but a bow and heels. Going out for a booty call?" he sneered.

"I'm married, you fuc—" I caught the words before I could insult him and slowly sat up on what appeared to be a dining table. I spread the quilt out across my body. Though it was nice and thick, it did little to warm me up.

"So?" He glanced at my wedding ring. "People have affairs all the time. Especially bored housewives." His red eyes glared at me.

"Not me." Fear prickled my spine.

I couldn't read his expression, but he continued to stare at me with those red, evil eyes. He had to be wearing colored contacts so he could intimidate his victims. It was certainly working on me.

I took a painful breath and lifted the quilt enough to look down my stomach and chest. I froze.

I expected to see blood flowing down my chest from all the pain. But I saw nothing. I reached up and touched my chest. I felt nothing unusual. No wound, no injury.

"My neck," I said more to myself than to the monster standing in the room. Maybe my neck wound was radiating out to my chest, and that's why it hurt so much.

I lifted the mirror to my face and neck. My mascara was running, and my lips were pale. My eyes were pink and swollen from crying. My cheeks had no color, probably due to how freaking cold the room was. Or maybe I was pale due to his ungodly body odor.

I hooked my fingers into the dingy, pink scarf wrapped around my neck. My fingers trembled as I pulled the material down and squeezed my eyes shut.

"The mirror isn't going to do any good if you don't actually look."

I gritted my teeth and reminded myself that my children needed me. I made a choice in that hopeless, horrible moment that I was going to live, no matter what.

I opened my eyes and forced myself to look at my reflection.

There was a red, scar-like mark around the base of my neck. Dried blood scabbed along the edges of the wound. The skin was uneven and puckered. Someone had done a hack-job of sewing me up.

Holy shit.

My heart thudded in my chest until it twisted and ached. I couldn't catch my breath.

"Why would you cut my throat and then sew me back up?" I couldn't stop looking at the nasty, horrible, puckered skin around my neck.

A horrified scream built in the back of my throat, but I swallowed it. I was afraid that it would hurt my neck even more.

"I didn't cut your throat. I only sewed you up." He narrowed his gaze at me.

"If you didn't cut it, who did?"

"A snowplow practically decapitated you." He glared.

"Decapitated? That's not possible." I pulled the quilt up around my body and dropped the mirror on the table. "I would be dead. Or at least paralyzed."

My head swam with tiny, white stars. An image of myself falling onto the road and then being blinded by headlights flashed through my mind.

"Why didn't you call 911? Or take me to the hospital? I need medical attention. I'm probably bleeding internally." I had to get out of here. I had to get away. I stood up and stared at him.

"There's no reason for an ambulance. You don't need medical treatment. Not anymore."

"Why not?"

A strange look crossed his face. "Because now you're a vampire."

CHAPTER 3

"*Y*ou're crazy." My eyes widened. My gaze darted around the dark room, silently searching for a way to escape. My heart hammered hard. Suddenly, terror replaced my pain. I was trapped with a homeless man, who was going to torture me for his own amusement before killing me.

My eyes adjusted to the darkness, and I could make out more of the room.

It was large with tall ceilings and elaborate crown molding. Judging from the peeling wallpaper and the overwhelming musty odor, we were in an older Victorian home that had seen better days. I racked my mind, trying to place where this house might be located. I was sure it would be in the rough part of town, the part of town I never frequented, the part of town I didn't know.

My kidnapper turned and squatted near the unlit fireplace. What was he going to use the fire for? To brand me? Cut off a piece of me? Roast my flesh over the coals and then eat me?

He positioned some logs in the hearth and threw a lit

match on the wood. I flinched. The flames sparked and slowly grew until there was a fire dancing in the fireplace.

A brick of panic settled in my gut. I scanned the area for an escape.

There were two large windows on one side of the room with thick, dark velvet curtains. The stranger was still between me and the door, but I figured if I could get to the window, I might be able to jump out—or at least yell for help. Anything was worth a try.

I took a step and immediately got light-headed. I reached back and grabbed the table for balance and squeezed my eyes until the dizziness went away.

When I opened my lids again, he was intently studying me.

"You should lie down." His gaze hardened.

"I'm fine." I lied. I needed to get out of here and back to my home, back to my kids.

He crossed his arms and leaned against the mantel, his stare never leaving me.

"Is this your home?" My mind raced for something to say. I'd read somewhere—or maybe I'd seen it on TV—that if a kidnapping victim connected to their captor, there was a higher chance of being released.

"It is."

"What part of town is it in?" I forced myself to keep my tone calm and unafraid.

"The part you wouldn't ever be caught dead in." He narrowed his gaze at me.

"That's pretty judgmental. You don't know me." I took a few careful steps towards the window.

"I know your type." Hatred practically dripped from his voice. If he despised me this much, he wouldn't hesitate to kill me.

"Ah, you're one of those." I tried to keep my voice light to avoid suspicion as I made my way to the window on shaky legs.

"One of what?" He uncrossed his arms and stood straight. I had his full attention.

"One of those men who hate all women." I shrugged my shoulders and continued walking towards the window. "Probably from some trauma you faced as a child or later in life. Maybe you felt ignored by a woman you loved very much. What do they call that?" I arched my brow and looked over my shoulder at him as I walked towards the window. "Unrequited love? Is that the correct term?"

"Yes." He hissed through his teeth and then shook his head violently. "I mean, yes that's the term. No, that has never happened to me." He looked offended that I had even brought it up.

"Okay, okay." I held up my hands and stopped when I got to the large windows. "No need to get all upset over it."

I didn't need to rile him up, so I turned back to the window.

"So, how long have you lived here?" I drew back the thick, velvet curtains with the crook of my finger. My heart dropped.

The windows were boarded up. Thick, wooden planks completely obscured the outside view, and there was no way I would be able to pry off the wood without a crowbar. Why the hell would he board up the windows of his own house?

Maybe he didn't plan on anyone leaving once they got inside.

Fear settled in the pit of my stomach once again, and I turned to look at him.

I jumped and screamed.

He was standing only a foot away, his intense gaze settling on me and making the hairs on the back of my arms stand at attention.

"Two hundred and fifty-nine." His deep voice seemed to vibrate in the room.

"What?" I asked breathlessly. I pressed my hand to my throat in an attempt to protect it from him.

"You asked me how long I've lived here." A smirk played on the corners of his mouth. "I've lived here exactly two hundred and fifty-nine years."

"That's impossible. That would make you...." I couldn't finish the sentence because it didn't compute in my brain. It wasn't possible.

His smirk grew. "That would make me a vampire. Just like you."

CHAPTER 4

"*T*hat's impossible. Vampires don't exist." I wrapped my arms around myself. Numbness spread through my body as I stared at the crazy man in front of me.

"You'll soon accept your new reality." He shrugged and turned his attention back to the fire.

My mouth dropped open. He actually believed what he was saying. I was trapped in a house with a delusional killer who thought he was a vampire. Considering my luck, he was probably schizophrenic, as well.

He glanced back and caught me staring. "How do you think you are standing after almost being beheaded by a snowplow? How could the bleeding around your neck completely stop? How do you explain the fact that there's no wound around your neck now?" He glared. "It's because you are a vampire.

My hand went under my scarf, and I gently pressed my fingers to where the wound should be. The puckered skin was now smooth flesh.

"That's not possible."

I headed to the table and snatched up the hand mirror. I tore off the scarf and held up the mirror to my neck, ready to see the injured flesh staring back at me.

My wound was completely healed. My skin wasn't red, and the puckering where I'd been sewn together was gone. I squinted and brought the mirror closer. In fact, the subtle age lines around my neck weren't there anymore, either.

I lifted my gaze to the stranger and pressed my hand over where my heart was. I breathed out a sigh of relief when I felt the steady rhythm of my heartbeat against my palm.

"Vampires are dead. And they don't have a pulse." I lifted my chin, challenging him.

"Not actually true. They have a pulse for a while. Once they have fully turned, they lose their heartbeat."

"What do you mean, *fully turned?*" I wasn't about to throw all my vampire information at him at once—all of which had come from romance novels and late-night movies. After reading one racy romance novel from a favorite author, I had gone searching on Google for everything about vampires. I knew all about stakes to the heart, their repulsion to garlic, and not having a reflection. I also knew that vampires would burn up in the sunlight and that they preyed on their victims at night.

When he stayed silent, I met his eyes and blinked. "How is a human turned into a vampire?"

"Slowly. And not all at once." He looked back into the dancing flames of the fire.

"I don't understand." I frowned and shook my head. His information went against everything I'd read. "I thought once you were bitten you immediately turned into a vampire."

He sighed heavily. "That's in the movies and stupid romance books written to give women the idea that vampires are romantic or worse, heroes."

The hairs on the back of my neck stood up, and I shivered. I needed to find a way out of here, and the only way I was going to do that was to keep him talking while I came up with a plan. I glanced around the room, searching for an escape from this prison.

"Explain it to me. Explain how a person becomes a..." I found the more I entertained the idea, the harder it became to say the word.

"A vampire. You need to get used to saying it. You might have to mark it on your driver's license as ethnicity."

Ah, so the psychotic kidnapper had a sense of humor.

"Why should I get used to it?" I snorted and shrugged my shoulders.

"Because that's what you are now. Or very soon will be." His eyes narrowed again.

"Explain what you mean." I cocked my head and gave him my full attention while my mind tried to come up with an escape plan. He was between me and the door, and I doubted that he was just going to let me walk right past him.

"The process of turning into a vampire is slow. It doesn't happen all at once. After the blood exchange has occurred, then the body begins to change. From the inside out."

I crossed my arms and studied him. My eyes drifted down his large body to his feet. I arched my brow. I wasn't sure, but from where I was standing, the black boots he wore appeared to be expensive leather. It didn't match his old trench coat, which looked cheap.

"It's different for everyone. But, eventually, everything changes. Your senses, your appearance, your heart, and then your complete dependence on blood." Excitement flashed through his eyes. His gaze landed on my throat.

I wrapped my hand around my naked neck. I could feel my pulse hammering against my fingers.

"Don't worry. I already had your blood. I don't want any more." He chuckled and turned his back.

"You bit me?" Emotion fluttered through my stomach.

"Yeah. Tasted like rich-bitch housewife. Not to my taste at all."

"You assh..." I clamped a hand over my mouth, shocked at my outburst. I didn't need to give this guy a reason to cut out my tongue.

It was probably the trauma of being kidnapped, bitten, and nearly decapitated.

"Get used to the aggression. Everything about you is about to change." He pushed away from the fireplace and turned to give me his full attention. "You'll find once you become a vampire, your true nature comes out."

"I have to get back to my house." I didn't want to talk about vampires or blood or anything else. All I wanted was to be inside my home, safe and protected.

I clasped my trembling hands together and held my breath to keep from screaming. I didn't recall ever feeling such an overwhelming need to run.

"You can't go back home. There is nothing left for you there." He shook his head and rested one hand on the mantel and looked back into the fire.

My children were there. That's all the reason I needed.

"Please, just let me go. I'll give you anything. I'll...do anything." I forced that last sentence out of my mouth and tried not to imagine him wanting anything sexual from me.

He was dirty, smelly, and scary. All really bad things.

He pushed off the mantel and swung around to me. "You act like I've kidnapped you and are holding you against your will. Do you know how much I wish I'd never seen you?" His gaze hardened on me again. "How badly I wish I hadn't saved you."

"So, why did you? If you hate me so much, why did you

pick me to turn into a vampire?" I carefully eased out of my high heels. If I were going to make a break for it, then I would need to do it barefoot so I could cover more ground.

"Because you stumbled out in front of my snowplow. You made me hit you." He turned away and propped his hands on his hips as he looked at the ceiling. "For someone with such a charmed life, you sure have a death wish."

"You were driving the snowplow?" Forgetting my fear, I walked over to him, grabbed his arm, and tugged him around. He flinched when I touched him and stepped back out of my space.

"It was all your fault. You're the one who fell in front of my snowplow. You had plenty of time to move, but you didn't." He looked at me as if I'd lost my mind.

"Why did you say I have a death wish?"

"Because I heard what you said before I hit you." His eyes narrowed.

I would remember the next sentence that came out of his mouth for the rest of my life.

"You looked straight at the blade and said, 'take away my pain.'"

CHAPTER 5

"*I* would never try to kill myself." I shook my head vigorously and backed away from him. My hand gripped the windowsill as my mouth went dry at his accusation. "I've never even had suicidal thoughts."

"You had time to get out of the way. But you didn't move. You laid there. I tried to stop, but couldn't in time. The snowplow caught your neck and nearly took your head off." His voice was low.

"I knew you wouldn't live if I didn't turn you. So, I took your blood and then fed you mine. I wrapped up your neck with my shirt and brought you here until I could sew your wound together." He glared.

"So, you turned me because you felt guilty for hitting me?" My mouth dropped open. First, my husband betrayed me. And now this *vampire* regretted turning me. Even a homeless psycho didn't want me.

"Pretty much." He turned and walked over to the table in the corner of the room. He kept his back to me as he picked up something.

It was now or never.

With my heartbeat pounding in my ears, I held the quilt close around my body and ran out the door. I heard him growl, and his heavy footsteps behind me, but I forced myself not to look back. I knew if I did, he would be on my heels.

It was dark in the house, but thankfully I could still see.

I tore down the hallway, running as fast as I ever had in my life. Hope flickered inside my chest when I spotted the front door, my escape from this hell I currently found myself in.

"You can't leave!" he screamed behind me, but I didn't stop. I knew if I stopped running, he'd capture me, and I would never leave that house in one piece.

I had to escape, or die trying.

I grabbed the doorknob, and my heart nearly seized in my chest. I expected it to be locked. Miraculously, it wasn't. I flung open the door. The cold wind slapped me in the face, but I didn't care. My body was running on adrenaline and fear.

I ran out into the snow-covered yard with nothing but my big red bow and the quilt to shield me from the elements.

I heard him growl behind me, but I didn't stop. Barefoot, I managed to put some distance between my kidnapper and myself. I had even left my Jimmy Choo's behind. They weren't worth my life.

My lungs sucked in icy air. I worked out religiously, so running was part of my everyday routine. I wasn't a fast runner by any means, but I knew that I was topping my best time tonight for sure. I suppose when you have a delusional kidnapper/killer/possible cannibal on your heels, you get motivated in a whole different way.

I ran out into the empty street. It was late, and there wasn't any traffic. I wasn't sure where I was, or which way to go, so I headed in the direction where the streetlights and restaurant signs lit up the night sky.

I continued running down the middle of the frozen street, hoping I could flag down a cop car.

The snow was still falling, and the flakes stuck to my long lashes. I blinked them away and tried to ignore the cold seeping into my bones and freezing my bare feet.

I turned into the parking lot of a well-lit convenience store. There were bars on the windows and the front door. Normally, I stayed away from places like this. Hell, I usually stayed on my side of the tracks.

Whatever was inside this store couldn't be any more dangerous than what I'd just escaped.

I flung open the door and ran inside. "Please, help me." I threw myself on the counter in front of the wide-eyed cashier. The quilt fell from my shoulders and puddled on the floor. The dark-skinned man backed away from me and reached under the counter.

"Please, you've got to help me. Someone kidnapped me and…"

"Kidnapped you?" He squinted his dark eyes. "Aren't you too old to be kidnapped?" His gaze skimmed down my body. The quilt slipped revealing the ridiculous red bow. His gaze moved back up to my face where his eyes narrowed.

I pulled the quilt tighter around me.

"Abducted, then. He abducted me and took me to his house." I looked around the store, but it was empty. I caught my reflection in the glass door of the cooler and almost gasped. My makeup had run down my face. There was a smear of blood across my neck from where I had, at least according to my kidnapper, almost been decapitated.

I looked like a deranged hooker.

I squatted, trying to keep my lady parts covered as I picked up the quilt. I wrapped the blanket around me like a protective shield and looked back at the clerk.

Suddenly, I wasn't sure if I felt safer here.

I took a step away from the clerk. The cashier kept his eyes on me and one hand under the counter.

I had an uneasy feeling that I had sprinted out of the pot and into the frying pan.

The door swung open, and two large men walked in. When they saw me, they stopped in their tracks.

My gut churned, and I wrapped my arms around myself.

"Hey, baby, are you lost?" One guy smiled, revealing a gold tooth. He was wearing a hoodie and low riding jeans. His friend was dressed in the same manner.

The other male cocked his head and eyed me suspiciously.

I hoped I looked like an undercover cop, or maybe even a high-class drug dealer. Instead, I knew I looked like a mentally insane prostitute.

"She says she's been kidnapped," the cashier spoke up.

I looked over my shoulder and noticed that his hand was still under the counter. The back of my neck tingled.

"Is that so?" The guy with the gold tooth smiled wider. Shivers raced up my spine.

I looked around. If I had to fight, I needed something to use as a weapon. I knew my limitations. Going to spin class and running didn't make me a lethal weapon.

"I'm just trying to get back home. Back to my children. I'm not looking for trouble." My voice hitched on the last word, and I took a step back.

"Well, you came to the wrong neighborhood, sweet thing." Gold-tooth guy took a step forward. "Trouble is all we got here."

My body tensed, and my throat ached.

"Don't come near me," I hissed and fisted my hands at my sides. I wasn't going down without a fight.

The thug reached out, and I jumped. He snagged a bag of chips off the rack beside me as his eyes raked over me.

"Easy, lady." His smile was gone. "Don't flatter yourself. I ain't that hard-up." He tossed some dollar bills on the counter before taking his leave and heading out the door. His large cohort stayed a second or two longer, staring me down with hard eyes. Without a word, he opened the door and followed his friend out into the night.

I looked back at the cashier, who now had his cell phone up to his ear.

I knew then that this had been a bad idea.

CHAPTER 6

I should have been happy that the cashier was finally calling the police. Assuming he was. I should have felt relief.

My mind raced with thoughts of what my neighbors would say when they found out I'd been kidnapped. They would likely all assume the worst, and I doubted I could persuade them otherwise. Worse, I worried about how people would treat my children when they found out what had happened.

And what about my husband?

Fear, terror, and pain seized my chest and crawled into my throat.

I blinked as images of my husband and my best friend in bed flashed through my mind.

I'd never associated my husband with fear or pain before. But now, every time I thought about him, those were the only emotions that welled up inside of me.

Then, that image, so vile and disgusting, blazed in front of my eyes again.

A scene that I knew would be forever scorched into my brain and on my soul.

Our bedroom.

My husband.

My best friend.

Those words didn't belong in a sentence, not together, and they didn't make sense.

"Impossible." Even as I whispered the words, the truth settled in my stomach like a lead weight.

I ran to the front of the shop.

"Where are you going? What about the police?" the cashier yelled after me.

I ran out the door and into the snowy night.

I skidded to a halt on the icy pavement and looked both ways. The streets were not familiar to me. I made the decision to keep heading right. It was better lit, and I figured it would eventually lead me into town where I could find my way home.

After thirty minutes of walking, my feet were numb from the cold.

"Maybe it was a dream." I reached up, and my fingers grazed the faint scar on my neck. I snatched my hand away and cringed.

It didn't make sense. Nothing about this whole fucking night made any sense.

I walked faster, my footsteps silent on the sidewalk. I looked around at the neighborhood I found myself in. Blanketed in snow, it didn't seem so intimidating.

I stopped at the next corner and felt a tiny flicker of hope.

Sedgeway Drive.

Hope burst forth in my chest. I knew that street! If I turned and continued walking down Sedgeway, I'd eventually run into Foster. From there, it was a fifteen-minute drive to my neighborhood.

On foot, however, it would probably take an hour.

I broke into a jog, careful not to step on any spots that might be black ice. The last thing I needed was to break my leg and be hauled to the hospital wrapped in a giant bow.

The stores soon gave way to older homes—once the *nicer* part of town. But years of neglect had taken its toll on the outdated, ranch-style houses.

I turned on Foster and continued running. I was surprised that I wasn't getting cold or that my lungs didn't ache like they usually did when I ran too fast.

I felt...different.

My eyes had adjusted well in the dark, and that was odd. Usually, I tried to avoid driving at night because the lights hurt my eyes and made it hard to see. I especially hated driving at night in the rain. I always avoided it when I could.

I was antsy, and I knew it must be the adrenaline pouring through my veins. After what I'd just been through, I was honestly surprised I was still on my feet and pushing forward.

My heart lurched for joy when I saw the gated entrance to our subdivision come into view. I was almost home.

I sprinted the rest of the way to the gate and stopped at the keypad. The gate hadn't been locked when I left, but it was always shut after nine p.m.

I quickly punched in the access code and held my breath for entrance.

I let it out a big sigh when the large gates swung open. Wasting no time, I jogged inside.

My house was located a mile into the subdivision, backed up to a wooded area. Our neighborhood had a golf course, but we hadn't built our house on the greens. Although my husband loved playing golf, he'd said he didn't want to actually live on the fairways where people would be in your backyard all the time. So, we'd bought and built on one of the larger plots of land away from the course.

I jogged past my neighbors, barely giving them a glance. Some I knew well; others, I didn't even know their names. Certain neighbors I'd only heard rumors about, and I steered clear of any of their drama.

A dog barked, and I jumped. I knew immediately who the bark belonged to. The white and tan beagle named Scooby. Scooby belonged to the Macys, who never put Scooby up. They believed that dogs weren't meant to be in pens or kept on a leash, but should run free. Scooby had been a neighborhood nuisance for years, getting into people's garbage, humping other dogs, and chasing after runners. I had my own encounters with Scooby nearly every time I went for a run. He'd tried to hump my leg twice and bite me once but, luckily, I was faster and had gotten away all three times.

It didn't do any good to complain to the Macys either. A bunch of the ladies had gotten on the neighborhood group text to voice their complaints about Scooby. But Mr. Macy had fired right back, saying that if they didn't like Scooby, then they should move.

After that, I fully expected the dog to turn up dead. But Scooby was still alive and humping his way through the neighborhood bitches.

The closer I got to my house, the faster I ran. My kids, Gabby and Arianna, would be home. I needed to see my girls.

No. That was wrong. The kids *wouldn't* be home. They were at a sleepover.

I slowed my pace when I saw my house.

The image of my husband and my best friend once again filled my head. My chest ached, and I thought it might explode from the pain inside.

Were they still inside my house? Was Nikki still naked and curled up in my bed?

Oh, God. Did the neighbors see her?

Of course, they probably saw her. She was my best friend. She came over practically every day.

I walked up my driveway.

I punched in the code to the garage. The doors slid up. My heartbeat amped up when I saw Miles' car inside.

I walked inside the garage, shivering with cold, adrenaline, and uncertainty. I reached for the door to the house.

The door swung open, and a wide-eyed Miles stood there, staring back at me.

CHAPTER 7

"*R*achel. What are you doing here? It's three o'clock in the morning. And why are you wearing a quilt?" Miles tightened the belt on his robe as his Adams' apple bobbed like a cork. He shifted his weight, and his eyes widened. "Good Lord, you don't have any shoes on. Are you naked under that dirty thing?"

Anger rushed from my chest and heated my face.

I didn't take my eyes off his. I couldn't. I needed to see what kind of man he was.

"I thought you were in Memphis." He blinked and looked out into the garage and frowned. "Where's your car?"

"I had car trouble." Wasn't exactly a lie. It was in the ditch somewhere. "I lied."

"What do you mean, you lied? About the car trouble?" He froze.

"No. I lied. I didn't go to Memphis. I said that so I could surprise you." I barely got the words out through my thick throat. "For your birthday." I blinked. "What have you been doing?"

He smiled the smile that I'd fallen in love with. Suddenly, everything felt wrong.

"I just got home around two. Surgery went late," he said easily.

My stomach lurched. He lied right to my face.

I grabbed my churning stomach and ran to the bathroom off the kitchen.

"Are you okay?"

I slammed the door behind me and locked it before kneeling in front of the toilet. Everything I had eaten that day came up. Tears streamed down my face. Agony twisted deep in my chest.

My husband lied to me.

I'd never trusted someone as much as I trusted—*had* trusted—Miles. And he'd betrayed me.

"Rachel, are you okay? Are you sick? What do you need?" He knocked, and for a second, the gentleness in his tone almost made me open the door. Almost.

"Leave me alone," I whispered and buried my face in my hands.

Sitting on the expensive marble flooring of my bathroom, I struggled to regulate my erratic breathing.

This would change me. In that heart-beat of a moment, I knew without a doubt, that I would be forever changed.

"Honey, let me in so I can help."

My heart cramped and convulsed. How could he be so calm and caring after what he'd just done? After what he'd done to his family? After what he'd done to us?

I grabbed the sink and forced myself to stand. I looked at my haggard face in the mirror and cringed. I turned on the faucet and splashed my face with water, hoping to conceal my expression. Miles always told me never to play poker, that my feelings were written all over my face.

I'd worked on it over the course of our marriage.

Feigning interest at parties with other housewives to advance his career and reputation while I slowly died of boredom inside as the conversations turned to how to put on the perfect child's party, or talk of the latest interior decorating styles.

My breathing increased. Surely, sleeping with Nikki was a one-time thing. Surely, this hadn't been going on forever. That's why he sounded so concerned. He was feeling guilty. Surely…

My gut twisted.

I tightened my hand on the sink, scared that I would fall into the invisible black abyss of pain and uncertainty beneath my feet if I let go. That I would fall away from my life that I no longer recognized.

My gaze shifted down my body. Shit, I was still wearing the stupid bow.

I grabbed my quilt and wrapped it tightly around myself.

I sucked in a deep breath, but it didn't help. My heart raced as I grasped the cold doorknob in my hand and twisted.

I opened the door to see Miles standing there. His handsome face was pinched with concern, and something else flashed behind his eyes. He shoved his hands into the pockets of his robe. "Are you all right?"

We were standing three feet apart, yet the distance felt like miles. I rubbed my hand over my aching chest and choked back tears.

I will not cry. I will not cry. I will not cry.

"I saw you." My voice quivered, and I looked away. I couldn't look at him anymore.

"I don't know what you are talking about." The remoteness in his voice confirmed my fears.

Anger…white-hot anger blazed up inside me like never before. I clenched my hands until they grew numb.

"I walked in on you and Nikki fucking in our bed."

His eyes widened, and he glanced away. He shook his head furiously. "You're crazy. That didn't happen."

My anger leveled up to rage. "You betrayed me, and now you're lying to my face? How could you?"

"Calm down, you don't know what you're talking about." He lowered his voice and began to blink rapidly like he was trying to come up with an explanation: any explanation that I would believe.

I stormed past him into the kitchen. I saw his phone lying on the counter and snatched it up.

"What are you doing?" Panic rose in his voice, and I knew I had him.

"If nothing is going on, then you won't mind me looking through your phone." The cell felt heavy in my hand, and I waited for him to tell me it was okay to look. The man I married never kept secrets from me. Never. We'd been together almost fifteen years. He was my best friend.

"Why are you acting like this, Rachel?" His gaze hardened.

"Acting like what?" My anger boiled in my gut, and I waited for his next few words.

"You're acting crazy. For God's sake, Rachel, you're naked with nothing but a quilt on. And where's the Volvo?"

"It's in a ditch. I had to walk home after I wrecked."

His eyes widened. "The neighbors didn't see you, did they?"

That pissed me off. He was more concerned about what the neighbors thought than if I were okay.

I held up the phone and swiped my finger across the screen. It wasn't locked. It didn't surprise me. He never kept his screen locked. But then again, I never looked at it. He never gave me a reason to.

"Rachel, give me back my phone." He took a step forward and held out his hand.

I skirted the granite kitchen island and pulled up his messages. I scanned them, noting the names. Me, the kids, various doctors he worked with all popped up on the screen.

"Why are you doing this?" His eyes widened, and the way he looked at me was strange.

He didn't look like a man angry at his wife for falsely accusing him. He looked like a man afraid of a secret coming out.

"Maybe I'm wrong." Was I going crazy? Had the whole thing been a nightmare?

"Of course, you are." His shoulders relaxed, and he held out his hand again for the phone.

Instead of giving it back, I clicked on Nikki's name.

"Maybe we should cool it. She may be on to us."

Hurt and panic and all-encompassing despair raced through my veins.

And then came the anger. As swift as a summer storm, the rage came upon me and swallowed me whole.

I looked up at him and held out the phone. "I'm crazy? Then why the fuck did Nikki send you this."

He blinked, went pale, and swallowed several times. I could tell he was racing to come up with an answer, something to satisfy me. At the same time, he knew he was in deep shit.

"It's not what you think. We're just friends."

"You're a fucking liar. Nikki is my best friend," I screamed at him and stormed out of the room toward my bedroom.

"It's not what you think," he said again, low and slow.

I stepped into the bedroom and rounded on him. "I don't believe anything you're saying. I walked in today and saw you and Nikki fucking in *our* bed." I pointed to the messed-up sheets. The assholes didn't even have the decency to change the fucking sheets.

"And now I find a text on your phone from her. "

His mouth dropped open, and his face went pale.

"Get your shit and get the fuck out of my house." The words came out bitter and slow, and I tasted every hateful syllable.

"Rachel, please…"

I swiped at the tears on my cheeks and looked at him. "Why? Why would you throw your family away like this?"

His eyes widened with fear. "Rachel, don't do anything rash."

His words struck my heart like a blade. He didn't deny it. He wasn't refuting anything. He wasn't even apologizing.

I shoved him in the chest, needing him out of my sight and out of my house before I did something bad.

I'd never hurt anyone in my life. Never been a violent person. But, so help me God, I wanted to hurt him. I wanted him to feel the pain of his heart being torn from his chest. I wanted him to feel what *I* was feeling.

"You threw away your family for a piece of ass. You chose her over your family." I nodded and looked him straight in the eye. "Well, congratulations. You are free of me." I ran into the walk-in closet and locked the door.

"Rachel, what do you mean? What did you mean by that?" He pounded on the closet door, but I'd locked it from the inside. It was a safety lock that we'd had installed in case of a break-in. Kind of like a panic room. Perfect for what I was feeling: panic and fear.

I sank to the hardwood floor of the closet that looked like a small boutique and tugged the robe off the back of the door. I bundled it up and shoved my face into it and screamed as loudly as I could. The soft fleece muffled my anguished cries.

"Please, Rachel, what did you mean by that?" Miles' tone was panicked. I'd never heard him like that. He was always in control, always the strong one, always my anchor in the storm.

But no more. He was a liar. Which meant our marriage had been a lie.

More frightening than all of that…everything I had ever believed was a lie.

$\mathcal{I}$ stayed curled up in a fetal position in my closet for what seemed like an eternity. The bow was crumpled and itchy, and I wanted it off, but I didn't have the energy to get up off the floor. Finally, I heard the garage door shut.

Miles had left.

I stood up and clawed at the ridiculous bow until it came off and slung on my soft, chenille robe. I bolted out of the closet, my heart pounding in my chest. I ran to the dining room. I pressed my face to the window just in time to see his taillights as he turned onto the main road headed out of the subdivision.

He didn't turn left. I let out a long sigh. That's where Nikki lived. I frowned. Why didn't he turn left? He was already fucking her, so why didn't he just go to her? Probably because Nikki's husband, Brad would wonder what Miles was doing at his house at such a late hour.

Did Nikki's husband suspect that anything was going on?

I couldn't worry about anyone else right now. I had my own nervous breakdown to attend to.

I curled my arms over my head and shook my head in denial. My hands trembled against my scalp, and my heart threatened to jump out of my chest.

I was utterly alone.

I ran to the girls' rooms, needing to see something that reminded me of my children. I flipped on the switch in Arianna's room first.

She was fourteen, the oldest, and getting more independent by the day. I'd had her room redone almost a year ago in soft pink walls with zebra-print bedding. The twin bed had different shades of silver throw pillows with sparkles. Her desk sat in the corner, littered with framed photos of Arianna and her friends. She used to have pictures of us from our family vacations, but last year she'd replaced them with photos of her friends.

I sank onto the bed and grabbed her pink pillow. I held it to my nose and inhaled. The sweet scent of strawberry shampoo washed over me as I soaked her pillowcase with my tears. I squeezed my eyes shut so tightly they hurt. And, for the first time in a long time, I prayed for God to help me.

The pain of Miles' betrayal was unbearable. How could I have been so stupid to trust my husband and my best friend? How had I not seen what was going on? How would I survive?

I threw the pillow back onto the bed and hurried out of Arianna's room and into Gabby's room. I switched on the light. Immediately, I was wrapped in a loving and soft glow from the sconces on either side of her castle bed.

Gabby, at ten, was my youngest, and she loved her castle bed. I'd had it built years ago and had offered to have her bedroom redecorated last year, but Gabby had said no. She'd said she wanted to stay in her castle bed forever. She said it made her dream of dragons and wizards and let her be a princess who saved the kingdom.

My Gabby. My independent dreamer. My strong child.

I stood in her room, staring at her castle and wishing it was real. If it were real, then I would run inside and hide from the pain that was wracking my body and tearing my heart in two.

But the castle wasn't real, and I had no safe place to hide from my pain.

I was here.

Alone.

My stomach rumbled in the empty room, yet I had no appetite. My eyes were heavy, but I knew if I lay down, I wouldn't be able to sleep.

I had all this anger inside, and I didn't know what to do with it. I walked past the mirror on the wall and froze.

My pale face and red-rimmed eyes echoed my pain. Gone was the makeup that I'd had professionally applied. I'd managed to wash it all off with my barrage of tears.

I swallowed and realized that my neck didn't hurt anymore. I carefully pulled my robe away and examined my throat.

The wound was healed. Not even a hint of a scar.

Nothing made sense anymore, and I didn't have the energy to try and figure it out.

I was going to get through this. I had to. For my children.

I stripped off my robe and stood under the spray. I let the shower fill with steam as the hot water washed over me.

I couldn't move, not even to pick up a washcloth. I was numb, drained of energy. My head felt the opposite, though. My brain raced with thoughts of the hows, whys, and what nows.

Home was the one thing that always felt secure.

It was my shelter against the world.

Home was where I felt safe.

Now, that feeling had been ripped from me, leaving an open wound. Painful, unexpected, shocking.

My kids. How was I going to support my girls? I'd met Miles in college, and we had quickly fallen in love. We married when we were broke and didn't have a cent between us. He'd desperately wanted to go to med school, so I'd agreed to drop out of college to support that dream. We figured between me getting a job as a secretary, and the student loans, medical school was within our reach.

At the time, I didn't mind the sacrifice. I figured every good wife wanted to support her husband as he fulfilled his dreams. Dropping out of college wasn't a big deal for me. I'd never really figured out what I was supposed to be or what I wanted to do. When I met Miles, we'd seemed to fit so well, that becoming a wife and mother became the important things I wanted in life.

Now, I was afraid. Afraid of how I would support myself and my kids.

Where Miles reached new heights in his medical career, I excelled at being a housewife and mother to my girls.

Stinging tears gathered behind my eyes and spilled down my cheeks. I hated crying. I couldn't remember the last time I had.

Now, I couldn't freaking stop.

I stayed in the shower until the water turned cold. I skipped grabbing a towel and stepped right into my plush, chenille robe instead. The material instantly soaked up the water and felt uncomfortably wet against my skin.

I didn't glance at my reflection in the bathroom mirror. I was too afraid that I would see a coward staring back at me. The stupid housewife who didn't have the sense to know that her husband had been cheating on her.

Averting my gaze, I walked into the large master

bedroom and laid on the hardwood floor. I stared up at the ceiling as the tears slid down my face and into my wet hair.

"God, please help me. Help me know what to do. I don't know what to do," I sobbed.

Anxiety and adrenaline rushed through my veins. I was tired, so very tired, yet I couldn't close my eyes, and I couldn't sit still.

I got to my feet and hurried to the bathroom.

Survival mode. I was in survival mode.

I went to my closet and shrugged out of my robe. I grabbed panties and a bra and didn't really care that they didn't match. I threw them on and then tugged on some yoga pants and a sweatshirt.

I always did my best thinking when I was cleaning.

I threw on my Ugg's and went to the laundry room to gather up the cleaning supplies.

The maid had just been there two days ago, and my house really didn't need another deep-cleaning. But it was the only thing I could think to do. It was the only thing I could control.

I started with the bathrooms, scrubbing the toilets until they shone. After that, I moved to the bedrooms, first the girls' and then the guest room. I couldn't clean the master yet. The memory of Miles and Nikki was still too fresh.

After the bedrooms, I moved on to the kitchen, cleaning out the refrigerator, polishing the cabinets, and then scrubbing the counters. When I was done, I went into the dining room to dust and polish the table before moving on to the two living areas we had in the house. I didn't clean Miles' office. I stopped at the door and tried to step inside, but I caught a hint of his cologne, and it stopped me short. Tears gathered in my eyes. I stepped back and slammed the door closed.

After cleaning all the rooms, I tackled the floors; sweeping and then mopping as I went.

As I worked, I focused my mind on the task at hand, on what was familiar, on my breathing, on things I could control. When images of my husband in bed with Nikki popped into my head, I sat back on my knees, squeezed my eyes shut, and replaced the vile pictures with a memory of my girls.

When I was done in the kitchen, I gathered up my supplies and went to my bedroom. As I cleaned, I cried the entire time. I dusted and rearranged furniture. I tore the sheets and comforter off the bed and threw them into the trash. I put new, clean sheets on the bed and ordered a new bedding set off my favorite website with express shipping. It would arrive in a couple of days.

Back in the kitchen, I reached for my phone on the counter and checked for messages.

None. No calls, either.

My gut churned, and I struggled to catch my breath. Miles and I had never had a fight we didn't resolve right away.

But in my heart, I knew this wasn't a regular fight.

This was life-changing.

What scared me most was that he was willing to let us go. Just like that. After fifteen years of building a life together and me supporting his medical practice, he was willing to let it all go, as if it meant nothing more than a disposable birthday card.

I was scared, frightened, and in pain; an agony like I had never experienced. I felt like I was going crazy. I looked down at my chest, expecting to see a crater-sized wound there, and my heart lying on the floor.

I didn't see that. I rubbed my hand over my sternum and pulled up Miles' number on my phone.

I dialed. I needed answers. I had to know.

Before he could pick up, I ended the call. I knew that if I were the first to call, then he would realize that he had control over me. My knees buckled, and I slid down the wall to the floor.

Half of me desperately wanted to see him, so much that my hands shook. The other half never wanted to see him again, hoping he would regret what he'd done to our family for the rest of his miserable life.

What scared me most: I didn't know which side would win out.

CHAPTER 9

I managed to drag myself to the guest room in the early morning hours before dawn. I was cold from lying on the floor and sobbing uncontrollably, so I relented and crawled into the guest bed.

I should have fallen asleep the second my head hit the pillow. But my brain wouldn't let me. I was too wired. Too jittery. I really thought I was losing my mind.

I pulled my phone out from under my pillow and checked the time.

I knew better than to stick my cell phone under my pillow. I'd seen the news reports of phones catching on fire or just blowing up. Considering everything that had happened, though, catching on fire was the least of my concerns.

I needed my phone close in case Miles called.

I squinted at the time on the phone. Six a.m.

It was Saturday, and the girls wouldn't be home until Sunday. I was facing the weekend alone.

I scrolled through my contacts, an overwhelming desire to call someone to confide in flooding me.

My heart jumped in my throat when I came to Nikki's number. My best friend. My *best friend*, who had stolen my husband.

I furiously scrolled until the screen showed no more names. I'd gone through my list of friends, the other soccer moms, the women I worked out with, went to church with, or shared wine nights with.

I couldn't call any of them. If I did, it would be all over town what a cheater my husband was.

I also knew they'd likely encourage me to leave him or kick him out and take everything.

The thought of being without Miles clawed at my heart.

He'd already made up his mind. That became obvious when he made the choice to sleep with Nikki.

He didn't want his family or his wife. He wanted something new and different.

I grabbed the pillow, held it against my mouth, and screamed.

Pain pulsed through my body.

What had I done for fate to punish me so much? I didn't deserve to be cheated on. Did I?

The doorbell rang. I jumped out of bed and raced down the hallway, not bothering to grab my robe. I glanced out the dining room window but couldn't see anyone.

It was still dark and too early for visitors.

My heart pounded in my chest as I fumbled with the locks. I flung the door open and froze.

The large man who'd kidnapped me filled the doorway.

I'd been drowning in thoughts of my husband's infidelity, too upset to spare my kidnapper any consideration.

My fingers instantly went to my neck, and my eyes widened.

"How did you know where I live?" I croaked out the words, my throat scratchy from screaming.

"I've had your blood. As your Maker, I can find you anywhere." His hard gaze didn't leave my face, and I suddenly wondered if I could slam the door before he tried to get inside.

"What do you want from me?" I reached for the door to shut it, but he stuck his booted foot in the doorframe and glared.

"I'm responsible for you now. You don't know how to live in your new world."

No shit, Sherlock. I felt like my whole marriage was a lie.

"While I appreciate your concern, I'm perfectly capable of taking care of myself. You need to leave." I left unsaid the *and never come back* part of the statement.

I saw movement behind him and glanced over his shoulder. My neighbor, Cal, was bundled up in his winter coat and rubber boots, making his way to the bottom of his driveway. He didn't bother looking up as he bent to grab the newspaper before hurrying back into the warmth of his house.

"You don't know the first thing about being a vampire." The man curled his nose in disgust.

"And you know nothing about personal hygiene." I poked my finger into his chest and stepped closer. Something inside me snapped, and anger bubbled up inside my chest. I was tired of not having any control over my life.

"You don't belong here. If you don't leave, I'll call the cops." I spat out the words. "And I will have you arrested."

His lips twitched before sliding into a smile that revealed his sharp fangs. His eyes were no longer red but a deep shade of turquoise blue, with a look as hard as stone. He leaned in closer. He still stank, but it wasn't his smell that I focused on, it was his teeth.

"Are you going to bite me?" I shocked myself by voicing the question.

"I already did."

"So, what does that mean? You don't double dip?"

His smile slid off his face and was replaced by a look of cold indifference.

I'd rather him hate me than treat me like I wasn't there. It was a surprising reaction.

"I'm not like you, you know. You may be a…vampire, but I'm not." I lifted my chin.

"You are delusional. The newly turned usually are. You'll come around, you've no choice. You'll accept your fate or die."

"Die? If I really am a vampire, how can I die?" The thought of death evoked a different set of emotions, something I wasn't ready to face.

"You'll have to learn how to survive. Your new life requires a certain skill set, which, as your Maker, I have to explain."

"I thought all you had to do was drink blood and…"—my gaze raked over his unkempt appearance—"not bathe."

His eyes narrowed. "It's not as simple as that. But, yes, we do require blood—human blood—to keep us strong."

"I don't drink blood, and I don't intend to start. Unless you can make me a vampire who survives on wine, then we have nothing to discuss."

"You don't understand," he hissed as he leaned down, obviously frustrated. "You don't have a choice about drinking blood. You'll long for it, have cravings stronger than anything you've ever experienced. You'll want blood more than anything, even sex."

My eyes widened with the ferocity of his words, and I was suddenly acutely aware of how little I was wearing. I'd slipped on booty shorts and a tight cami before I went to bed.

A tingle swept up the back of my neck, and heat crept across my face as I crossed my arms to glare at him.

"You may try to resist at first. Seeing how hard-headed you are,"—his gaze slid down my body before meeting my eyes—"you probably will. In the end, stubbornness won't matter. At first, you will feel weak and lethargic, but then it will get worse. You'll have the worst cramps you've ever had. It's your body's way of demanding you feed it blood."

I shook my head. "Nope." I pursed my lips together. "No way, no how."

"We'll see." He dangled a set of keys under my nose. "Your Volvo is in the driveway. There was a dent in the front fender that I straightened out. Hardly noticeable."

"You brought my car back?" I took the keys and blinked. "Why would you do that?"

He ignored my question and continued glaring at me.

"You need to wake up. You're a spoiled housewife who wouldn't survive a minute alone in the real world. You're going to need my help whether you like it or not." He turned on his heel and strode out into the street without looking back.

He was the second man in a twelve-hour period that had walked out on me.

CHAPTER 10

I rested my face against the cold, dining-room window. Dawn spread across the sky, illuminating the blindingly bright white blanket of snow that stretched across every lawn and rooftop in my neighborhood. Every tree limb was heavily frosted, while yellow daffodils sagged toward the ground. It was only a little after eight, but the neighborhood kids were already bundled up in bright jackets and hats, dragging their sleds behind them as dogs tiptoed carefully through the unfamiliar white stuff. I wondered how many moms had set out bowls in the backyard to catch some clean snow for snow ice cream.

In the South, when it snowed, we took advantage of it: from sledding and snowmen to snow ice cream.

My heart cramped. I wished my girls were home so we could play in the snow together. The last time it had snowed, I hadn't been a very good sport about it. I hadn't put on the right kind of socks, and the wet snow had seeped into my boots. I'd tried sledding, but Scooby came barreling toward me and knocked me off the sled. I'd face-planted right in the snow. The kids and Miles had thought it was funny, but that was it for me. I'd gone inside and made hot chocolate while they played.

Scooby raced across my yard, barking at the neighborhood kids and marring my perfect blanket of snow with his paw prints.

The girls always wanted a dog, but Miles didn't want an animal in the house. I was secretly relieved when he told them no. With my obsessive-compulsive nature, I think I would have gone crazy trying to sweep up the dog fur.

I had no idea how long I was standing at the window, but it was long enough for my feet to ache.

I dragged a chair over to the glass and sat down, placing my cell phone in my lap and checking to make sure I had the ringer on.

I told myself that I was just enjoying watching the kids play in the snow. I was just checking to make sure the girls hadn't called. I was a strong woman. No matter what happened, everything would be all right.

But the lies I told myself burned away like paper in a fire.

I was sitting there, watching for Miles' familiar Tesla to turn down our road and come home.

I was waiting on a miracle.

When noon hit, I gave up and dragged myself back to the guest bed. I was emotionally and mentally exhausted. The adrenaline had finally worn off, and it was all I could do to make it to the bedroom. I squinted and used my hand to shield my eyes from the sunlight coming through the slats in the blinds. I tugged the heavy curtains closed to block out the light.

I needed sleep. Once I woke, I would shower and dress. I would put on makeup and do my hair. I would be ready for Miles when he came home. Because I knew, in my heart of hearts, that he would come back.

CHAPTER 11

*J*woke up shrouded in darkness. I sat up in the bed and glanced at the window. The outdoor lights were on.

Damn. I'd slept the entire day away.

The doorbell chimed, and I scrambled out of bed.

I glanced at my reflection and stopped in my tracks.

Despite not having any makeup on, my skin looked fabulous, and my eyes sparkled. My eyes were still red from crying, otherwise I looked pretty damn good. I threw on some yoga pants and a white, long-sleeved shirt.

I hurried to the front door and caught myself before rounding the corner. I stopped and took a deep breath.

Maybe Miles was back to say how sorry he was with a bouquet of roses and tears in his eyes. Perhaps he was utterly and truly apologetic and hated himself more than he could say. He didn't want to lose our family. He didn't want to lose me.

I forced myself to walk slowly to the door. He needed to wait as much as I needed to see his face. He needed to wait on me.

I tried looking through the glass but couldn't see clearly. I'd forgotten to turn on the front lights, and the shadowy figure was impossible to make out. I grabbed the doorknob, took a deep breath, and opened the door.

"Rachel, thank God. I was beginning to think you weren't going to answer." Liz Thomas, my neighbor and the head of the neighborhood book club stood in a long, red wool coat and brown boots. She held up two bottles of wine and pushed her way inside before I could stop her. Liz's husband Michael was an anesthesiologist that worked at the hospital with Miles.

Holy shit. It was book club night. The one night a month where the ladies in our neighborhood gathered with wine to discuss the book we'd read.

The book discussion usually only took ten minutes. The wine drinking took two hours. Basically, it was a wine club disguised as a book club. Calling it a book club looked better to the Baptists in the neighborhood, though.

"Liz…I completely forgot about book club." I stood like a deer in headlights.

"I figured you did. With this freak snowstorm in the middle of March, you probably thought no one would show up." She grinned, showing a set of perfect, white teeth. "Don't worry. I called the other girls, and they are on their way. Everyone has to walk over since they can't get their cars out of the driveway." Liz narrowed her eyes suspiciously. "Rachel, are you feeling okay? Your eyes are all red."

"I…I have a cold." My brain kicked in, and I answered quickly. If they thought I was sick, then maybe they would go home.

Liz was a free spirit, a stay-at-home wife who loved to paint abstract art and practice yoga. She usually dressed in boho chic fashion, the only woman I knew who could pull that look off. Paired with her short, jet-black hair and large, blue eyes, the style totally worked for her.

The doorbell rang again. Liz shoved the wine bottles at me and pulled off her coat to reveal a flowing, floral-print dress paired with tights. She turned and opened the door.

"Thank God, book club is back on." Meredith Groves sauntered in, wearing a knit hat with an oversized camouflage jacket. She'd pulled her blond hair up into a ponytail and had forgone any makeup. She pulled off her coat, revealing a sweatshirt and jeans. She had tucked her jeans into polka-dot rain boots. Meredith's husband, Allen, was a drug rep.

"If I had to spend ten more minutes with my kids, I was going to lose my mind." Meredith didn't smile as she spoke. She had three children all under the age of five. She was one of the few moms in the neighborhood that didn't dress to impress. She hated Pinterest, freely spoke her mind, and didn't give a rat's ass who she offended. I secretly wished I could be more like her and not try to please everyone.

"Why isn't the wine open?" Meredith shot me a death stare. I didn't mind. At least she hadn't commented on my appearance, unlike Liz, who noticed everything.

"I'm not feeling well. I think I'm getting a cold." The quicker they left, the better.

"Perfect. If you get sick, then I get sick. Bobby will be forced to take a day off and take care of the kids," Meredith said dryly. "Pour the wine, and I'll drink after you to make sure I catch whatever you have."

Liz cringed and gave Meredith a serious side-eye. Meredith didn't notice because she was already making her way into my kitchen to the cabinet where I kept my wine glasses.

"I was telling Meredith that I forgot about book club

tonight. I'm sorry." I coughed for good measure. "Plus, I'm not feeling well."

"Here, just sit over there." Meredith pointed to my barstool. "I'll fix you a glass of wine. You'll feel better after that. Or, you'll throw up. Not sure which."

Before I could say another word, the doorbell rang again. Female voices and laughter filled the house.

Judith Beckett, Michelle Adams, and Gina Randle walked into the kitchen, all bundled up in their winter coats and laughing at something Gina had said.

"Rachel, I brought my famous sugar cookies. You know the ones with the decorative icing." Judith smiled and opened the lid on her box as she waited on compliments from the other women. Judith was married to John, who was the President of the bank. Judith was a housewife who made Martha Stewart look like a slacker. Everything she did was perfection.

I could only stare at the cookies. They were gorgeous, something one might only see in a famous French bakery. They looked like Victorian embroidery with tiny flowers and snowflakes. It must have taken her days to decorate them. They were too pretty to eat.

"How many calories do these have? Are they gluten-free?" Gina picked up an intricately decorated snowflake with white and pale blue icing and studied it carefully. Gina pulled off her coat, revealing black yoga pants and a matching zip-up top with thumb holes in the sleeves. Gina was the athlete of our book club. She had shoulder-length, blond hair, soft brown eyes, and an incredibly slim body, which she achieved from miles of running and taking a spin class every day. She counted every calorie and fat gram in everything she put into her mouth. Gina was married to Harvey who was an investment manager.

"I don't know how you do it." Michelle shook her head. "I

barely have time to get a shower every day. I'd never have time to make cookies as beautiful as those."

Michelle's light brown hair hung in loose waves over her shoulder. She'd worn a pretty red blouse that flowed with each movement, and black jeans tucked into tall boots. Michelle always looked stylish, but she was also on the run all the time, hurrying from one child's activity to the next, so she kept things basic and rarely accessorized. She had twin boys in second grade. She was married to Stanley who own the local furniture store in Charming.

"I got the idea off Pinterest." Judith placed the box of cookies down on my kitchen counter and turned to me with a frown. "Rachel, are you feeling okay? You look a bit pale."

Out of all the housewives, Judith was my least favorite. It wasn't because she always showed up looking picture-perfect with her beautiful, long, brown hair and professional makeup, and her designer jeans, heels, and strand of pearls. It wasn't the fact that, unlike the majority of us, she worked outside the house as an interior decorator. Even with that, she managed to keep her home neat as a pin, and her two girls dressed like they were going to Sunday brunch. It wasn't even the fact that her husband doted on her like she was a queen. The reason I resented Judith was because she was always so full of energy. It both annoyed and drained me at the same time.

But, right now, in my moment of desperation with my world falling apart, I loved Judith. I knew that, out of all these women, Judith would do the right thing and send me to bed and make everyone leave. Judith would do the perfect thing because that's what she was. Perfect.

"Actually, I'm not feeling well. I think I got whatever's going around." I knew I could be vague about my illness. There was always something going around school when you had kids.

Michelle frowned and took a step back.

I liked Michelle because she made no bones about not being the perfect mom. If she managed to feed her kids without someone going into a meltdown or gluing the dog's tail to the floor, she counted it as a win. Michelle's husband wasn't much for helping around the house, especially when it came to cleaning up. In truth, Michelle was raising and taking care of three kids instead of two.

Gina shook her head and took the glass of wine that Meredith shoved into her hand.

"This should make you feel better." Meredith handed me a glass and poured a liberal amount of red wine into it. "Alcohol will kill anything. Trust me." Meredith frowned and then looked at me. "Wait, we're missing Nikki."

"She's not coming tonight," I managed to speak. That bitch would never be allowed inside my house ever again.

"Too bad. Let's move into the dining room and get started, shall we?" Judith smiled and waved everyone into the room like it was her home. Usually, I was a much better hostess, but after the last twenty-four hours and with my life now in shambles, I figured I was doing well just to have avoided a nervous breakdown in front of the group. If that happened, my secret would be out, and everyone would know that my perfect husband had cheated on me.

"So, our book this month is Karen Marie Moning's *DARK FEVER*." Meredith held up the book on her Kindle. "Did everyone read it?" She narrowed her eyes and looked around the room.

Everyone's head was down.

It was a well-known fact that a lot of our group lied. I looked at Michelle and already knew that bitch hadn't even opened the first page. She was looking intently at her wine glass instead of making eye contact. Half the time, she didn't even show up for book club, or when she did, it usually came out that she really hadn't read the book. She needed book club more than most of us, though, as it was a couple of hours away from the mayhem that was her life.

Judith took a tiny bite of her cookie and gave Meredith her full attention. Judith read the book. I knew because Judith was a perfectionist. She wouldn't just read the book, she'd write a review online about it and listen to the audio version, as well. Judith was an overachiever. And probably secretly hated by the rest of the women because none of us measured up to her lofty standards.

I looked at Gina. Gina was hard to figure out. But because she was so disciplined, I figured she probably read the whole book. Or at least enough to know what the hell the plot was about.

I looked at Meredith. She pulled some paper out of her purse. I arched my brow. She had questions written up. I was surprised. Meredith wasn't usually this prepared. I craned my neck and noticed that she'd pulled the list from the internet.

A smile played on my lips. I knew then that Meredith hadn't read the book. She'd probably just read the blurb to get an idea of what it was about. That's why she had the questions from the internet: to distract us.

"Rachel, what did you think about the book?" Meredith looked directly at me.

"I loved it. I've read her entire series. I know that we don't usually read paranormal, so that's why I picked this book." I looked at the other women. For just a moment, talking about books and being forced to interact with these ladies made me forget my problems.

"I love Karen Marie Moning. I'll read anything by her," I added. I meant it, too. Right then, I wished I had some powerful magic of my own to make the nightmare of my life go away.

"What about you, Michelle?" Meredith looked at her and took a sip of wine.

Michelle went wide-eyed and then blinked several times. I kind of felt bad for her.

"I loved the heroine. Very unique." She grabbed a decorative sugar cookie and shoved the whole thing into her mouth.

"What about the character did you like?" Meredith cocked her head.

Michelle pointed to her mouth and held up a finger as she slowly chewed the cookie.

"Well, I loved the book," Judith spoke up and set her glass of wine down on my dining room table. She stood so everyone could focus their attention on her.

"I found the plot intriguing and interesting. And the hero, very sexy. She tells the story in a way that is magical. The way she pulls you into the story and makes you want more is the touch of a true artist." She grew serious and nodded at the rest of us. "You know, in that respect, I find I have a lot in common with Karen Marie."

"You do?" Gina frowned.

"I truly do." Judith placed her hand over her heart. "You see, we are both creative artists. We just work in different mediums. She crafts the perfectly honed word, while I, well. I use…"

"Dough?" Meredith snorted.

Judith's smile faltered, but she quickly recovered. "You see, an artist's way is different for different people. While Karen Marie touches people with her words and worlds, I touch people with my time-consuming crafts that bring a smile to everyone's face."

"Why the hell is she referring to the author as 'Karen Marie?'" Gina leaned over and whispered to me. "I'm pretty sure she doesn't know her personally."

I bit my lip. I felt a chuckle growing deep in my gut and knew what would happen if it just rolled out. For the first time in twenty-four hours, ever since my life had gone to hell in a handbasket, I was on the verge of laughing. Not just laughing but laughing my ass off until I hurt.

"Yes, well, I'm sure what you just described is wine. Wine brings a smile to everyone's face." Meredith snorted.

"I found that this book touched me in a way that made me want to connect more deeply with these characters." Judith ignored Meredith's comment and kept talking.

Michelle shrugged and took another cookie and dipped it into her wine before taking a bite.

Judith's eyes grew wide at the irreverent act Michelle had just committed against her confectionary art.

"Judith, why are you referring to the author as Karen Marie? Do you know her?" Gina arched her brow.

"How about we stay on track." Meredith clutched her paper and scanned it for her next question.

"How about we just drink wine. Wine is what I need." Michelle stared into her glass and then took a large drink.

"Easy, girl, you still have to make it home. Don't need you stumbling and falling in the street. You might get run over." Gina laughed.

I froze. An image flew through my mind, one of being in the street and cold.

Of seeing Miles with someone else. In our bed.

I grabbed my wine glass and downed it. The harsh oaky taste burned my throat, but I didn't care. I'd rather that pain instead of the one in my heart.

"Gosh, Rachel. You must really feel bad." Michelle gaped at me.

"I do." I cleared my throat and did my best to give everyone a sheepish smile. I didn't feel embarrassed. I felt like a fraud and a fool.

Worst of all, I felt utterly alone.

"Poor thing." Judith's mouth dropped into a frown, and she grabbed my faux fur throw off the ottoman in the living room. She hurried over to me, draped it over my shoulders, and then patted my back.

I fought a cringe. I didn't want anyone to touch me. I felt raw and sore.

"I know just what you need," Judith said.

"To go to bed," I said. I didn't care if they thought me rude or not.

"First, you need a toddy." Gina cocked her head and studied me.

"Why don't I just go to bed." I honestly didn't feel like drinking anything. I was afraid it would come up.

"You need to get something warm in your stomach. It will help you sleep." Meredith walked into the kitchen.

I stood and followed after her, my throw slipping off my shoulders and falling to the floor on the way. It was my years of being a hostess that made me get up. I still felt like I needed to be serving them. It was my house, after all.

"You need some soup." Meredith stopped and turned to me. "Where do you keep your canned goods?"

"Oh, you really shouldn't eat anything from a can." Gina's eyes widened. "Too many additives. You should only eat whole, clean foods."

Meredith snorted. "When there's chicken noodle soup available without a can, let me know. Until then, I'm eating my soup from a can."

"In the pantry. Middle shelf." I didn't feel like putting up a fight anymore. At least if they thought I was sick, they wouldn't expect much from me.

Michelle and Judith joined us in the kitchen with their wine and cookies. Michelle had half a cookie dangling out of her mouth. She had a second cookie in her right hand, and her glass of wine in her left.

I'd heard Michelle complain too many times that the kids always ate her favorite cookies before she got a chance to have one. I guessed tonight she was over-compensating to make up for lost time. It would probably have to last her until next month's book club meeting.

Meredith had gathered a can of chicken noodle soup and dug out a pot from my cabinet. She began mixing the condensed contents with water over the stove to get it to the right consistency.

I didn't want soup. I didn't want wine. I didn't want book club.

I was heartbroken and dying inside, yet I knew I had to keep it together until they left.

"Here, honey. Sit down, and I'll get this served up." Judith smiled and gently pushed me down onto the barstool.

Her words were more irritating than comforting, and I had to bite my tongue.

Meredith ladled some chicken noodle soup into a pot and heated it on the stove. She then poured the soup into one of my decorative bowls. Judith swept in and took it out of her hands before Meredith could hand it to me. Meredith narrowed her gaze on the woman, and for a second, I thought she was going to say something.

"Here we go." Judith set the bowl in front of me and took the seat to my right.

"I think we should go." Gina glanced at the smartwatch on her wrist. I didn't know if she wanted to leave because she wanted to let me rest, or if she wanted to go because her watch was reminding her to get her steps in.

I didn't care. At that moment, Gina was my favorite.

"Do we have to? I don't think the kids are asleep yet." Michelle gave me puppy-dog eyes and then shoveled another cookie into her mouth. I knew she didn't have much of a life and never put herself first. So, just getting cookies without having to hide them from her kids was a big deal. "Anyone know any gossip?"

I forgot to breathe.

"No, but I did hear on the news that a woman is missing. Samantha Sims is her name." Judith shook her head. "She's a student at Ole Miss."

"I heard about that on the radio. Said she went missing last night during the snowstorm," Gina said. "Can you imagine what her poor parents are going through?"

I managed to relax a little. The conversation had turned from me, and that's all I cared about.

"Poor girl. I bet they're going to find her car in a ditch somewhere. And her, frozen to death," Michelle said.

"I'm going to add her to my prayer list, "Judith stated and gave a solemn nod.

"Well, while you're at it, you might as well add Dr. Franks to the list." Meredith snorted. "His wife just left him for her yoga instructor."

"But isn't the yoga instructor a woman?" Michelle asked.

"Oh, yeah. They said Dr. Franks nearly had a heart attack. The wife cleaned out his bank account and filed for divorce, right before flying to New York."

"Damn. That's rough," Gina said.

I could feel the heat rising in my face. If they knew about Dr. Franks, then they would surely find out about Miles.

"Rachel, are you okay? You really don't look so good," Liz stated. "Maybe we should go."

"Book club is for two hours, minimum. That's the rule." Meredith looked at Liz, waiting for her to challenge the statement. "When we started this group, we knew things were going to crop up and demand our attention. The rule is two hours. We've only been here thirty minutes."

I felt nauseated to the point of passing out. I wasn't going to make it ten minutes with these ladies, let alone two hours.

I clutched my stomach and shoved away from the island. I ran to the closest bathroom.

I was going to be sick.

I locked the door and knelt in front of the toilet.

"Honey, are you okay?" Judith's sugary-sweet voice called from the other side of the door.

"No. I think I have the flu." I sat on the floor and leaned against the cold wall, slamming my eyes shut.

"We need to go," Gina insisted. "I'm training for a marathon, and I don't need the flu."

"Yeah. She's right," I said. "If your kids catch this, it's going to mean cleaning up vomit twenty-four-seven."

I heard collective gasps from the other side of the door. I could picture Michelle's look of horror as she thought about mopping up vomit from her three little ones. A door slammed, and I was pretty sure Gina was the first to leave.

"You're right, Rachel. I'm heading home. Feel better," Michelle said as she rushed past the bathroom door.

"Bye, Rachel," Liz called out.

"I'll call and check on you in the morning," Judith said. I knew she was going home to Clorox her entire house.

"Fine. Fine," Meredith said. "Hope you feel better, Rachel. Remember, book club is at Gina's next month. She still has to pick the book."

I didn't dare move from my position on the floor until I heard the last footstep followed by the door closing.

I reached up, opened the door, and peeked out.

I was, once again, alone.

I should have felt relieved, but I didn't. Loneliness descended on me so quickly that it stole my breath away. I scrambled up from the floor and headed into the kitchen to grab my phone off the counter and check my messages.

Nothing. Miles hadn't called.

I had no one to call and talk to. No one that would understand.

I punched in some numbers and held the phone to my ear. I held my breath until my daughter's sweet phone voice came over the phone line.

"Hello?"

"Arianna. Hey, sweetie." I swallowed back the lump in my throat and tried to sound happy. I didn't want my daughter to sense anything weird going on.

"Hey, Mom. What's up?" Her bored tone made me smile.

"What are you guys doing?" I swiped at the tears trailing down my face and took a deep breath.

"We're on Snapchat."

"What's Snapchat?"

"It's an app. Where you take selfies. You can morph the pictures or make yourself look like a rabbit and stuff."

"Ah, sounds like fun." Just when I had mastered Facebook, there was another app to learn.

"Well, not when you say it like that." Again, her boredom came through the phone loud and clear. "What's wrong? You sound weird."

"Ah, nothing. Just missing you and Gabby."

"Well, she went to bed early because she clearly can't hang with the big girls. One movie, and she was down for the count." Arianna snorted.

"Be nice to your sister, Arianna."

"I will." I heard the hesitation in her voice. "Mom, is everything okay? Are you home alone?"

"Well, I am now. Just finished up book club."

"You mean wine club. Let's not kid ourselves, shall we?"

A laugh bubbled out of me at my daughter's words. If anyone in the world could make me feel better, it was her.

"We had to cut the meeting short."

"Someone get too wasted?"

"Arianna, no." I forced the authority back to my voice. "I just wasn't feeling well. So, we cut it short. I'm sure it's just a bug, and I'll be right as rain in the morning."

"Well, if you're not, and I catch it, can I stay home from school Monday?

"Only if you're really sick," I said. "And, like I said, I'm sure it will be gone by the time you come home. So, you need to make sure you have all your homework done on Sunday night."

"Ugh. You're no fun." She groaned just as a girl's giggle came over the phone. "I've got to go. I'll see you tomorrow."

"Okay, sweetie, love you."

"Ditto, Mom." She hung up the phone.

She never would say she loved me back when she was around her friends. I understood that, but tonight I needed to hear it more than ever.

All I wanted to do was put on my PJs and climb into bed.

I made my way through the empty house, turning off the lights as I went. I walked into my bedroom and refused to look at my bed. I didn't think I could ever look at it the same way. Instead, I looked at my reflection in the mirror. Despite my broken heart and lack of makeup, I still looked pretty. My eyes were shining, and my skin looked even more youthful. I stepped closer and turned my face to look at my crow's feet.

They were gone.

I'd always done my best to moisturize, use sunscreen, and do the occasional preventative Botox. I knew I was approaching my forties, and I didn't want to go down without a fight.

While those things had helped, they hadn't erased the tiny lines around my eyes when I smiled.

Now, they were gone.

I unbuttoned my shirt and shimmied out of my jeans. I

threw them both on the floor and walked over to the full-length mirror in my walk-in closet.

I gasped.

When I got dressed, I'd noticed that I had lost weight. Now, my body looked firmer, and my stretch marks were gone. I turned to look at my butt. And...oh my God, my butt! It was small and firm and looked amazing.

I looked absolutely amazing.

"What the hell? How can this be?" I stepped closer and pulled off my bra and panties and let them fall to the floor.

I reached down and touched my breasts. They were full but firm. And very sensitive. I hissed as I ran my fingers across my nipple.

"It's like I'm aging in reverse." I blinked. Maybe I was hallucinating. When I woke up in the morning, I'd probably have gained twenty pounds and have my crow's feet back. Perhaps even my husband.

The doorbell chimed, and I jumped. Miles. He must be coming back to me.

I grabbed my robe and threw it on. I ran my hands through my hair and quickly tied the sash. I ran out of the bedroom and straight into a wall of steely brawn.

I didn't remember Miles having so much muscle on him.

I blinked as the wall of muscle grew arms and reached down to steady me.

I looked up and froze at the sight of my kidnapper.

"What the hell are you doing here?" I stepped back and tried to look fierce. "And how the hell did you get inside? I locked all the doors."

"I have a key." He held up the extra set that I kept in my purse in case I ever got locked out of my car.

"You asshole. Give me those." I made a grab for them, but he held them out of my reach. The dude was as tall as a mountain. "How the hell did you get those?"

"I swiped them the last time I was here." He shrugged.

"You what?" I cringed at his smell and covered my nose with my hand. "You really should think about stepping up your hygiene game. I'm not sure how I didn't smell you coming from a mile away when you kidnapped me."

"That's because you were splattered on the highway, like roadkill," he replied casually.

"Which reminds me, I need to call the cops." I turned, but he caught me by my arm and spun me around.

"You won't do that." A slight smile played at the corner of his lips, and his eyes darkened.

"Don't think I won't." I tried to act brave, but my quivering voice betrayed me.

"All right, then. Go right ahead. And while you're at it, you should tell them that you were beheaded and that I saved you by giving you my blood and now you're a vampire."

I gritted my teeth. "I think you're full of shit. If I was a vampire, I'd be drinking blood. And the only thing I've had tonight was wine."

"That's because you're not fully turned yet. Becoming a vampire is a process." He shook his head. "Don't you listen when people talk? I already told you this. Maybe if you weren't so self-absorbed, you would listen when others speak."

"You don't know anything about me, you overgrown, smelly, skunk guy." I shoved my finger into his muscled chest with each word, wincing at the resistance. I think I jammed my knuckle.

"I know everything I need to. Housewives like you are a dime a dozen." He narrowed his gaze on me. I could feel the hatred pouring off him.

"You know nothing about me." Something inside me cracked, not out of fear but from sadness.

"You don't have to work because your husband is a doctor

or lawyer. You stay home with the kids, you probably have two, and you drive a luxury car. You fill your days with meaningless activities like chauffeuring your children to activities, and in between that, you go to exercise classes then meet up with your other skinny-ass friends for Starbucks, where you order a drink and substitute everything in it when you should have ordered a black coffee. You don't leave your house without having all your makeup on and dressed to the nines. You host parties where you serve up wine, appetizers, and insults. You spend your days worrying over every little line in your face and fighting time in the mirror. You bring nothing to society except your disdain for others who make less than thirty-five thousand a year, and you wouldn't be caught dead in anything sold at Target." He said all of this as if ticking the items off a list.

The air whooshed out of my lungs at his harsh assessment. I blinked back tears that were stinging the backs of my eyes as loneliness overwhelmed my heart.

I swallowed and met his gaze.

"If I'm so worthless, why are you here?" I lifted my chin and fought to keep my lip from quivering. I felt as if he'd just stabbed me in the chest.

"Because I'm your Maker now. And under vampire law, I'm obligated to help you. You have to leave your human life and come live as a vampire. It's my duty to show you how to survive."

"Obligation. Duty." The words sliced through my chest and I wasn't sure why. I hated this man. He'd kidnapped me. He'd turned my life upside down. He'd taken my humanity —*if* I believed him.

So why did it hurt to hear him be so dismissive?

I began to tremble, and I wasn't sure if I was going to start crying or hitting. Either choice would be bad.

Gathering up my anger and desperation like armor, I looked him in the eye and swallowed the lump in my throat.

"I'm no one's obligation or duty. I release you of any responsibility you have for me. From here on out, you are free." I turned on my heel and headed for the bedroom.

Like Miles, I listened to see if he followed.

And like Miles, the stranger did not.

CHAPTER 12

I did not sleep in my bedroom last night. Instead, I lay in the guest bed, staring at the ceiling and contemplating what I had done to deserve being betrayed. I must have drifted off right before dawn because, when the alarm went off at six, I didn't want to get out of bed. I must have hit the alarm at least five times before forcing my feet to the floor.

As much as I wanted to sleep, the crippling fear of losing everything: my family, my marriage, and my home had me crawling out of bed and into the shower.

After showering, I made an effort and put on makeup and get dressed. I didn't feel more put-together, and every movement was painful. But I knew if Miles were to come home, I wanted to look my best—not necessarily for him, but for me.

I stood near the Italian coffeepot and waited until the coffee was finished brewing. I grabbed my cup and poured in equal parts sugar and cream.

I took a sip and immediately spit it out, spraying coffee all over my white quartz countertop.

I cringed and looked down into my cup. I poured that cup

of coffee down the drain and sniffed the carton of creamer. It didn't smell sour. Maybe my stomach couldn't handle the sugar.

I rinsed out my cup and set it back under the coffee maker. I thought about just adding creamer, but the thought turned my stomach. Instead, I lifted the freshly brewed black coffee to my lips.

It slid down my throat in a cozy, warm rush.

I liked it. That was odd since I preferred my coffee doctored with ample cream and sugar. But drinking it this way would save me calories so I wouldn't complain.

I quickly cleaned up the spilled coffee from the counter and sat on a stool at the kitchen island.

Despite my physical exhaustion, my mind raced. I knew I couldn't just wait around for Miles to come home. I had to do something. Anything. I got up and headed for my laptop. I turned it on and settled on my couch, scouring the internet, looking up statistics on infidelity and divorce. A lot of the advice was stuff I'd heard before: once a cheater, always a cheater.

The statistics on how many husbands cheat floored me, though. Some sites offered hope, saying that an affair was an indicator that something had broken within the marriage.

That information hit me like a ton of bricks. Had I been so blind as to not notice that something was wrong? Had I done this to us?

There was so much information on affairs that it was staggering. There were different kinds of dalliances, and not all of them meant the end of a marriage. Some couples said their marriage was even stronger after the indiscretion.

I had gotten on the internet to find hope, yet I only found my anger.

It made no sense. If Miles were unhappy, why hadn't he said anything? Why not *tell* me that he wanted a different life? And how did I think he could have an affair and then just come home?

I was torturing myself, yet I couldn't help it. I was like an addict craving another hit, but instead of drugs, I needed information. I needed to know everything, or I wouldn't be able to get over it. Hell, who was I fooling? I may not get over it even *after* learning everything.

What Miles did was unfathomable and unforgivable.

The phone rang, jerking me out of my self-inflicted torture. I answered it before even looking to see who it was.

"Hello?"

"Rachel." Miles' voice came over the phone, slow and low.

My stomach tumbled into a nauseating freefall.

"Yes?" I couldn't think of anything else to say. As much as I wanted answers, that simple greeting was the only thing I could force myself to voice.

"We need to talk."

"Okay." My mouth went dry, and my heart raced. I wasn't feeling hopeful, I feared the unknown. I cleared my throat. "Do you want to come over this afternoon?"

"Yes. I'd like that."

"Okay." I didn't say anything else. I waited for him to say "I love you" like he always did.

"I'll see you then."

The line went dead.

My heart ached, and I knew that whatever happened tonight would set the stage for the rest of my life.

* * *

AFTER MILES HAD HUNG UP, I moved to search on the internet for a different topic. I typed in *how to react when your husband reveals an affair*. Knowing Miles, who never took responsibility for anything, I also typed in *how to prepare for a divorce when you find out your husband is cheating.*

There were several betrayed wives' sites with more details than I wanted to know. The first point they all shared was to secure the money. Apparently, once your husband cheats, it makes him a liar. Cheating doesn't exist without lies. Miles was now both a cheater and a liar.

The article stated that a liar will do anything to hide their assets in the event it looks like a divorce is on the horizon.

Financial security had always been important to me. Not because I wanted Louboutin's and Rolex watches. No, I'd grown up in the foster care system, where I never knew where my next meal was coming from or if I would have shoes to wear. Financial security was *necessary* to me. As important as air.

I pulled up the bank accounts and studied them, looking for large expenditures or withdrawals. I breathed out a sigh of relief when the balances looked right.

I still had a couple of hours until Miles arrived, so I made a list of questions to ask him, to get the details of the affair.

My cell phone rang, and I looked at the caller ID.

Nikki.

My blood ran cold, and the anger resurfaced.

Nikki. My ex-best friend, who had fucked my husband.

I wanted to hear her voice, wanted to see how she would explain sleeping with Miles. To find out exactly what kind of person did that to their best friend. More than that, I wanted to hear her apologize for tearing my family apart.

I held my finger over the *Accept* button. I really wanted to push it. I really, really, really wanted to hear what the bitch had to say. While I was trying to get my anger under control, the call went to voicemail.

I lowered my head and counted the seconds it would take

to leave a message before pulling up the voicemail on my phone.

"You have no new messages."

I screamed. The bitch didn't even have the decency to leave a voicemail.

I glanced at the time.

I wanted nothing more than to go over to Nikki's house and tell her husband, Brad what she'd done. He would be devastated. But, hell, apparently everyone in this situation would end up devastated except the cheaters.

I warred with what I wanted versus what I needed to do.

My sensible side won out. The part that said I needed to get all my ducks in a row.

So, I went back to my research on the internet. I found information on how to make your marriage work after infidelity, along with a list of things the betrayed spouse needed from the cheater. It said that boundaries were important.

I quickly printed off all that info so I could study it while I prepared for my meeting with Miles.

CHAPTER 13

I'd dressed in black jeans and a fitted cream blouse that clung to my new, slender body. I carefully applied my makeup and straightened my long, black hair. While the other moms sported cute, shorter locks, I'd stuck with long hair because Miles had always preferred it that way.

My mind went right back to Nikki. She and I were as different in appearance as apples and oranges.

I had long, dark hair that almost looked black, while she sported short, blond hair. My eyes were dark blue, and hers were brown. I was a little on the tall side, while she was short.

It made me sick to think that someone I knew so well could betray me—in the most horrific way possible.

I heard the garage door open, and my heart jumped into my throat.

I wanted to be prepared for this meeting. I needed to be. If I lost it, then I would lose whatever footing I had.

I quickly slipped into my red heels and headed out of the bathroom. Once again, I avoided looking at the bed.

My heels made sharp tapping sounds on the hardwood floors and became even louder when I headed into the kitchen.

Miles was standing in the kitchen with his hands in his pockets when I walked in. He hadn't bothered to shave and had a thick five-o'clock shadow that contrasted with his neatly pressed shirt.

Just looking at him made my heart ache. I held my breath, waiting for him to open his arms. I wanted to run into them, to feel his sorrow and then feel safe again.

"Hi," he said.

"Hi." My voice was but a whisper. My hopes dwindled as Miles stood there, unmoving. His voice sounded foreign to me. He felt like a stranger to me.

I swallowed and forced back my tears. I didn't want him to see me cry. Didn't want him to think me weak. I was going to stay strong. I had to.

He walked towards me, and my heart swelled with hope. This was it. He was going to tell me how sorry he was and how much he loved me.

He ducked his head and went around me to the wine refrigerator. He bent down and pulled out a bottle of cabernet.

"Let's have some wine," he said.

Wine? Who the hell wanted wine? We never had wine in the afternoon.

Fear rose up in my chest and marched up my throat. I braced myself while he pulled out two wine glasses from the cabinet and opened the bottle of red.

My legs felt weak. I slid onto a stool at the island to stop from falling down.

And I waited.

He poured the wine and slid a glass towards me.

The distance between us frightened me.

Miles took a sip of the wine and shoved his free hand back into his jeans' pocket. He glanced out the window into the backyard, never once meeting my eyes.

My stomach was rock-hard. Questions rose up in my mind, and I was afraid I might split open like an overripe watermelon.

"Where did you spend the night?" I vomited the words because he wasn't offering me anything.

"I got a hotel room." His reply was measured, calm.

"Have you talked to Nikki?" I hated even saying her name. It felt like a knife to my heart, knowing that someone I loved like a sister had betrayed me.

He didn't meet my eyes but stared straight ahead. "It was a one-time thing. It won't ever happen again."

Disgust swelled and rose in my stomach. "That's it? That's all you have to say?"

"What do you want me to say?" He looked at me. There was nothing in his eyes. Not guilt. Not sorrow. Not regret. All I saw was irritation.

"I'm supposed to do what? Sweep it under the rug and forget all about it?"

"Look, Rachel, we have a good life together. It won't happen again. Let's move on." He casually took a drink of his wine then met my gaze.

In this moment, Miles was more of a monster than the guy who'd kidnapped me. At least that asshole had brought my car back.

Fury swelled inside me until I thought I might burst. I picked up my wine and threw it in his face.

"Are you crazy?" he sputtered and wiped the red liquid out of his incredulous eyes.

"Get the fuck out of my house," I said, low and lethal. Visions of impaling him on the gate of our subdivision danced in my head. I wanted him to feel pain. I wanted to hurt him like he'd hurt me.

"Rachel, don't be rash," he warned.

"If you don't get the fuck out of my house, I'm going to shoot your ass." I meant it. So, help me God, I meant every single word.

"Rachel." He took a step towards me.

I ran back to the guest bedroom and locked the door behind me. I picked up the pillow I'd slept on and stuffed my face into it as I screamed.

The foam muffled the sound, but nothing could disguise the way my heart had seemingly shattered into shards of thin, red glass in my chest.

"Rachel, open the door." Miles banged on the wood, and I was tempted to open it. But, I knew if I did, I would likely inflict bodily harm on him. I'd never been so angry in my life.

Then again, I'd never been so betrayed before.

I laid down on the floor and curled up into a ball. Tears streamed down my face as I sobbed loudly, not caring who heard.

I wanted him to break down the door, to see what he had done to me, to see the pain he had caused.

He never did. Instead, I heard his car pull out of the garage, leaving me alone to drown in my pain.

* * *

I STARED up at the ceiling until my eyes ached from crying so much. I wasn't sure how much time had passed. I wanted to go to sleep and wake up to discover that this had been nothing more than a nightmare.

My heart, however, told me that this was not a dream and I wouldn't just wake up and find that everything was fine.

I'd just stepped into a waking nightmare.

I turned my head, and my gaze found a small picture of me, Arianna, and Gabby that Miles had taken while we were on vacation. We were at an amusement park and standing in front of a castle. The princess had stepped out and stopped to talk to my girls. My daughters both told me how much I looked like that princess. And in response, I had said their father was my prince.

I'd been wrong. He was no prince. He was a monster.

My heart squeezed and ached for my girls. What would happen to us? What would happen to our home?

Those articles I'd seen had said that once a man had been caught cheating, he would either deny it completely or admit everything because he wanted to get caught so the marriage would end.

Miles hadn't apologized. Nor had he really admitted anything. Of course, he wouldn't take responsibility.

The doorbell rang, jolting me out of my circling thoughts.

I stayed on the floor, hoping that whoever it was would go away.

The chime sounded again and again and again. If it were a neighbor, they would have gone away by now. It was probably a salesperson. There was nothing I hated more than door-to-door salespeople.

I forced myself off the floor and ran my hands through my hair. I didn't bother looking at my reflection as I passed the mirror. I could care less what anyone thought. Maybe if I looked as bad as I felt, they would go away sooner.

I barely noticed the cold hardwood under my feet. All I wanted was to get rid of whoever was ringing my doorbell. I just wanted to be alone.

I grabbed the door handle and threw open the door, glaring at the intruder on my stoop.

My kidnapper glared back at me.

My anger intensified. "Go away."

I shut the door, but he stuck his large boot in the doorway like he had the night before and forced his way inside.

I no longer cared. I turned to walk away, but he grabbed my arm.

"You look like hell, Roadkill."

"No shit, Sherlock. I feel like hell," I shouted. I wrenched out of his grasp. "Go away." I could feel the threat of tears behind my eyes again, and I didn't want to cry in front of him.

"What's wrong?" His voice, deep and low, sparked something in my chest.

I didn't know if it was the stress I was under or the fact that my own cheating husband didn't have the decency to ask about my emotional needs. Maybe it was because I had, apparently, been decapitated, only to be turned into a vampire by a rancid stranger.

But the second the guy said those two words, I fell apart.

Tears streamed down my face as I sobbed. I buried my face in my hands and slid to the floor in a heap.

The cold winter air whipped in from the open front door. I didn't have the strength to crawl over and shut it.

I didn't care about anything at that moment.

I barely noticed when the guy silently walked over to the door and closed it, shutting out the winter wind and shielding me from the cold.

I didn't flinch when he walked back over to me and knelt, putting his arm around my back and under my legs to lift me into his arms.

I didn't even fight when he stood and carried me to the master bedroom.

"No, not there."

He didn't say a word. Instead, he turned away and headed to the guest bedroom where'd I'd taken up residence ever since my life had turned upside down.

He gently laid me down and pulled the unmade covers over me.

I didn't say anything about his odor, despite him smelling very skunky and dirty because he was the only person who'd shown me any kindness.

And he had been my kidnapper.

"You need to eat," he said, looking down at me and tugging the covers up to my chin.

"I can't eat. I can't see how I'll ever survive this."

His eyes narrowed. "You are now more powerful than you were. You'll survive this."

"Have you ever had someone betray you? Someone you thought you could trust with your heart and your life?" I looked at him through tearstained eyes.

"Yes."

"How did you go on?"

"I became a vampire." He shrugged. "I outlived them."

"Tell me something."

"I may not have the answer."

"You're a man. I need to hear a man's perspective."

He waited for my question.

"Why do men cheat on their wives? Why do they risk their families, their marriage, and ignore their vows for sex?"

He blinked and looked at me. "Not all men cheat."

"I used to think that." I laughed. "Now, I know I was wrong."

"Not all men cheat, just the weak ones. There are still men who refuse to harm someone they love. Men who would take their last breath to remain faithful. Perhaps you should be asking why you are still with a man who would cheat?" He stood.

His words struck me, wounded me.

"He wasn't like this when we got married." I lifted my quivering chin.

"Wasn't he?" He turned to go out the door. "Go to sleep. You will soon have to start sleeping in the day and getting up at night. You have a few more weeks before your body starts to demand it. Might as well start now."

"Wait." I turned to look at him.

He stopped and looked at me over his shoulder. "What?"

He turned fully then, giving me his undivided attention.

"Why did you come here?"

"I could feel your pain. It was all-consuming, and I couldn't sleep."

"You feel what I feel?" My eyes widened.

"Only if it's a powerful emotion."

"So, you came to check on me?"

"I came to make it stop so I could get some rest." His eyes blazed.

His words stung, and I decided it made me like him less. Not that I liked him a whole lot to begin with.

"Are you going to keep showing up at my house unannounced?"

"Yes, until you decide to leave this life and come live with me so I can show you how to be a vampire."

"Not happening," I pouted.

He said nothing, just turned to go.

"I have another question."

"What?" he snarled as he stopped, but he didn't turn to look at me this time.

"What's your name?"

He stayed quiet, and I wondered if he'd answer.

"If you don't tell me, then I'll have to come up with a name like…Vinny the Vampire."

He turned and glared at me. I was unfazed. At least I'd gotten a reaction out of him. It was more than I'd gotten from Miles.

"My name is Khalan."

86

I watched him leave and listened as the door shut. Once again, I was alone.

I looked at the ceiling and laughed. For some reason, I was more disturbed that my husband had cheated on me than becoming a vampire.

* * *

THE RINGING of my phone jolted me out of a sound sleep.

I blinked and looked around. I was in the guest bedroom. Unease settled in my stomach at the new reality of my life.

I glanced toward the windows. It was just getting dark outside. The ringing phone pulled my attention back to the present, and I searched the bed for my cell.

My fingers finally found it tangled up in the comforter. I hit the button to answer without looking at the screen. I hated to admit it, but I was holding out hope that Miles was calling to apologize—or to at least check on me.

"Hello?"

"Mom, where are you? You were supposed to come pick us up two hours ago?" Arianna whined.

I glanced at the clock on the nightstand. Shit. I'd slept the whole damn day away and had forgotten to pick up my daughters. What the hell kind of mother did that?

"I'm on my way, sweetie. Make sure you and Gabby have everything packed."

"Can we stop by the Sugar Shack and get some ice cream?"

"Sure, sure." I ran to my closet to throw on some clothes.

"Mom, are you okay? You sound different?"

"I'm fine. Just grabbing my purse. I'll be there in a few minutes." I hung up the phone and stuffed my legs into some black yoga pants. I pulled on a long-sleeved T-shirt that said *Let It Snow* across the front.

I ran a brush through my hair and slid on my boots. I didn't have time for makeup, and at this point, I really didn't care. I needed to see my girls.

More than that, I needed to pull it together. I didn't know what I was going to tell them about their father. I didn't know what the future held. I didn't want them to worry.

I grabbed my keys and dropped them into my purse. I was halfway out the garage door when I realized I didn't have a coat on.

I ran back inside and grabbed my North Face jacket. It wasn't a snow coat, but it would have to do.

I walked into the garage and stopped. I had forgotten that Khalan had brought my Volvo back.

I climbed into my car and glanced at the passenger's seat. There sat the Jimmy Choo shoes I'd left at Khalan's when I escaped.

I turned down our street, and a wave of sadness swept over me. I looked from house to house, remembering how excited we had been when we first built our home in this neighborhood.

It was the most expensive neighborhood in the city and the only gated subdivision. We had struggled financially to get Miles through medical school, and when we picked the plot where we were going to build our house, I'd finally felt like things were looking up.

We'd been here for twelve years now. We'd made friends that would last a lifetime. Or so I thought.

I turned into the driveway of Maggie's house. Arianna and Lilly Rose had been friends since kindergarten. They did everything together. Had the same classes, same friends, even played the same sports. I hadn't been very athletic growing up, but both my girls had inherited their love of sports from their father and took both dance and soccer.

I stayed on the road, taking them from activity to activity while Miles built his career and made a name for himself.

It had felt like we were a team, working together for our family.

Now, that team was fractured.

I pulled into the driveway and checked my reflection one last time. I was relieved to see that my eyes weren't red from all the crying. Instead, I looked bright and alert.

I slid out of the car. The wind whipped around me, and I noticed that yesterday's snow had melted a little. Now with the temps dropping, the ice would freeze, and I doubted that the kids would have school in the morning. That was one thing about the South. When it snowed, everything shut down.

I didn't snuggle down into my coat like I normally did. Tonight, I embraced the cold, hoping it would numb the pain in my heart.

I knocked on the front door of the sprawling two-story, brick house.

Maggie Nelson had decorated her home to the hilt for spring. A large wreath of brightly colored flowers and Easter eggs adorned the door. Two human-sized white bunnies stood sentry on either side of the porch, and large, pink, blue, and purple eggs were stuck in the landscaping around the front of the house.

Usually, Maggie's house made me feel all warm and cozy.

Now, looking at all the garish decorations made me sad. It felt as fake as my marriage.

Tears welled in my eyes, and I blinked them back before pressing the doorbell. The kids didn't need to see me like this. I had to stay strong for them.

The door swung open.

"Rachel! Come in, come in. You must be freezing." Maggie

smiled and waved me inside. She gave me a quick hug before scurrying off to the kitchen.

"As you can see, the girls had a great time." She nodded at the kitchen island littered with decorated Easter cookies, glittery, hard-boiled eggs, and a row of chocolate Easter baskets.

"I see that." I forced a smile and looked away. "I'm sorry I'm late."

"No worries. Lilly and Rose loved having your girls over for the weekend." Maggie grinned. "So tell me. Was Miles surprised to see you home?"

I froze. I'd forgotten that she knew I planned to surprise him.

"You have no idea." I swallowed

"Mom! You're here! We need to go if we're going to grab some ice cream before the Sugar Shack closes." Arianna gave me a worried look as she stuck her arms into her coat sleeves.

"That's right. They close early on Sunday." I gathered her against me and hugged her. She pulled away.

"Tell Gabby to hurry up." She frowned. "I told her fifteen minutes ago to get her shoes on, and she's still shoeless."

"Gabby, we need to go." I looked up at the top of the stairs and saw my youngest peeking at me over the banister.

She bounded down the stairs, dragging her coat and carrying her boots under her arms.

"You're late, Mommy," she said as I kissed her cheek.

"Sorry, sweetie. Time got away from me."

"It's okay. I got to play longer." She gave me her beautiful smile.

My heart ached with all the love swelling in my chest. I loved my girls more than anything.

And I feared that what Miles had done would destroy them.

Looking into the depths of my daughter's eyes, I knew I had to work this out, for them.

"Thanks for watching them, Maggie." I smiled at my friend. "I totally owe you one."

"Anytime." She smiled. Her husband Harry came around the corner and waved as he spotted me before snatching up a cookie.

The sight of their happiness was almost too much to bear. I herded my children out the front door into the cold night.

"Mommy, why don't we have bunnies like this?" Gabby brushed her fingers across one of the rabbit's arms as we walked by.

"Because Mom does a Christian theme at Easter, you know with crosses and lilies and stuff. She doesn't do rabbits and eggs." Arianna sighed and shook her head like she was trying to explain algebra to a child.

"So why don't we change it?" Gabby looked up at me, sniffed, and swiped her arm across her nose.

"Maybe I will." Maybe that's what we needed. To shake things up, try something different.

If Miles saw that I wasn't stuck in a rut and could bring some excitement back, maybe he'd be willing to work on our family.

What about what I wanted?

I wasn't sure what I wanted. I felt like I was trapped inside someone with multiple personalities. One minute I wanted to kill him; the next, I desperately wanted to see him.

"I guess the reason you're late is because you and Dad had a 'nap,'"—Arianna made air quotations with her fingers —"and you fell asleep."

"If they're taking a nap, of course, they fell asleep." Gabby glared at her sister.

"Not if it's an adult nap." Arianna smirked.

"What's an adult nap?" Gabby asked.

"Okay, okay. No more talk about adult naps." I tried to keep the laughter out of my voice. As much as I tried, it was hard. I was emotionally exhausted, and that was the first thing I'd found funny since my life had changed.

"Don't forget about the ice cream," Gabby insisted.

"I won't." And I frowned. "Are you sure you have enough room for something sweet? There were enough treats in that kitchen to kill a horse."

"Oh, we didn't eat those." Arianna cringed.

"I ate the cookie dough. Before they put it in the oven." Gabby confessed and then gave me a big smile. "But I have room for ice cream. Especially with caramel on top."

We loaded into the car, and I eased out of the driveway and onto the street. I turned onto the main road that led to the ice cream shop. The Sugar Shack was our favorite place to grab a scoop. Homemade ice cream with thirty different toppings to choose from. They even served burgers. The good kind, with real meat fried in a skillet.

The Sugar Shack was a tradition in our family.

I wondered how much longer we would be a family.

I swallowed back the lump trying to form in the back of my throat as I turned into the parking lot. My headlights illuminated a couple seated in a booth by the window as I pulled into the parking space.

I glanced up at the couple and froze. All the air whooshed out of my lungs, and I found that I couldn't breathe. I blinked, trying to make sense of what the hell I was looking at.

Miles was sitting in the booth with Nikki. He was holding her hand and looking like he was comforting her.

Anger surged in my veins and burst my heart right open. How the fuck could he take that whore to our place, right in front of our family? In front of our girls?

"Look, it's Daddy," Gabby said.

"It sure is," I whispered under my breath. I snatched up my purse and slid out of the car. I waited for the girls to get out, all the while keeping my gaze trained on Miles.

Nikki shook her head and pulled her hand away. I wished I could be a fly on the table to hear what they were saying to each other.

I hurried toward the entrance, shoving the door open as the tiny bell jangled happily.

"Daddy! I didn't know you were going to meet us here." Gabby ran to her father.

Miles looked up and quickly scrambled out of the booth. His face went white and for a second, I thought he might pass out. I hoped he would hit his head and get a bad concussion that would lead to brain death.

I wondered if I would donate his organs. I probably would since I'm generous like that.

"Arianna, Gabby. What are you two doing here?" He hugged Gabby who launched herself at him and then smiled at Arianna.

"You didn't know we were coming?" Gabby asked and then looked at Nikki and frowned. "Then what are you doing here?"

Nikki's face was white, and her eyes were wide with shock. She didn't dare look at me. Probably in fear of me outing her in front of the girls.

I wanted her to look at me. I really wanted her to look me straight in the eye.

"I was just getting off work and stopped in for ice cream. Nikki was already here when I got here."

I wasn't buying it. From the looks of it, Arianna wasn't buying it either.

My girl was smart.

"Hi, Nikki." Gabby ran to give her a hug, but I grabbed her by the arm.

"Oh, sweetie. No. Don't hug Nikki. She's sick."

"She doesn't look sick." Gabby looked up at me.

"I know. It's a stomach bug that gives you horrible diarrhea and very bad gas."

"Like that hippo we saw at the zoo?" Gabby blinked up at me. "The one whose tail flew around in a circle while it pooped everywhere?"

"Exactly like that hippo." I knelt down to her.

"Gross." Arianna stepped back and wrinkled up her nose. She grabbed her sister's hand. "Come on, Gabby, let's go order."

The girls walked over to the counter, animatedly talking to the server. I looked back at my husband and ex-best friend.

"Are you following me?" he asked.

"Excuse me?"

"Are you following me? How did you know I was here?"

Anger made me tremble. I curled my fingers into fists and glared at him and then Nikki.

"No, I didn't follow you. The girls wanted ice cream, so I brought them here for a treat. You do remember that this is where we go. *As a family.*" I hissed out the last three words and noticed that my spittle had landed on Nikki's nose.

I wished I could infect Nikki with some hippo diarrhea that would last for weeks.

"I'm sorry." Nikki grabbed her purse and hurried out of the ice cream shop. Miles didn't watch her leave.

"Are you fucking kidding me?" I hissed and then glanced around the near-empty store. "Meeting your fuck buddy out in the open like that?" Nausea rolled around my stomach. "Does the whole town know?"

My eyes widened. Holy shit! *Did* the whole town know? Was I the last idiot on the face of the planet to realize what was going on?

"No, nobody knows." Miles' eyes widened, and he waved me back down to the booth where he'd been sitting with Nikki.

"I'm not sitting there."

He said nothing but moved to the next booth down and sat. His gaze wandered from me back to the kids. A thin sheen of sweat had gathered on his top lip.

His discomfort actually made me happy.

I justified that he should suffer after everything he'd done.

"Have you told them?" he whispered.

"Tell them what? That Daddy is fucking around with my ex-best friend?" I hissed.

"Keep your voice down." His gaze darted back to our girls.

My heart was pounding in my chest, and I wasn't sure what would come out of my mouth next.

"I'm coming home tonight." He looked back at Gabby, who gave him a funny face as they served up her ice cream in a waffle bowl.

I felt defeated. "That's it. No apology, no remorse? Just that you're coming home." Anger was an emotion I was starting to embrace.

"We'll talk about this later." He got up from the booth and went over to pay for the girls' ice cream.

I watched his back as he walked, considering how a human being could be so cruel and evil to do what he'd done to his spouse, to his children, and to his future.

I could not understand why he would cheat and then feel no remorse. My mind went back to the numerous web pages that had said that spouses sometimes won't show remorse because they are compartmentalizing their emotions. They put the affair in a different box, away from marriage and family, and they don't think the two have anything to do with each other.

I forced a smile as the girls walked over to me, holding large waffle bowls of ice cream with their favorite toppings.

I slid out of the booth and stood up. I couldn't sit there with Miles and pretend that everything was okay. I needed something to do, so I walked over to the ice cream counter and pretended to look at their flavors.

"Hello, Mrs. Rachel." Sam Seyler, the owner, smiled. His weathered face and white hair stood on end as if he'd forgotten to comb it after taking off his hat. Sam had owned the Sugar Shack for years. He'd started it with his wife in the fifties, and it was still going strong.

"Hi, Sam." I returned the smile without feeling. "Looks pretty empty in here tonight."

"Yes, with all that snow, no one is wanting ice cream. They are home playing in the snow and making hot chocolate. No one wants anything cold to eat."

"I'll always come here, Sam. Even after a snowstorm." I looked up and gave him a genuine smile.

"You are good people, Mrs. Rachel. A good mother, a good wife." His gaze flicked to Miles and then back to me.

My heart nearly stopped. Did Sam know? Had he suspected something from Nikki and Miles sitting together?

Holy shit.

"I'll let you look. Let me know what you decide." He nodded and walked to the end of the counter to wash out his scoops.

The doorbell chimed, and immediately the hair on the back of my neck stood at attention.

I didn't have to turn around to know who I'd be smelling soon enough.

I wrinkled my nose as his scent hit me. There was still a

faint whiff of skunk, but something else had been added to the odor. He smelled a lot like cat pee.

He didn't say anything, just stood next to me and looked down at the ice cream.

"What are you doing here?" I whispered under my breath. I glanced over my shoulder at the girls. They were each sharing a spoonful of ice cream with their father and laughing at something Gabby had said.

"What are you doing here? Following me?" I narrowed my eyes at him.

"Keep your emotions under control. The rage you keep putting off is making it hard for me to concentrate on my work."

"What work is that? Decapitating and kidnapping?" I snapped back.

He glanced at me with a little smile on his lips. "Maybe, Roadkill."

"Don't call me that. It sounds horrendous."

"Your emotions are horrendous." He arched his brow and glanced in the direction of where my family sat. "Is that the Cheater?

"Yes." I crossed my arms and studied the rocky road.

"Want me to kill him?" Khalan looked into the freezer.

I looked at him and blinked. "Maybe later." I looked back down at the ice cream. "Right now, you need to leave. People can't see us together," I hissed.

"Whatever, Roadkill. Keep those emotions under control so I can continue living my undead life." He glared, then turned and walked out the door without a word.

What the hell had I done to him? It wasn't like I had asked his stinky ass to turn me into a vampire.

Vampire. That was a topic I was so not ready to deal with. First mental breakdown was going to be dealing with my cheating husband. I'd deal with the whole vampire stuff later.

"Mom, are you getting something?" Gabby called out.

I turned and smiled. "Nope. Can't decide," I lied. My stomach couldn't handle anything in it. Especially not anything sweet.

I slid into the seat next to Arianna. I was thankful that Gabby sat next to her father. There was no way I could stand being inches away from him without plowing my fist into his face.

"Mom, spill," Arianna said between bites of her ice cream. "I know something is different. You might as well tell me now."

I froze and, for a second, thought my heart had stopped beating in my chest. My gaze flittered around the near-empty store to see if we had drawn any attention.

Sam was busy washing up the ice cream scoopers and bowls. A couple sat huddled together, obviously either dating or newlyweds, sharing a banana split, while a small family of three stood near the counter, trying to decide which flavor to get.

No one was looking at me except my daughters and Miles.

"What do you mean?" Miles asked, his voice tight.

I was relieved that I wasn't the only one who was nervous.

"Oh my God." Arianna rolled her eyes. "It's so obvi." She pointed her spoon at my face. "You look different, Mom. You look…younger." She stuck her spoon back into her scoop of ice cream and narrowed her eyes. "How much Botox did you get done this weekend?"

A laugh bubbled out of me as the tension slid like butter off my shoulders.

"I mean, come on, Mom." She leaned forward. "Whoever did your Botox this time did a really good job. Those little lines around your eyes are completely gone. Not to mention your elevens."

Elevens?" Gabby frowned. "What's elevens?"

"I think she means the lines you get between your eyes when you frown all the time." I pulled Gabby up against me and snuggled her blond head.

"My teacher, Mrs. Smith, must have equal marks." She giggled. "But she frowns all the time, especially when Billy acts up in class."

"No doubt." I laughed.

"Spill, Mom. You had more than just Botox." Gabby cocked her head. "You've lost weight, too."

"I just had a very busy weekend and haven't had time to eat very much," I assured her with my lie.

"Well, you look really great," Arianna said and picked up a spoonful of rocky road. She looked at Miles. "Doesn't she, Dad?"

My eyes flashed to Miles. He hadn't said anything about my appearance since the shit hit the fan this weekend. I didn't think he'd even notice. He was too busy trying to cover his ass.

"She looks beautiful as always." He smiled at Arianna.

His words fell flat.

I remembered in church one time, we'd taken a test in our couple's class. It had talked about how to better relate to one another. The material talked about how everyone speaks a different love language. Miles' love language was acts of service. It made sense to me. He loved coming home to a clean house and a hot-cooked meal, especially after working late hours at the hospital.

My love language was different. I needed words of affirmation. Miles had told me it probably came from the fact that I was orphaned at an early age and put into foster care after my parents had been killed. He'd said that words of affirmation made me feel worthy.

Tonight, his words didn't make me feel anything but sad.

Because tonight they were coming out of the mouth of a liar.

"Mommy always looks beautiful," Gabby said to her sister.

"Thank you, sweetie." I bit the inside of my cheek to stop the tears from flowing. The words from my child's mouth held a different meaning. They meant the world to me because *they* were my world.

"Finish up so we can go home," Miles said. He gathered his coat from the back of the booth.

My stomach clenched. I didn't know if things were going to get better or worse once we got home. I didn't want to start a scene in front of the girls. They didn't deserve that. Miles had broken our family.

It was up to me to put it back together.

CHAPTER 14

My stomach cramped all the way home. The girls had ridden back with me while Miles followed behind us.

I opened the kitchen door, and the girls rushed past me and dropped their bags on the floor before heading to their rooms.

"Pick up your stuff," I called after them. I didn't count on them to obey, nor did I care at this moment. Miles would be walking in soon, and I needed the distraction of everyday life.

The cramps grew worse. I placed my hand over my stomach and hissed in a breath at the pain.

"You okay?" Miles narrowed his eyes at me. I hated his look of concern because I didn't trust it.

"Probably just that time of the month," I said and straightened.

"When's the last time you ate?"

"Friday morning," I said. I didn't want to tell him anything about me. I felt like I was divulging secrets to a stranger.

"No wonder your stomach hurts. You're probably hungry." He shrugged.

"I probably have an ulcer." I glared.

"I'm going to take a shower." He ignored my last barb and headed towards the bedroom.

The pain swept across my stomach again, and I wasn't sure why. These cramps felt worse than anything I'd ever experienced. Even labor pains.

I bounded to the bathroom and locked the door behind me.

White-hot pain spread across my stomach. I sank to my knees and cradled my belly. I bit my lip to keep from crying out.

"Mom, tell Gabby to stop going in my room," Arianna called out from the other side of the door.

I gripped the sink and forced my feet under me. I couldn't let her see me like this. I had to get this under control.

"Just a second." I tried to keep my voice calm and even, but it hitched when another round of pain sliced through me.

"God, I'm dying," I murmured as I lifted my eyes to the mirror.

I saw my reflection, eyes tight with pain, and lips pressed into a thin, white line. My breathing had turned to pants as I tried to keep from crying out.

I stared at the mirror.

My reflection in the mirror began to shift and change until, suddenly, I was looking into the face of Khalan.

Shit. I was really losing it.

"You're not losing it," he said.

I screamed and jumped back from the mirror.

"Mom, you okay in there?" Arianna called out.

"Yes, yes. Just thought I saw a spider." I narrowed my eyes at Khalan.

"Gross. Well, kill it before it makes spider babies in the wall." Arianna's footsteps headed away from the door.

"What are you doing? How can I see you in the mirror?" I hissed and grimaced at the pain.

"Because I can feel what you're feeling. Remember?" He cocked his head, looking none too pleased. "You're in pain because your body needs blood."

"What?" My eyes widened slightly. The second he mentioned the word *blood*, my stomach cramped again, and a sudden craving washed over me. I licked my lips, and Khalan smiled.

"Admit it. You want blood." He grinned, looking very predatory.

My craving intensified.

"Stop saying that," I hissed.

"Stop saying what? Blood?" he taunted and cocked his head. He was clearly enjoying my discomfort.

"Yes." I dug my nails into the counter of the sink and squeezed my eyes shut.

"Rachel." His voice, deep and controlled, made me obey him, and I opened my eyes.

"What do you want from me?" Tears gathered in my eyes and slid out of the corners and down my cheeks.

"Why do you fight this?" This time, his voice was harsher, and I knew from the tone that he was angry.

"In a few hours, my life has been destroyed, devastated, and burned to the fucking ground. I'm in my house with my children, and I'm trying to protect them from what their father has done. My heart is shattered, and now I'm in the worst pain of my life. I fight what you claim I am because I'm a mother and I will always fight to protect my children."

Khalan held my gaze, not saying anything.

"Do something," I said through gritted teeth.

He sighed heavily. "Fine. Go out in your backyard. I left

you something that will stop the pain. But hurry up. You don't want it to cool off."

And just like that, his face was gone, and I was staring at my own reflection again.

I opened the bathroom door and peered out. I didn't see anyone, so I silently made my way to the back door. I stepped out into the backyard.

The pool was uncovered, and snow still lingered in the flower beds. We'd just had the pool people come out to get it ready for spring break. When the freak snowstorm hit, I hadn't thought to re-cover it. Now, worrying about the pool was the furthest thing from my mind.

The cold wind caressed my skin as I stepped farther into the backyard. I glanced around, trying to see what Khalan had left for me. Near one of the columns of the outdoor living space sat a small, blue cooler.

I glanced back at the house to make sure my family wasn't looking at me through the windows. I could see Arianna in the kitchen, grabbing something to drink.

I hurried over to the cooler, the snow crunching under my shoes.

I squatted and opened the lid.

Inside was a stainless-steel coffee cup with a lid.

I picked up the container and noticed that it felt warm in my hands. I tried to pry the plastic lid off the cup, but it was sealed tight.

I lifted it to my nose and sniffed.

The tempting, sweet scent filled my nose and made my mouth water. An intense craving shot through my stomach, and before I knew it, I was placing my lips against the small opening and tilting up the cup.

Liquid, warm and sweet, slid into my mouth and down my throat. The silky-smooth texture coated my tongue, and I nearly groaned as I swallowed the sweet elixir.

It tasted like red roses and dark chocolate.

I held the cup to my lips and drank deeply until I emptied the cup.

I lifted my head to the sky and sighed with pleasure.

"Mom, what are you doing out there?" Gabby called out from the door.

I turned my head and smiled. "Just looking at the night."

My body felt warm and tingly all over, and my stomach cramps were gone.

I didn't think I'd ever felt so good.

Gabby bounded outside in her PJs and boots, giggling as she ran to me.

I bent and gathered her in my arms and held her close.

"I like the snow." She laid her head on my shoulder and sighed. "I pretend that I have a castle in the mountains covered with snow. I have a dragon, and we fly over the trees at night when the moon is full."

"Sounds like fun." I smiled and hugged her tightly.

"I wish I could fly, Mommy." She lifted her head and looked at me.

"If you could fly, where would you go? If you could fly, you might keep flying and never come back to me. And that would make me very sad."

"I'll always come back to you, Mommy." Gabby giggled and pressed her hands to either side of my face. "I'll even take you flying with me."

"You will?" I grinned and rubbed my nose against hers.

"Yes! You could hold my hand, and I'd be strong enough to take you with me. We will fly above the trees, so high that we could touch the moon." Her eyes sparkled as she talked.

Gabby was my dreamer, my girl with her head in the clouds. While other girls her age wanted to fit in, she was determined to stand out. Miles was always trying to rein her in, but I secretly loved it.

My princess rebel. I wished I had her optimism, her fearlessness. I needed that now more than ever.

"What are you doing outside in your PJs? You're going to get pneumonia," Miles called out from the door.

I turned and studied his expression. He was squinting as he tried to see what we were doing.

"We're looking at the sky, Daddy." Gabby giggled.

"Well, there's snow on the ground. You two need to get inside before you both get sick. The flu is going around, you know." He narrowed his eyes and walked back inside, shutting the door.

Gabby looked at me and rolled her eyes.

"He needs to have a little fun," she said.

A laugh bubbled out of me and was swallowed up by the dark night.

It felt good to laugh. Even if I knew the happiness wouldn't last. I needed it. I needed Gabby's innocence to remind me of the good things.

"We better go inside," I whispered near her ear.

"All right. But, tonight, can you read me that story? You know the one about the girl and the dragon."

I blinked. "Of course. It's been a while since you asked me to read you a story." She usually stayed up late reading under her covers with a flashlight.

If Miles got up in the middle of the night to go to the hospital, he would usually catch her still reading and get on her. But I didn't mind. A girl who loved to read would become a powerful woman.

She giggled and jumped down. She ran toward the house with her dark hair bouncing in the light of the moon.

I smiled as she ran into the house, leaving the door open for me to follow.

My Gabby.

I picked up the stainless-steel coffee mug and pried off the top. Despite the dark, my eyes adjusted very well.

Odd. I usually hated driving at night because the headlights made my vision blur. Now, I could see the bottom of the cup and the red drops of liquid left behind.

I frowned and lifted the cup to my nose and inhaled.

It still smelled of roses and chocolate, but there was another scent mingled with it.

A coppery scent.

My stomach had stopped cramping, and I'd just drunk something red and thick.

My heart nearly stopped.

It couldn't be.

I clutched the cup to my chest and ran for the house. I bounded inside, forgetting to shut the door behind me. I set the cup down on the quartz countertop in the kitchen and scraped my finger along the inside wall.

I pulled out my finger and looked at the red smear.

"Geez, Mom, is that blood? Did you cut yourself?" Arianna froze in her tracks and wrinkled her nose.

"I...ah..." Words wouldn't form on my tongue, and something dark settled in my gut. I didn't want to think about what I had just drunk. But the evidence was there on my finger.

"Dad, Mom cut herself," Arianna called out. Miles came into the kitchen, concern stretched across his face when he saw the blood on my finger.

"What happened?" He grabbed a dishtowel and covered my finger. He held it up above my heart to stop the bleeding.

I couldn't tell him that I wasn't bleeding, nor that it wasn't my blood. Oh, God...that thought settled over me in a nauseating rush.

I drank blood. A lot of it. I didn't even know whose or what kind it was.

I could have contracted some kind of disease like Hepatitis or HIV.

"I'm fine." I snatched my finger out of Miles' grip and hurried toward my bathroom.

"Rachel, I need to see if you need stitches," Miles called after me.

I didn't slow my speed but headed into the bathroom and locked the door behind me.

I whipped the towel off my finger and stuck my finger into my mouth. I moaned at the sweet taste of the blood on my tongue.

It couldn't be. I couldn't be craving blood. This was not happening.

I opened my eyes and stared at my reflection. The image began to blur, just like before, and suddenly, I was staring at Khalan again.

A little smirk played on his bearded lips.

"What did you give me? Tell me it wasn't…" I couldn't say the word out loud. If I said it aloud, it would make it real.

"Blood. Yes, you just downed a sixteen-ounce tumbler of blood."

"Oh, God." My knees felt wobbly as white stars danced in front of my eyes.

"Stop your bitching," he groused. "You feel better, right? The cramps are gone, yes?" He crossed his large arms over his chest and glared.

"Yes, but I didn't want to drink blood to feel better." I narrowed my eyes at him.

"Too bad. It's what you do now. You drink blood."

"Where did you get it?" I needed to know.

"Let's say a donor." He snorted. He had smiled more in the past ten seconds than in all the time I'd known him.

"You killed someone." I shook my head. "Why didn't you just kill a chicken or deer or…?"

"An animal? Kill an animal so you can live? You are so fucking selfish." His smile slid off his face.

"So it was human blood?" I swallowed. I hated to admit that the thought didn't repulse me like it should. It should have made me queasy. But, no. Here, I was literally drooling thinking about sucking on some poor human's neck.

"Of course, it was human blood. Human blood is much stronger than animals' blood."

"What will it do to me? I mean, it didn't have any disease like Hepatitis or worse, did it?" My heart thumped faster in my chest.

"Of course, not. I wouldn't have given you corrupted blood."

"Would corrupt blood have killed me?"

"No. It'd just make you sick to your stomach. Not that you would have drunk the whole thing anyway. You would have smelled the taint before you took the first sip."

I blew out a breath. At least that was good news.

"What would animal blood do to me?"

"You can't drink animal blood." He shook his head. "You need human. It's stronger. And you can last a lot longer on it."

"How long?"

He shrugged. "It's different for everyone. It could last you a few days or a week. No way to tell just yet."

"What about animal blood?"

He glared. "You wouldn't last a day on it."

"Fine, fine." I knew when to drop the subject.

"When are you bringing me more?" I cringed after I'd said it. I hated how I was already dependent on blood.

"Bring you more?" He threw back his head and laughed. "I'm not your little bitch. You have to go out and get your own." He held my gaze and, suddenly, his image was gone, and I was looking at my reflection once more.

I stood there for a while, unsure.

On one hand, I felt incredible, and I looked absolutely gorgeous. I looked better than I had at twenty. And now that my cramps were gone, I felt like I had energy for days.

"Mom, are you coming?" Arianna called out from the other side of the door.

I took a deep breath and composed myself. I had my children to take care of before I could figure out the rest of this craziness. Like being a vampire.

"I'm coming," I said and looked at my reflection again.

I may be a vampire now, but first and foremost, I was a mom.

CHAPTER 15

"Hurry up," I groused at the coffee pot as it slowly filled my cup. I had stayed up all night, unable to sleep, and now that it was time to get the girls to school, I was dragging.

"I thought school would be canceled," Arianna huffed and glared into her bowl of cereal.

"Nope. I checked and double-checked. The roads are clear, so school is in. Sorry, kiddo." I gave her a sympathetic smile and turned back to wait for my coffee.

"What did you do last night?" Gabby asked as she walked into the kitchen.

I froze.

"Sounded like you were up half the night." Gabby plopped down on the kitchen stool and poured herself a bowl of cereal. "Cereal? We never get to have cereal."

She was right. I usually cooked breakfast for them every morning. But after staying up all night, I didn't feel like cooking. I felt like going to bed and sleeping all day.

"I couldn't sleep, so I decided to declutter the Christmas ornaments." I turned and faced them.

"But there are about twenty boxes of them." Arianna frowned.

"Actually, twenty-six." I had dug everything out of every Christmas box we had and had gone through it all with a fine-tooth comb. "There were a lot of boxes with lights that were tangled or had bulbs out."

"You must have thrown away half of them," Arianna said.

I grinned. I didn't tell her that I had untangled hundreds of feet of white Christmas lights. I then went and tested each light and replaced the ones that didn't work. I'm not sure why. I could have thrown them away and bought new ones. But I couldn't do that. I didn't want to throw things away just because they had gotten old or outdated.

It would have been like throwing myself away.

"Hurry and eat. We have to leave in a few minutes." I glanced at the time on the microwave and then picked up my coffee cup. I was usually a two-cup-a-day woman. I had a feeling that today I'd need more caffeine to get rolling.

I quickly glanced at the newspaper that I'd gotten off our doorstep. The headline was the freak snowstorm that had struck Mississippi, followed by a small mention of a missing college girl from Ole Miss. She was a senior at college and majoring advertising. Her boyfriend had not heard from her since the night of the snowstorm. And her car was nowhere to be found.

The hairs on the back of my neck stood on end. I couldn't imagine not knowing where my daughters were. The mere thought of something happening to them made me sick to my stomach. Crime rarely happened in Charming and there hadn't been a missing person's case in years. Hopefully the girl would be found soon.

"Soccer practice is going to be canceled." I glanced at my cell phone and read the group text.

"Damp, Hit" Arianna said.

"Arianna, no cussing." I turned and glared at her.

"Geez, it's not like I said the real thing." She shrugged. She'd been using words that sounded like curse words without actually cursing. I was on to her, though, and I didn't like it.

"Well, it's close enough to damnit. Don't say it again." I held her gaze to let her know I was serious.

"Ugh, Melanie's mom lets her say the real thing," Arianna pouted.

"I have never heard Melanie say damn."

"She says worse." Gabby giggled.

I took a deep breath and looked at both of my girls. "I'm not Melanie's mom. I'm your mom. And neither of you will curse. Got it?"

"Got it." Gabby nodded once, and her dark bangs fell over her eyes. Laughing, she pushed them out of the way.

I looked at Arianna.

"Yes, Mom. I got it." Arianna gave me a long-suffering sigh and hopped off the barstool. She gathered up her bowl and spoon and put them in the sink.

"You know, you're lucky." Arianna turned to me.

"Oh, yeah. How's that?"

"Because Melanie doesn't even put her dishes in the sink. And she doesn't clean her room." Arianna crossed her arms.

I should have been sterner with her, but for some reason, I couldn't. My life had tilted on its axis and shifted in ways that would never be the same. But I had my girls, and that wouldn't change. For that, I was grateful.

"You're right. I'm lucky that I have you and Gabby as my beautiful daughters." I reached out and stroked Arianna's dark hair.

"Ugh, Mom." Arianna ducked away from my touch and hurried to the foyer to get her backpack.

Gabby hopped off the stool and placed her dishes in the sink with a clatter.

She looked up at me and grinned. "Sorry, Mommy."

"It's okay, sweetie. Go brush your teeth and make sure Arianna has brushed hers, too. We have to get going, or we'll be late for school."

Gabby hurried off to find her sister. Words were exchanged in the hallway, followed by footsteps running toward the bathroom.

I sighed and grabbed my coffee and picked up the creamer. I stopped. I'd almost forgotten. I didn't like cream in my coffee. Not anymore.

I lifted the black brew to my lips and took a tentative sip, expecting not to like it.

The hot liquid slid down my throat in a heated rush. I sighed with joy that I still liked coffee. I just preferred it prepared differently.

"Good morning." Miles came up behind me and reached for a coffee cup. I quickly got out of his way. He gave me a look but said nothing more.

"I figured you'd be at the hospital early today," I said over my coffee cup.

"I don't have surgery today. Just making rounds at the hospital and then off to the office this afternoon." He waited while the coffee maker filled his cup.

I didn't answer him. I didn't really want to be around him until I figured things out. My emotions were settled a bit this morning, and I didn't have that strong urge to draw and quarter him for what he'd done. What scared me was the fact that I was beginning to feel numb. Like I saw him for what he was, and I didn't want that in my life anymore.

Hell, maybe it was the blood that I had consumed. Perhaps it was making me delirious. Maybe Khalan had put something into the blood to calm me down so he could sleep. That could be why I was so freaking tired this morning.

"Let's go, Mom!" Arianna called out from the foyer.

"I'm coming." I grabbed my coffee cup with one hand and swiped my purse off the kitchen island with the other.

"Rachel," Miles said.

"Yes?" I turned and looked at him.

"I just want you to know I love you," he said softly.

I blinked and nodded, then headed toward the door where my girls were waiting on me.

They scrambled into the back of my Volvo. I climbed into the driver's seat and turned on the car and opened the garage door.

It was still early, but the sun was bright and just starting to come up over the horizon. I loved sunrises, and the colorful streaks of pink and orange and blue looked like an artist's canvas across the sky.

It always made me happy.

I grinned as I backed out of the garage, thinking to myself that this was something Miles couldn't ruin for me, couldn't take away from me.

The sun seemed brighter today, more intense, and I cringed and flipped the visor down to block the light.

I stopped and squinted as I dug around in my purse for my sunglasses and slipped them on. Before I continued down my street Cal stepped in front of my car. I slammed on the brakes to keep from hitting him.

My stomach dropped. He didn't say anything, just stared at me for a full five seconds before crossing the street.

He didn't have to say anything. I knew he knew. He'd seen me almost naked, driving like a madwoman the night of the snowstorm. He could tell the whole neighborhood if he wanted.

"What are you doing? The sun's not up yet," Gabby asked.

"It may not be all the way in the sky, but it sure is bright this morning." I cleared my throat and pulled away slowly. My gaze landed on the landscaped mascot in our yard, and I frowned. After the snow had killed the foliage and flowers, the Ole Miss Landshark was unrecognizable. The flowers were all distorted into a shape that resembled a limp penis.

I turned onto the main street heading toward the school. A beam of early morning sunlight came through the window.

"Ugh." I cringed and scooted farther down in my seat. I held up my hand to shield myself from the brightness.

"Mom, what's the deal? Please tell me you're not going diva on me," Arianna said from the back seat.

"What are you talking about?" I snarled and batted the visor to position it so the sun wasn't blinding my eyes.

"You act like you're scared of the sun. Like you're one of *those* people."

My heart thumped hard in my chest. "One of what people?" My voice cracked as I spoke.

"The moms who think the sun is going to give them crow's feet or other wrinkles or sun spots," Arianna said.

Maybe that's why the sun was so hard on my eyes this morning. Maybe after drinking that blood, I had started hating the sun.

"Maybe Mommy had too much wine last night." Gabby giggled.

"She was up all night. That could be it," Arianna added.

"I assure you, I didn't drink last night." I hissed when another beam of sunlight came through the windshield.

I was going to have to get some darker shades. What I had on was not cutting it.

I turned into the carpool line in front of the school and came to a stop. I always made the girls wait until we were right in front of the school before getting out of the car. I didn't take chances when it came to their safety. I knew that something could happen in the blink of an eye. Someone could hit them with their car, or someone could kidnap them.

The line was moving at a snail's pace this morning. I'd never minded before and usually used the time to remind the girls of what activities they had that afternoon. Whether it was soccer, dance, or church, they were constantly busy. They didn't seem to mind either. Both had high energy levels and seemed to thrive on the challenges.

But today with the sun trying to get into the car, and my body literally exhausted from staying up all night, all I wanted to do was make it home to my bed for a well-deserved nap.

When I was almost to the beginning of the line, I looked at the girls in the rearview mirror. "You know, I'm not feeling very well. I think, just for today, it would be okay if you guys got out here."

"Yes!" Arianna pumped her hand in the air and grabbed her bag. "I love you," she whispered as she got out of the car and slammed the door behind her.

"You okay, Mommy?" Gabby's furrowed brow made my heart clench "I could stay home and take care of you."

"I'm okay, sweetie." I forced a smile. "But thank you for the offer. I'll take you up on it next time."

She nodded and unbuckled her seatbelt. She opened the door and stuck her arms through her backpack straps before slamming the car door. She ran for the school entrance, her dark hair swinging from side to side.

I pulled out of the car line and, immediately, someone behind me honked.

I growled but chose to ignore them as I headed toward the street.

The ride back home was the longest drive ever. I had to turn on the air conditioner to try and stay awake. Even with the air on sixty and blowing in my face, all I wanted to do was pull over and go to sleep.

But I resisted. The last thing I needed was some cop knocking on my door and the whole town whispering that I was the new town drunk.

I wanted to weep when I finally saw my house. I pulled into the garage and dragged myself inside. I tossed my purse onto the counter and headed toward the bedroom.

As tired as I was, I could not bring myself to sleep in my bed. So I turned and headed toward the guest bedroom and slid under the covers.

Before closing my eyes, I set my alarm, just in case, so I wouldn't forget to pick up the girls.

CHAPTER 16

The annoying sound of an alarm had me patting the bedside table in an attempt to turn it off. When I couldn't find it, I pried my eyes open and reached for the cell in the bed.

Squinting, I looked at the screen.

It was the alarm. I'd slept nearly the whole day away. Again.

And now I only had twenty minutes to get up and get the kids.

"Shit." I groaned and forced myself to crawl out from the comfort of the sheets.

Sunlight streamed through the blinds, leaving a pattern of light on the hardwood floor.

Startled, I stepped around it.

I plodded into the bathroom and splashed some water on my face. I didn't have time for a shower, so I rubbed on deodorant and brushed my teeth, then headed downstairs.

I slipped my feet into my boots and grabbed my purse off the kitchen island, then with my hand on the kitchen door, I stopped. I couldn't forget my sunglasses.

I dug around in my purse and stuck them on, then headed to the closet for a long coat that provided the most coverage. My hand landed on the fur coat that Miles had given me when he first opened his practice. He'd said it was to show his appreciation for how much I had sacrificed so he could live his dreams.

I never really wore it because it wasn't my style. It looked like something a pimp or socialite on the Upper East Side of New York would wear. No self-respecting Southerner would wear it. Plus, I was always afraid PETA would track me down and picket my house or throw paint on me.

Now, I didn't care.

I slid my arms along the silk lining and then snuggled down into the soft fur of the coat. I glanced out the window to see the sun beaming down on the quickly melting snow. By tomorrow, there wouldn't be any signs of the freak March snowstorm.

The sun seemed brighter, and I knew I needed bigger sunglasses. I hurried to my closet and pulled open the drawer where I kept my accessories, sifting through my designer sunglasses until I found what I was looking for. A pair of square-shaped, oversized shades. The only time I wore them had been on vacation in the Bahamas. They looked pretty ridiculous, but they kept the sun out.

I slid them on and started to leave, but my gaze lingered on a pair of long, black gloves. Silk gloves that had been worn to some black-tie event hosted by the hospital.

I hesitated for about a second, then my sensible side won out. I grabbed them and tucked them into the pocket of my fur coat.

I was out the door and into my car in a flash.

I opened the garage and cringed as I backed out. I expected the sun to be glaring down on me with blistering heat, but between the protection of my coat and the obnoxiously large sunglasses, the light was manageable.

I pulled out onto the street and headed toward the school.

I sighed with relief and pulled into the carpool line, grateful that school had not let out just yet.

A brisk knock on the window nearly made me jump out of my skin.

I turned and scowled at the intruder knocking on the driver's side window.

I groaned when I saw her. Veronica Counts.

She was the biggest gossip in town. She showed up at every school event, birthday party, and charity fundraiser. Every time people saw her, they ran the other way.

People avoided her like the plague. She didn't really have any friends. She would volunteer for every event just so people would be forced to interact with her. She'd find out who you knew and then start gossiping about them. It didn't matter if it was your mother, she'd smirk and then launch right into the kind of filthy gossip designed to ruin reputations. It didn't matter that the majority of what she said was false, or was no one's business. She even gossiped about her best friend's children. Nothing was off-limits with Veronica.

I'd learned to never tell her anything that might be misconstrued. She thrived off other people's misery.

She wasn't going to thrive off mine.

I let out a sigh and rolled down the window about six inches.

"Rachel! I was wondering if that was you behind those ridiculous sunglasses," she screeched. People three cars down could likely hear how loud she was.

"Hello, Veronica." I cringed. I couldn't bring myself to give her a smile. I felt that gracing her with my time was sacrifice enough.

"Why are you dressed like that? Are you *hiding* from

someone?" Her smirk grew as her eyes narrowed. Very reminiscent of the Grinch when he decided to steal Christmas.

"No, Veronica. That's ridiculous." I hit the button, and the window slid upward, but she stuck her claw-like fingers in at the top of the glass to stop me.

I wondered what would happen if I continued to close the window. Would her fingers snap off like the legs of a gingerbread man, or would they just get squished? I decided I didn't want the bother of cleaning up and stopped the window before it caught her digits.

"What do you need, Veronica?" I said in a bored voice.

"I'm just checking on you. I haven't seen you in a while. How's everything?" She leaned in as if I were going to tell her a big secret.

"Everything is going wonderfully. And your family?" I glanced over at the time on the clock. The bell should have rung by now. The kids would soon be pouring out of the building like ants.

"Well, you know Elizabeth Grace won first place in the science fair, and she'll be going to Nationals in a few weeks for band. She's also garnered some interest from two Ivy League schools." Veronica smirked and lifted her chin.

I lifted my brow. "She's only fourteen. I didn't realize colleges started recruiting so early." I didn't believe a word coming out of this woman's mouth. She had lied so many times about so many things that no one ever believed anything she said.

"Well, they do if you have a prodigy." She chuckled. "How are Arianna and Gabby? You know it's not too late to put them in band. Studies show that kids that take band are smarter and make better career choices."

"You don't say?" I looked a few car-lengths ahead of me and saw my friend Liz from book club. She had gotten out of her vehicle and was waving at me.

I lifted my hand in greeting, and Veronica turned to see who I was waving at.

Liz spotted Veronica, her eyes narrowed as she wrinkled her nose in disgust, quickly getting back into her Range Rover. I grinned, thinking I heard her lock her car even from where I was.

"Liz!" Veronica screeched and rushed over to Liz's car.

I rolled up my window and locked the door in case the bitch got bold and tried to get into my car. She'd done it before and nearly scared the hell out of me.

Kids were now trickling out of the building, and I quickly spotted Arianna.

I let out a sigh and waved to her. She nodded but didn't wave back. She was with her friends, and I didn't want to embarrass her.

I cut my eyes to Liz's car. Veronica was talking loudly through Liz's closed window. My friend wouldn't even roll hers down. Smart girl.

My phone buzzed. I glanced down and grinned at Liz's text.

This crazy woman won't leave me alone. Can you run her over for me? I'll buy you Starbucks if you do.

Arianna opened the back door of the Volvo and got inside.

"Hey, pumpkin. How was school?" I smiled at her in the rearview mirror.

"It's school. Same old, same old." Arianna didn't even bother looking up from her phone, concentrating on whoever it was she was texting.

I picked up my cell and sent a text back to Liz.

Don't tempt me. That woman is a whole lot of crazy. Besides, you'd owe me 2 coffees at Starbucks. Not one.

I looked up when the car door opened, and Gabby scrambled inside.

"Hey, sweetie! How was your day?"

"Great." Gabby cocked her head. "Mommy, you look like a movie star with your big sunglasses and fur coat."

Arianna looked up from her phone. "Fur coat? Since when do you wear a fur coat?"

"It's the one your father gave me years ago. I found it in the closet and thought I'd wear it since it's gotten cold and snowed." I shrugged and started the car.

"What about those ridiculous glasses?" Arianna leaned forward. "Geez, you look like a pimp."

"What's a pimp?" Gabby asked with wide-eyed innocence.

"I'll tell you when you're older," I said and shot Arianna a stern look. I knew she couldn't see it, but she knew from my tone that I wasn't happy.

She smirked and went back to her phone.

I pulled out of line. Veronica waved like mad, but I pretended I didn't see her and merged onto the street. My phone buzzed again, and I was pretty sure it was Liz to rant about Veronica's conversation.

I would look at it when I got home.

We made the short drive and were back at the house within fifteen minutes.

The girls got out of the car and were into the house before I could even get my door open. I hit the garage button and sealed out the light before exiting my vehicle.

I frowned as I noticed Miles' car in the garage. He was supposed to be working.

I shrugged out of the coat and stowed my sunglasses in my purse before walking into the house.

I followed my daughters' voices into the kitchen. I stopped short when I saw Miles standing there in his scrubs, talking to Gabby about her day.

"We don't have soccer practice because of the soggy

ground." Gabby hopped on the barstool at the kitchen island and grabbed a banana from the crystal bowl.

"Why do you have that fur coat out?" Miles asked.

"It was the first thing I grabbed to go pick up the girls," I said quickly.

"Mommy looks great. " Gabby offered.

"Thanks, sweetie." I gave her a smile, and my heart lifted at the sight of her. My girls always had that effect on me.

I scooted out of the kitchen and went to the closet to hang up the coat. I made sure to stay out of the spots where the sun was shining on the hardwood floors.

I grimaced as I glanced around the living room. I hadn't realized how large the windows were in my house. When we built the house, I'd made sure that there were plenty of windows to let in natural light. I loved how it made me feel optimistic and joyful.

Now, I wished there were fewer windows—so many made me feel vulnerable.

What I needed were curtains. Long, thick curtains.

I opened the closet and quickly stowed away the fur coat. I went through the rest of the outerwear and sweaters, checking to see if any of them would provide full coverage and not look as ridiculous as the fur. Walking around in a fur coat in March was sure to set tongues wagging in Charming.

"What's for dinner?" Miles' voice made me jump.

I spun around and shot him a glare.

"Sorry, didn't mean to scare you." He reached out and touched my arm. I recoiled and took a step back.

"What are you doing home? I thought you had work?" I frowned.

He dropped his hand. "I did. I finished up early."

He was never home early. If he came home by six, that was early. He always said he was working late at the office, seeing patients or in surgery.

Now, I was beginning to wonder if he'd lied and had actually been with Nikki the entire time.

"You're never home this early," I stated. I turned and closed the closet door.

"I wanted to be home with my family." I barely heard his low response.

My gut tugged. I felt sorry for him. Actually felt *sorry* for him. Yet it still wasn't enough for me to forgive him. Not yet. I knew myself, knew what I was made of, and I wasn't sure I was capable of pardoning him for what he'd done to our family.

In my eyes, he'd murdered our family bond and burned our future. I still wasn't sure how he could stand in front of me and act like everything would be okay.

"Mom, look what I made in English today." Arianna bounded into the kitchen, her face shining brightly. "Mrs. Grisham said I was the only one who had all the spelling right and who got the three bonus spelling words correct." Arianna held out her sheet and smiled brightly. There was a grade of *103* written in red ink at the top. "Even Elizabeth Grace didn't get a perfect score."

Elizabeth Grace. Veronica's daughter. She was a know-it-all, just like her mother. She was all polite and sincere when around me, complimenting me on everything from my clothes to my home. I'd never met a child who was such a brown-noser. My gut told me Elizabeth Grace was probably a troublemaker.

"That's wonderful, Arianna. And what an achievement." I smiled.

"Well, remember, honey, it's not nice to brag," Miles countered.

My spine stiffened. "She's not bragging. She's just telling us about her achievement." I looked back at Arianna. "You're a smart girl, Arianna. And there's nothing wrong with being proud of your achievements."

"Thanks, Mom." She gave me a sheepish smile before leaving me alone with Miles.

Irritation burned in my gut, and I looked at him.

"Rachel, you don't want people thinking you are trying to be better than them. It's best not to encourage her too much," Miles said.

"First of all, she's my daughter, and I will always encourage her and be proud of her accomplishments. She did the work. She earned it. Second of all, I give zero fucks what anyone else thinks." I shook my head. "Thirdly, you are the last person to be giving advice or worrying about what people think right now." I turned on my heel and headed to my bedroom.

"Be reasonable, Rachel." He hurried behind me.

"Your hypocrisy is overwhelming, Miles." Something in my chest hardened like the coating on a candy apple.

"Think about our family." He grabbed my arm, stopping my retreat.

The words boiled over in my chest.

"Don't you dare say that," I spit out, curling my fingers into fists so tightly that my fingernails dug trenches into my palms. "Don't you dare tell *me* to think about our family." I shoved my finger against his chest in disgust and anger. "You are the one who should have thought about our family before you started having an affair."

"Rachel, you need to stop rehashing that. You need to move on," Miles said.

"What's going on?" Gabby asked.

"Nothing." Miles turned and smiled at our daughter.

My chest clenched. I wasn't sure how long she had been standing there.

Her dark blue gaze landed on me as if for reassurance.

"Everything is okay, Gabby. I'll be back in the kitchen to start on dinner in a minute. Any preferences?" I kept my voice cheery and light, hoping to cover up the mess that was now my marriage. I'd sworn to always protect my children. I didn't intend to break that promise now.

"Tacos sound good. With that Mexican rice that you make," she said.

"I haven't made tacos in a while. I'll change shoes then grab some meat out of the freezer and get started."

"What about key lime pie for dessert?"

"I don't know if it will be ready in time. But I can make some banana pudding." I grinned.

"Yes! Even better." She turned and headed toward the kitchen.

My smile faded as I looked at Miles. "You need to watch what you say around the girls."

"I'm trying to move on. You're the one who keeps bringing it up. You need to let it go, Rachel." He released a long-suffering sigh and turned. "I've got some paperwork to catch up on. I'll be in my office."

I watched his retreating back as anger rose so swiftly, I thought it would burst out like lava.

I headed into my closet and shucked off my shoes then slipped on my comfy pair with the fur on the inside as I sank down on the overstuffed ottoman.

In a few short hours, I had gone from crying over my husband and hoping he'd come to his senses and stay with me, to an emotion I was unfamiliar with: hatred.

I told myself I didn't really hate him. I was hurt and wanted to see remorse from him. Maybe he was in denial over what he'd done.

All that mattered to me was my girls and keeping what was left of my family intact.

I stood and headed into the kitchen, determined to make a wonderful meal and not let Miles get to me again.

I grabbed the meat out of the freezer and stuck it into the sink in hot water to defrost. I went to the large pantry and gathered up the items for the banana pudding.

I placed my supplies and bowl on the kitchen counter. While the meat thawed in the sink, I began to fix the dessert.

As I mixed ingredients together, I quickly got lost in my task. The scent of vanilla pudding and bananas filled the kitchen. When I was finally done, I popped the dish into the refrigerator.

I touched the ground beef in the sink of hot water. It was still frozen in the middle, so I popped it into the microwave for a few seconds to finish thawing out.

The doorbell rang. I quickly wiped my hands on a dish-towel and headed for the front door.

My stomach clenched, and I prayed it wasn't one of the neighborhood kids trying to sell something. In a neighborhood the size of ours, everyone's kids were selling something. Football players in the fall, Girl Scouts in the spring, Christian Summer Camp in the summer, and we can't forget band in the winter.

Out of all of them, I had a love-hate relationship with the Girl Scouts. I loved their cookies. I hated the extra weight I put on after a box or two.

I tried looking through the glass doors. Whoever was standing on the other side was too big to be a child. This was bad. If it were a kid selling something, I could throw money at them, and they'd be gone. If it were an adult, getting rid of them wouldn't be so easy.

I took a deep breath, blew it out, and then opened the door.

"Hi, Mrs. Jones." My landscaper, gave me a smile.

"Mr. McIntyre. I completely forgot you were coming by." My eyes widened.

"Well, I'm a few days late. Had trouble getting out of my garage with all that ice and snow. Let's have a look, shall we?" He kept smiling and waited for me to walk outside. I glanced up at the sun hanging low in the sky. I knew it wouldn't be much longer before it set.

"Let me grab a coat," I said.

"Of course." He nodded and walked back down the porch steps to wait for me.

I closed the door and headed for the coat closet. My hand went straight to the fur coat before I stopped. I could only imagine what the neighbors would say if they caught me outside looking like a grizzly bear.

I poked around until I found the heavy coat I usually wore when we went skiing. It was thick and had a hood to cover my head. I grabbed my sunglasses and looked at my reflection in the mirror. I tucked my head farther back into the hood, hoping the sun wouldn't bother me too much.

I opened the door and walked out into the front yard.

Mr. McIntyre's eyebrows shot up when he saw me.

"I'm very cold," I said.

"I understand. My wife is the same way. She's usually curled up in a quilt even when she's inside in the summer." He shook his head and grinned. "Let's take a look at your flowers."

"To be honest, I haven't really looked since I called the other night." I had been too busy trying to figure out my new life.

We stopped in front of the landscaping. He groaned.

"Oh, goodness. I see what you mean." Mr. McIntyre cleared his throat and rubbed his chin. "You know that petunias aren't meant to survive a snowstorm. I could redo it for you, but I'm going to have to charge you for the flowers." He looked back at me.

I stared down at the landscaping. It was right in front of the house in the middle of the yard. Because our house was on a hill, the garden with the college mascot was the first thing everyone saw.

"What's going on?" Miles asked behind me.

"Mr. Jones, I was just coming over to talk to your wife about how we're going to fix the landscaping problem." The landscaper shoved his fingers through his hair and studied the ground. "I sure am sorry the snow ruined your surprise. It was supposed to be the Ole Miss mascot, but now it looks like…"

"Jesus. It looks like some guy's junk." Miles' eyes went wide.

I'd forgotten that Miles hadn't seen it yet. I stifled a giggle.

Both men looked at me.

"It was supposed to be the Ole Miss Landshark. Your wife wanted it to be special, for your birthday. She said it had to be perfect and, well, that darn snowstorm just ruined it." He shook his head.

"Well, it can't stay like that." Miles looked over his shoulder as a car passed by and honked.

"I told Mrs. Jones that I could fix it. But I'll have to replace the flowers."

"Why don't you go inside, Miles, I'll talk to Mr. McIntyre," I offered. I couldn't help but be pleased with how uncomfortable Miles was about the neighbors seeing something that wasn't up to his standards. He always cared way too much about what people thought. It was a constant battle and, to be completely honest, it was exhausting.

"You sure?" He gave me a worried look and then looked back at the street.

"I got this." I gave him what I hoped at least appeared to be a sincere smile.

He nodded and hurried inside.

I turned and looked back at Mr. McIntyre. "Why don't we wait about a week. I want to make sure there are no more surprises from Mother Nature. I sure would hate to plant more flowers and have them destroyed, as well.

"But what about Mr. Jones? He looked like he wanted this taken care of right away." He frowned, knowing if Miles weren't happy, he'd let his friends know. Mr. McIntyre was all about the bottom line.

"I think he wants it done the right way. No use in a big rush." I leaned closer and lifted my sunglasses from my eyes. I held his gaze. "Let's just wait on replanting everything." I grinned.

Mr. McIntyre's smile slid off his face, and he stared at me. His pupils dilated, and he leaned into my personal space. For a second, I thought he might try to kiss me. I'd never seen him look at me like that.

"I've got to go inside." I took a step back.

He only nodded and continued to stare at me without blinking. He looked like he was in some kind of trance. I turned to walk inside, and he just stood there like some kind of idiot. I shrugged. I wasn't sure what the hell was wrong with him, but he wasn't my problem. I had enough issues of my own.

When I reached the front door, I turned. Mr. McIntyre was still standing in the front yard, staring at me with that same stupid look on his face. I squinted. He actually looked like he had a bit of drool dangling from one corner of his mouth.

"Mr. McIntyre. Go home. I'll call you and let you know what to do about the flower bed later, okay?" I gnawed on the corner of my fingernail, a little worried. I'd never seen the man like this. Maybe he was having a stroke.

He blinked then smiled and nodded. "Yes, Mrs. Jones."

I watched as he made his way to his truck. He backed out and then pulled onto the street before making his way out of the subdivision.

"That was weird," I muttered, shaking my head.

Once inside, I went back to the kitchen to finish making dinner. I couldn't help but wonder just how this *family* dinner would go.

CHAPTER 17

*D*inner went off without a hitch. We fell into our routine of talking with the girls about their day, and for a moment, it almost seemed like we were a family again.

Until Miles got a text. He got up from the table and grabbed his phone. I followed him into the kitchen while the girls finished their dinner.

"Who is that?" I asked once we were alone.

"Just work." He shrugged and stuffed the phone into his pocket.

"Let me see." I held out my hand.

"Seriously, Rachel?" He cocked his eyebrow at me like I'd asked him what color the sky was.

"If you want this marriage to work, you need to be honest. Let me see your phone." I kept my hand out. My stomach clenched when he handed it over. I almost dreaded to see what was on the text.

I glanced down and read the group message from the doctors at the hospital. It was about an upcoming golf match for charity.

I held Miles' gaze and then handed it back to him.

"We aren't going to make it if you don't trust me." He cocked his head to the side.

Guilt pooled in my stomach. A marriage had to be built on trust. I knew that.

"I don't know how to trust you. Not after…" I couldn't bring myself to say the words. The two bites of Mexican rice I'd eaten at dinner threatened to come up.

"That's the only way this is going to work. Trust." He stepped closer and took his phone back. "You know I love you, and I love our family."

His eyes seemed sincere. It still didn't change what he'd done, or who he'd done it with.

"It's going to take time," I said. I turned and headed back to the dining room.

Ever since the girls were born, the rule was that the family ate dinner in the dining room. I knew that dining rooms were going out of fashion, and a lot of families didn't eat together anymore at all, but it was one habit I didn't want to break. I liked the focus that came from eating together as a unit, I felt like it brought us closer.

As the girls got older, they complained, but I didn't care. I knew once they grew up, it would be something they'd remember and hopefully carry on when they got married and started families of their own.

I grabbed the banana pudding out of the fridge and took it into the dining room.

"Yay, dessert!!" Gabby clapped her hands together.

"I don't want any," Arianna said none-too-convincingly. "I'm trying to watch what I eat."

"Honey, you don't need to worry about that. You barely weigh anything as it is." I snorted.

"Well, I'm eating a big old bowl," Gabby said. "I don't care if it makes me fat as an elephant."

I snorted at Gabby's description and scooped a helping into a bowl before handing it to her.

Arianna bit her bottom lip and eyed Gabby's bowl with envy.

"How about just a little taste?" I asked Arianna. I didn't want my girls to have body-image issues. I figured they shouldn't be worrying about that until they hit at least sixteen—if ever.

"Just a little." Arianna pressed her lips together.

"I'll put in more banana than vanilla wafer. Banana is a fruit, so it's like a healthy dessert." I scooped some pudding into a bowl and handed it to her.

"Yeah, it's healthy." Gabby nodded and scooped more pudding into her mouth.

"How about you? Aren't you having any?" Arianna looked at me and picked up her spoon.

"Of course." I smiled. I really didn't think I could eat another bite of food, but if it made my girls happy, I'd do it. I'd do anything for them if it made them happy. Including staying with their cheating father.

"That looks good." Miles came back into the dining room and sat down.

I fixed him a bowl and handed it to him.

"Did you know that Lori's parents are getting a divorce?" Gabby said between licks of her spoon.

I froze. Lori's parents had been married for years and had waited until they were in their thirties to have children.

"What?" I looked at Gabby. "How do you know that?"

"Lori told me at school today. She said that her daddy has a girlfriend. Her mommy told her daddy he had to pick between her and the girlfriend. So, her daddy packed up his stuff and moved out."

My hand flew to my mouth, and I felt nauseated. Sheila and Doug Armell seemed so happy.

"That's awful." I swallowed back the bile that rose up in the back of my throat and eased into my seat.

"I never liked Lori's dad. I'm glad he's gone." Gabby licked her spoon. "He was always grumpy and didn't like when Lori had friends over. He said we laughed too much and were too silly."

I narrowed my eyes. "You're girls. You are supposed to laugh and be silly." I cut my eyes to Miles, but he didn't look up from his bowl of banana pudding.

"Is Lori very upset?" I watched Gabby's face to read her expression.

"She says she's not, but I can tell she is. She hasn't cried or anything. But she's really quiet and won't join in when we are playing on the monkey bars." Gabby looked at me with a scowl on her face. "I mean, how am I going to play dragons and fairies if I can't get the dragon to get on the monkey bars?"

I grinned. "Just give her time, sweetie. Maybe you should invite her over to spend the night in a few weeks. Maybe it would help make her feel better."

"Can I?" Gabby's face brightened.

"Of course." I smiled. It made me happy to see her happy. "Maybe we can do some fun stuff."

"Like Manis and pedis?" Arianna asked and cut her eyes at me.

"Yeah. Like Manis and pedis." Gabby looked at me.

"Let me check and make sure there's nothing planned first." I put my spoon down without touching my banana pudding.

"Maybe you guys can have it on a weekend I'll be on call," Miles joked.

My chest clenched. Was he really on call? Or was he just saying that so he could go meet Nikki?

"Aww, Daddy. You're always working. You're never home anymore," Gabby whined.

I froze at her words and waited to see his response.

"I'm going to try to be home more, Pumpkin. I can't get out of being on call, but I'm really going to make more of an effort, I promise." He gave her a genuine smile.

Despite all the hell he'd put me through over the past few days I really wanted to believe that he would make good on his promise. For his family. For me.

After dinner, the girls went to their rooms, and I went into the kitchen to clean up. It had been the same routine for years. Tonight, it was hard to load the dishwasher properly because I had so much on my mind.

Lori's parents getting divorced was a shocker. From the outside looking in, I thought they had the perfect marriage. Doug brought her flowers all the time, and Sheila always bragged about what a great guy he was.

It hit too close to home, and the similarity to my own life was scary.

"I'll do these. Why don't you go relax?" Miles came up behind me and took the plate I had been rinsing out of my hand.

I looked at him with surprise. Miles never helped in the kitchen. Never.

"Are you sure?" I studied his expression, trying to see how sincere he was.

"Yes. Go take a hot bath and relax." He smiled.

His smile used to make my heart stop. Now, it made my chest hurt.

"Thanks. I'll do that." I grabbed my purse off the kitchen island and headed back to the bedroom. My stomach dropped when I spotted our bed. I reminded myself to look and see when that new comforter I'd ordered would arrive. I wasn't sure I could ever sleep in that bed again, but at least I could have new linens.

I grabbed my favorite robe out of the closet and hung it on the hook by my soaking tub. I sat on the edge and turned on the hot water and added my favorite jasmine-scented bath crystals. As I waited for the tub to fill, I grabbed my cell phone to check my messages.

My phone buzzed in my hand with an incoming call.

The number was unfamiliar to me, and I debated whether or not to answer it.

But the number was local, and it could be an appointment reminder.

"Hello?"

"I need to see you." the familiar voice of my kidnapper, Khalan, came over the line.

"What the hell are you doing calling me?" I frowned. "How did you even get my number?"

"I am your Maker. I make it my business to know everything about you. Including your number."

I flinched at the tone of his voice. I could picture him on the other end, rolling his eyes at my question.

"I can't meet you, I'm in the middle of something." I scowled.

"A bath is something that can wait."

"How did you know I was going to take a bath?" I glanced around and looked at the mirror but, this time, I didn't see his reflection.

"I can hear the water. Either you're running water for a bath, or an elephant is taking a piss," he snarked.

I clenched my teeth. "What do you want?"

"We need to talk. We need to meet so you can transition out of your human life and into your life as a vampire."

"That's not going to happen. I have a life here. A good life with a family and two girls that need me."

"It doesn't sound so good with a husband that is cheating on you. Besides, the girls really don't need you, they'll have their father to take care of them."

Anger rose up inside me like a wildfire. The thought of abandoning my daughters was unimaginable.

"Fuck that. And fuck you." I spat out the crude words. "Let's be very clear. I will not abandon my girls. Not now. Not ever. You can get that shit out of your head right now."

"You are making a very stupid mistake, Roadkill." His menacing tone pissed me off.

"Stop calling me that. I have a name. It's Rachel."

"You are losing your humanity. It may be a slow process, but you will eventually lose it and become something else entirely. You will become a vampire, and you need to learn to live like one. In the next few hours, your body will crave blood in order to satisfy your hunger."

White spots danced before my eyes. "Why did the blood taste like dark chocolate and roses?"

"Blood tastes different to every vampire. The things you loved as a human are how blood will taste on your tongue. Just nature's way of making the transition a little easier."

"Listen, buddy, there's nothing easy about any of this. I still have a heartbeat, and I still eat real food. Nothing is changing."

"What about the sun? Did you question why you had to cover up when you went outside?"

My heart jumped into my throat. "Have you been following me? Did you follow me today?"

"Absolutely not." He sniffed. "I'm a vampire. I know better than to stay outside all day."

"I've been outside, and I didn't burn up or burst into flames. I didn't even sparkle." I lifted my chin defiantly, even though he couldn't see me.

"God, you are so pathetic." He sighed heavily. "Vampires

don't burst into flames in sunlight. And don't you dare bring up sparkling to me ever again. We can go outside during the day, but it drains our energy. The only way to combat that is to drink blood."

"Drains us?"

"Yes. And if you keep going outside in the daylight without replenishing your body with blood, the results will be catastrophic."

"Like what?"

"This is exactly why you need to meet me, so we can talk." He growled into the phone.

"Well, it's not like I can just up and leave right now. I've got kids to put to bed, and I have to..."

"Meet me after midnight."

"Have you lost your mind? I'll be in bed by ten. There's no way I'm hauling my butt out of bed after midnight." I shook my head and reached over and turned off the water to the tub.

"That's all about to change." He laughed.

The line went dead.

I blinked and looked down at the cell phone in my hand.

"He didn't even say goodbye." I clenched my teeth and tossed the phone onto the bathroom counter. I quickly shed my clothes and stepped into the hot bathwater.

I sank down and closed my eyes, letting the hot water slip across my body like a cocoon. I tried to relax and not think about that conversation, but my mind wouldn't let me.

I'd lost a lot these past few days: my marriage, my trust in my husband, and according to Khalan, my humanity.

I laid my head back against the edge of the tub. Where had Khalan come from? I'd never seen him out and about in town, not even at night. The house he was in was in an older part of town where the rich used to live. Some people were currently trying to buy up the homes and remodel them to revitalize that area.

It was clear that he didn't like people. He made no effort to bathe. The dude smelled to high Heaven, and his clothes were constantly dirty. He wore the same black wool duster coat and black pants each time I saw him. Even his button-up shirt was black.

If he really were a vampire, I wondered how old he was. I made a mental note to ask him the next time I saw him.

"Ugh. I'm not going to see him again. This whole thing is a bad freaking idea." I shook my head and grabbed the towel. I stood and dried off before grabbing my robe.

I went to the bedroom and tugged open the drawers in my dresser. I immediately reached for comfy, fuzzy pajamas that I always slept in. I froze, wondering. When Miles and I were first married, I'd always worn something sexy to bed. I'd made an effort. But once the children came along, I chose comfort over seduction. Had Miles cheated because I'd stopped making an effort?

I reached for the white silk gown with its plunging neckline and the slit up the thigh. I slipped on the sexy material and looked at myself in the full-length mirror in the closet.

The last time I'd tried it on, it was tight around the hips. But now it flowed over my slender body and made me look as if I'd stepped out of a Victoria's Secret catalogue.

I grinned and then slipped my robe over the top of my gown. I wasn't ready to be intimate with Miles, but I was more than willing to show him what he couldn't have.

I never thought I was vain. I knew I was attractive, and plenty of men had tried to get my attention over the years. Even the bag boy at the grocery store seemed to get flustered when I checked out.

But now, I looked gorgeous.

I stared at my reflection, and then it hit me.

"I have a reflection," I said to myself.

Vampires didn't have reflections. I stepped closer to the mirror and reached out my hand.

"Yep, definite reflection," I said and arched my brow.

I slipped on my comfy house shoes and headed back to the kitchen.

The dishes had been put in the dishwasher, but Miles hadn't bothered to turn it on. Nor had he put away the skillet. Typical. I shook my head and finished setting the kitchen to rights.

My mind raced with thoughts of Miles' betrayal. If someone could have seen inside my head at that moment, they would have thought I was crazy.

I was mad, sad, hurt, and devastated. But, I also had a flicker of hope that maybe we could work this out. Miles hadn't left the house, and he seemed like he wanted to make things work. But something kept gnawing at me. He didn't seem remorseful.

With a shrug, I started the dishwasher and headed toward the girls' rooms.

I peeked in on Arianna. She was lying on her bed with her feet up on the wall as she chatted away on her cell. I wasn't keen on her having a phone because she was too young, but Miles had given in and bought it for her.

I knocked on her open door.

"Start getting ready for bed." I waited until she nodded before heading toward Gabby's room.

I heard Gabby's voice before I even made it to her room. I smiled. She was always talking to herself when she was alone, playing games of dragons and princesses and fairy tales. I loved that about her. I wished I could be adventurous like her.

My Gabby was going to change the world.

"Hey, sweetie." I stepped inside her room.

Gabby looked up from her kneeling position on the floor beside her bed. She had a plastic knight's helmet on her head and a book in her hand.

"How about this book, Mommy?" Gabby's eyes sparkled with excitement.

"Sure." I smiled and sat on the bed. She pulled off the helmet and tossed it onto the floor.

She scrambled under the covers and snuggled close. I closed my eyes and sighed. This feeling of being needed warmed my heart and seeped into my lungs. I lived and died for my children. I decided then, in the space of mere seconds, that I would do whatever it took to save my marriage. For the girls' sakes.

I opened the book and began reading the tale of a brave knight rescuing a princess from the cave of a dragon. It was Gabby's favorite. Not because it had a princess. It was her favorite because it had a knight and a dragon.

When I had finished the last line, I closed the book and looked down at my daughter.

"I feel bad for that dragon." Gabby looked up at me with her big, brown eyes.

"But the dragon kept the princess captive and wouldn't let her leave." I frowned.

"He only did that because he was lonely and didn't have anyone to talk to." Her brow creased as she continued. "I think he was probably bullied in school and didn't have any friends. He had to go find a friend, it just happened to be the princess."

"Ah, so that's what you think." I grinned at her. I loved the way she looked at the world.

"It's what I *know*, Mom." She lifted her chin. "Besides, I think that princess was way too whiny. I mean, she didn't even thank the dragon for all the food, jewels, and things he bought her." She narrowed her gaze.

"I think he stole those things, honey. He didn't buy them." I bit my lip to keep from smiling.

"Whatever. The point is, the princess was a spoiled brat who was used to living in the castle and getting whatever she wanted. She should have thanked the dragon for taking her away. I mean, she got to fly on his back for Pete's sake!" Gabby waved her hands in the air to make her point. "Do you know what I would give to fly on a dragon's back?"

"No. What would you do?" I grinned and waited for her answer.

"I would love that dragon forever. I would be his best friend, and I wouldn't ever leave him. That's what I would do." She held up her hand. "Oh, and I would bring him people to eat."

"Gabby, that's very graphic, and it's not a nice thing to do."

"I didn't mean nice people. I would only bring him the bad ones."

"What do you think qualifies as a bad person?" A part of me wondered how she would describe Khalan.

She tapped her finger to her chin and looked up at the ceiling, seemingly lost in thought. She grinned and then met my gaze again.

"A bad person would be anyone who does anything bad. Like people who hurt other people. Or people that bully those who are weak."

I nodded, carefully choosing my words. "I see. What about forgiveness? Do you think someone who has hurt someone else and not say they're sorry should be fed to a dragon?"

She frowned. "If someone hurt someone, that means they did it on purpose." She shook her head. "Saying you're sorry doesn't mean squat."

"Gabby. Language," I warned. I had to admit, what she said intrigued me.

"People make mistakes. Nobody is perfect," I said.

"I know. But when you do something to hurt someone, you are making a choice to do it. It means, not only do you have no heart, it means you are very selfish." She narrowed her eyes. "Like that princess. I think the dragon should have eaten her."

A laugh rolled out of me, and I glanced at the bedside clock.

"Okay, my beautiful dragon. It's time to go to sleep." I slid out of bed and leaned down to tuck her in.

She smiled up at me. I touched my lips to her soft cheek.

"I love you," I said.

"I love you too, Mommy. And would you mind calling me dragon from now on?" She crossed her arms over her chest. "I wish I were a real dragon with scales and large wings. Then, when someone at school hurts Arianna's feelings, I could breathe fire on them until they are fried chicken." She shrugged. "And then I just might eat them."

My smiled faltered. Something about her playful words felt off.

"Honey, is everything okay with Arianna? Has she said something about someone being mean to her at school?" My stomach clenched.

Gabby blinked and shook her head. "No, not that I've seen." She slid under the covers and pulled the comforter up to her chin.

"You know, if something ever happens or someone does something mean to either of you…"

"I know, Mommy. I'm supposed to tell you." She gave a long-suffering sigh.

I nodded and decided to let it go. I knew Arianna would

tell me if I should worry. She'd always been good about telling me everything.

"I love you, sweetie." I leaned over and kissed her cheek. The warmth of her skin made my heart clench as a sense of loss washed over me. I wanted a family for my girls.

"Love you, Mommy." Gabby smiled and shut her eyes. Her long lashes rested against her pink cheeks. She was the picture of innocence and all that was good in my life.

I left her room and headed down the hallway to Arianna's room. She spotted me in the doorway and quickly sent a text and put her phone on the bedside table.

"Everything okay?" I glanced from her phone to her.

"Yep." She arched her brow. "Is everything okay with you?"

My throat tightened. "Yeah. Why do you ask?" I managed to squeak out.

"I don't know. You're just acting weird." She sat up in bed and crossed her arms over her chest and eyed me. "Plus, you lost all that weight."

"All that weight? You act like I was an elephant." I scowled.

"Come on, Mom. You definitely lost like…twenty pounds."

I glanced down at my body and then back at her.

"I didn't mean it that way, Mom. You look really great. You really do. I'm just wondering if something happened to make you lose so much weight so fast."

I forced a smile. "No, honey, I just had a little bit of the stomach flu and didn't eat for a few days." I shrugged. "I guess I should have gotten sick years ago."

"Nah. You've always been gorgeous. But you know that." Arianna's face fell a little.

"Thanks, honey. But you're way better-looking than me." I lifted my chin. "I mean, you are beautiful now. Just wait until you turn eighteen. I'll have to beat the boys off with a stick."

That pulled a ghost of a smile from her lips. "Really?"

"Without a doubt." I nodded slowly. "It's a day I'm dreading."

"Thanks, Mom." She smiled and scrambled under the covers.

I walked over and sat on the bed then leaned down and kissed her cheek.

"You know you can always tell me anything, right?"

"I know." She scowled and then looked at me under her thick lashes. "You can talk to me too, Mom."

My heart nearly shattered in my chest at her words. I blinked back the quick tears that had gathered behind my eyes.

"Thanks, Arianna. I needed that, sweetheart." I gave her a kiss and stood. I hurried out the door before the tears spilled down my cheeks. I closed the door and leaned against the wall as I cried freely. My oldest daughter had been the one to offer words that had broken down my walls and struck my heart.

Even when I felt like I had lost everything, I knew I still had my daughters.

CHAPTER 18

*J*brushed my teeth, and then brushed them again. I stared at my reflection in the bathroom mirror. Then I picked up the hairbrush and ran it through my tresses.

Miles was already in bed reading, as was his usual bedtime routine. I looked at the light spilling from under the door, and my stomach dropped.

I knew I was stalling, doing everything I could think of before I had to get into bed with him. I wasn't sure if I could even do it. Not the mattress where he'd had sex with Nikki.

Anger flared in my stomach as the image once again flashed in my head. Hatred settled in my gut.

The light from under the door went dark.

Miles was done reading and was ready for sleep.

I looked back at my reflection and narrowed my eyes.

I opened the door.

"Hey. Ready for bed?" Miles' gaze roamed down my body. I recognized the tone. It was the same one he used before he made love to me. It used to excite me, now it only pissed me off.

"No. I can't sleep," I said and stormed out of the bedroom back into the living room. I flung myself onto the couch and lay on my back, looking up at the ceiling.

"Ugh," I groaned to the dark, empty room.

Half of me wanted Miles to come and check on me. The other half wanted to be left alone. Either way, I was irritated and agitated. A state I wasn't used to.

"Stop being so dramatic," a dark voice whispered.

Khalan.

I sat up and looked around, searching for his large figure in my house.

"Are you ready to talk?" he asked.

I glanced over at the corner of the living room. The bright moonlight cast a glow over Khalan's large frame. He stepped forward, and his smell hit me.

"Jesus. You can't just come into my house whenever you choose. It's called breaking and entering," I hissed through my teeth.

I looked around to make sure Miles wasn't coming down the hall.

"How the hell did you get in here anyway? You gave me my keys back." I glared.

"I had a copy made," he stated in his usual bored tone.

"You can't do that. It's illegal. For a vampire who's been around for a while, you certainly don't know a lot about etiquette or the law." I narrowed my eyes.

"And for someone so eager to stay in your old life, you do a whole lot of bitching." He took a step closer and glared.

"Well, you make a shitty vampire," I shot back.

He said nothing as he arched a brow. When I saw that he wasn't making an effort to leave, I sighed and then walked over to open the French doors that led out to the backyard.

I motioned with my hand for him to follow me. I carefully closed the door and then froze.

"The alarm didn't chime when I opened the door."

"I turned it off," he said simply.

"How did you turn it off...never mind," I huffed out. I crossed my arms and looked at him. "You can't just walk in my house like that. It's rude."

"I needed to talk to you. I figured you would be on your second bottle of wine by now, drowning your sorrows because of your cheating husband."

My heart clenched. His words found their mark.

"I need you to come with me," he said.

"How do I know you won't try to hurt me?"

"Because I'm your Maker. A Maker would never hurt their progeny, unless..." His words trailed off, and he looked off to the side.

"Unless what?" I asked.

"Doesn't matter." His gaze drifted back to me.

I stared into his eyes. The color had changed to deep blue. Something about the color held me captive, and try as I might, I couldn't look away.

"Come." The words fell out of his mouth. A shiver ran through my body, and an erotic image of me naked on the ground with my hand between my legs flashed through my head.

I gasped. Had Khalan put that image in my mind?

"What?" He frowned.

I could tell from his expression that he hadn't.

"Nothing." I rubbed my hand over my collarbone and pressed my lips together. "I guess you expect me to follow you without any idea of where we are going."

"That's exactly what I expect." He leaned close to me, and his smell caught me off guard. It was different. This time, he smelled like gym socks and pine needles.

I opened my mouth to argue but was too caught off guard by the pull of his eyes.

"I get the feeling you're doing something to me," I said quietly.

"I am. I'm compelling you to follow me. I don't have time to stand here and argue," Khalan said and turned.

I wanted to stand my ground, but my feet had a mind of their own. First, my left foot, then my right until I was a few feet away from Khalan, following him out of the yard and into the dark night.

"You're an ass. I can't believe you are using your evil mind control on me," I spat.

"It's not evil mind control. It's called a glamour. And it has nothing to do with evil."

"Do all vampires glamour their victims?" The cold hit my face, but it didn't bother me.

"You act like I'm luring you to your death."

"You probably are." I glanced down at my feet and sucked in a deep breath.

"What is it now?' He glared at me over his shoulder.

"I don't understand." I held out my arms to my sides. "And I'm only wearing my pajamas. It's got to be around thirty degrees out here, and I'm not even cold. I'm usually freezing when the temperature is below sixty."

"That's because your body is acclimating to being a vampire. You'll grow to love the night and the cold and hate the day and the sun. After you fully turn, you'll only go out at night."

"What do you mean I can only go out at night? I can't do that. I have girls who play soccer. They do that during the day."

"Make them quit." He spoke without looking over his shoulder.

"Are you crazy?"

"Not that I'm aware."

"I can't make them quit. They love playing soccer. They've played ever since they were little."

"And I suppose they'll die if they can't play." His sarcasm wasn't lost on me.

Anger curdled in my gut. "You obviously have never been around children."

"I make it a point to never be around humans of any age. Unless they're food." He opened the back gate, walked through it, and moved into the woods that backed up to my house.

"Yet, here you are with me," I snarked. "You picked me up off the road and brought me to your house. Odd behavior for a vampire who hates humans."

"I didn't bring a human to my house. I brought you to my home because you were roadkill."

The only sound in the woods was my angry breathing and his heavy footsteps on broken twigs.

"Has anyone ever told you what an ass you are?" I was staring holes into his back.

"Only you. But, like I said, I try to stay away from humans. Animals are much more pleasant to be around."

"They probably think you're an ass, too. But they can't tell you because they can't speak.'" I felt my face heating. I wasn't sure why he was pushing my buttons. I didn't even know him.

"No, they don't." He shot a glare over his shoulder. "Animals like me. And I like them."

"Whatever helps you sleep at night."

I glanced around the forest and noticed how silent everything was. I'd never been out in the woods, and certainly not at night. It was out of my comfort zone.

"Here." He stopped suddenly and turned to me. "Wait here."

"I have better things to do than stand out in the woods at night with a stranger."

"Actually, you don't." His bored tone pissed me off.

I clenched my hands to keep from hitting him. Not that I could inflict much—if any—damage. He was as wide as a professional football player and outweighed me by at least one hundred pounds. Not to mention, he looked like he was made of pure muscle.

"There." He pointed toward the base of a large tree.

"Where? I can't see anything?" I squinted.

"Try harder," he insisted.

I narrowed my eyes and, surprisingly enough, my vision began to change. I could actually see clearly in the dark.

I looked at him. He smirked. "It's your vampire-enhanced vision."

"But..." I shook my head.

"You can try to keep pretending you're not turning into a vampire, but that won't change the reality."

My heart sped up. I didn't like him telling me this.

"So, why am I out here again?"

"I need to show you how to take blood."

"Take blood? Please tell me you mean from a blood bank."

He snarled. "You need to learn how to take blood from a human so you can survive."

"But I thought vampires didn't die."

"There are certain things that can kill a vampire."

"Not getting blood is one of them?" A shiver ran through my body.

He turned around and faced me, giving me his full attention. "If you don't get blood, you will certainly *want* to die. You'll become so consumed with bloodlust that you will attack anything with a pulse." He narrowed his eyes. "Even your children."

"No. I would never do that." I shook my head and

wrapped my arms around my chest. I wasn't cold, but his words had me shaking.

"You are young and naive. But once your body has fully turned, you won't retain any of your humanity. What you are now is not what you will be when you've fully converted."

"No. I will always be the same person I am now." I dropped my hands to my sides and fisted my fingers. I refused to be a monster.

He snorted and turned back to the tree. Without looking at me, he grabbed my hand and pulled me forward until I was standing by his side.

"Look over there by the tree." He nodded.

I sighed and looked over by the large pine. The breeze ruffled the needles on the low-hanging branches. A large, dark object sat at the base of the trunk. I thought it looked like someone had bundled some clothes up and left them on the ground. Until I saw it move.

I gasped and took a step back. "Is that a person?"

"Yes."

"What the hell is wrong with him? You didn't hurt him, did you?" My blood turned cold in my veins, and my eyes went wide.

"He's not hurt. Just glamoured." Khalan turned and looked at me. "Go over to him and tell him to give you his neck." He glared at me. "Make sure you look him in the eyes when you speak."

"I'm not doing that." I stepped away from him.

He lifted his chin and stared hard at me. "Do you want to survive? To stay with your children?"

I nodded.

"Then you will need to learn how to take blood." He looked at the guy. "Do it, now."

"Fine. But I don't think we have the same power. I'm not like you."

"Thank God for that." He snorted.

I bit my lip before I could return a blistering comment. Right now, I needed to get this done so I could get back to the house before my family woke up to discover me gone.

"Fine." I clenched my hands and slowly made my way to the tree. I stopped about two feet away from the man and looked down.

He was propped up against the base of the trunk with his knees tucked under his chin. He didn't even look up when I stopped in front of him

"Did you drug him?" I cut my eyes to Khalan.

"Of course, not. That would make the blood taste bad." He let out another long sigh and then walked over to me. "As I said, he's glamoured."

I wasn't sure I trusted Khalan; after all, he did turn me into a vampire. Or so he claimed. For all I knew, I could be experiencing some kind of psychotic delusion after seeing my husband in bed with another woman. At the moment, I was more concerned about the stranger in the woods behind my house.

I took a deep breath and blew it out.

"Excuse me," I said quietly.

The man looked up.

"Oh my God. That's my neighbor, Cal." I knelt on the ground in front of him. "Hey, are you okay?"

Cal stared at me, unblinking. He looked like he was in some kind of daze or that he'd been drinking a little too much.

"He's fine," Khalan said.

I stood up and spun around to face Khalan. "What the hell are you doing, bringing my neighbors here? He could tell everyone in the neighborhood about this."

"He won't," Khalan stated.

I stepped back from Khalan. "Oh my God. Was it his

blood you gave me in the cup the other night? You're going to kill him, aren't you?"

Khalan pinched the bridge of his nose and screwed up his face.

"No. It wasn't his blood you had the other night, and *no*, I hadn't planned on killing him." He looked at me.

"So, how do you know he's not going to spill the beans? What if I really do take his blood? He could go running back to his wife, Carla, and it will be all over the neighborhood that I'm trying to steal someone's husband."

"Has anyone ever told you that you're paranoid as fuck?"

"No." I glared. Actually, Miles had said I was a bit over-protective. But not paranoid. Never that.

"The sooner you get this done, the sooner we can both get back home." He crossed his arms and waited.

"Fine," I growled. "What do I do?"

"Tell him to stand up."

I took a deep breath and looked back at Cal. My entire body was trembling, but it wasn't fear I felt. It was antic-ipation.

"Cal, stand up." My voice was a little above a whisper, but it sounded so much louder in the dark. I felt like the entire woods was watching and judging me.

Cal's brown hair dipped upward, and his brown gaze locked on mine. His mouth was slightly ajar, and he had a dazed look.

"Tell him again. This time, louder," Khalan commanded.

My gut flared in irritation. I didn't like being ordered around.

"Cal, stand up." This time, my voice was more author-itative.

Cal didn't say a word, just stretched his legs out in front of him and got to his feet, all while keeping his eyes on me.

Cal wasn't a very tall guy, so we were pretty much at eye level.

"Now what? It's not like I have fangs," I spoke out of the corner of my mouth.

"You don't need fangs. Not yet. Now, tell him to give you his neck."

I jerked my head to Khalan. "I just want you to know that I'm very uncomfortable with all of this. I have never so much as kissed another man since I got married, and to do all this seems very inappropriate. Not to mention the whole blood thing."

"You are so weak." Khalan sighed.

His words caused a flare in my chest, and the irritation morphed straight to rage.

"I'm not weak, you asshole." My tone darkened with my current mood.

Khalan snorted, obviously not believing me.

I turned back to Cal, who was staring at me. He had a little bit of drool coming out of the side of his mouth.

It was now or never.

"Cal, give me your neck."

Cal said nothing but bent his head to the side, exposing his jugular.

I'd never really noticed people's necks before. I mean, I saw their eyes, mouths, and even their hairstyles. They were prominent features of a person's appearance and part of what made them so unique. Cal was a middle-aged man of average build with light brown hair and eyes. He'd never really stood out to me. And if I had to be honest, he was a person who just...blended in. He was neither great-looking nor ugly. Just average.

But in this moment under the dim light of the moon, Cal's thick neck beckoned me. I could see his pulse throbbing. I squinted my eyes as the skin seemed to tick with his blood, pulsing with each heartbeat.

My mouth watered, and I couldn't help myself. I took a step closer, fascinated by Cal's neck.

I took a deep breath, and that's when it hit me. The scent. The sweet smell of his blood filled my nose and made my mouth water. I let out a growl.

"Your first time is going to be rough," Khalan said behind me.

I must have been too intent on Cal's neck to notice that Khalan had walked up behind me. I could feel his breath on my neck, and I shivered.

"I don't want to hurt him," I admitted.

"Once you start, you're not going to be able to stop. I need you to listen to my voice and follow my instructions. When you start, you need to pay attention to your body so you'll know when to stop. Otherwise, you'll rip his throat out."

I heard Khalan's words and wanted to be frightened, but I couldn't. I was too mesmerized by Cal's throbbing vein.

I stepped closer and wrapped my hand around Cal's neck. His skin was warm under my fingers, I knew his blood would taste good.

I closed my eyes and inhaled deeply, letting the scent of his blood wash over me.

My breathing quickened. I bent my head to Cal's neck and opened my mouth.

I bit down.

Cal groaned but didn't fight. He stayed perfectly still while my teeth sank into his flesh. There was a pop. The edge of one of my teeth broke his skin, and the coppery taste of blood seeped into my mouth.

I tightened my grip on his neck and sucked hard.

Cal didn't fight or flinch, just stood where he was and let

out a low moan. As I drank from his neck, my body began to tremble, and I craved more.

I lost track of time.

"Rachel, you need to stop," Khalan said.

I heard him, but my body would not obey. I didn't want to listen. I wanted to drink every last drop of Cal's blood until he was dry. Oddly enough, I didn't feel any guilt over that thought.

Khalan rested his hand on my shoulder, and I shrugged him off, tightening my hold on Cal. I cut my eyes to the side and growled like a dog with a bone.

"You will kill him if you don't stop." Khalan made no move to stop me or pull me away from my feast. Instead, he stepped to the side and studied me, waiting to see if I would pass the test.

I closed my eyes, struggling with myself. I craved more of Cal's blood. It was like a fine wine, and I was a starving alcoholic.

With trembling hands, I released my hold on Cal and shoved him away from me. He stumbled backward into the tree. Blood trickled down his neck to his white shirt. He turned his gaze back to me.

I wiped my mouth with the back of my hand and studied the ground, too embarrassed to look him in the eyes.

"Is he going to be okay?" I cut my eyes to Cal, worried about how weak and pale he appeared. I didn't trust myself to go near him.

"You need to finish him," Khalan demanded.

"Finish him?" I gave Khalan a wide-eyed look and pointed my finger at his chest. "You said I didn't have to kill him."

Khalan blew out a breath. "I don't mean kill him. I mean make him forget what just happened."

"How do I do that?"

"Glamour him. Look him in the eyes and tell him the

story of an event, something other than what happened here."

"What do you mean?"

"Give him a new memory."

"Like what? I mean, we live in a gated subdivision, there's no reason for us to be out in the woods this late at night?"

"Oh my God. You are the most ridiculous person I have ever met. I should have left you in the road." Khalan glared at me. I could feel his disdain like hot wind.

"Right back at you," I shouted.

I turned my attention back to Cal and held his gaze. "Cal, you won't remember this. You will remember hearing something outside, and going to check it out. You thought you saw someone running away from your house and you chased them into the woods." I peered at the wound on his neck. The bleeding had stopped, but it still looked bad.

"You ran past a tree, and a low-lying branch scratched your neck. That's why you have blood on your shirt. When you go home, you'll change your clothes, wash up, and go to bed. If Carla asks about your neck, tell her about the limb."

"That's very detailed. You should have just said, 'you won't remember this night, and you won't remember me.'" Khalan scrubbed his hand down his face.

"I guess you should have been more specific." I glared. I turned my attention back to Cal. If this really worked, then now was my time to cover my tracks. "Cal, you won't remember anything about the night of the snowstorm."

I looked back at Khalan. "How do I know he isn't going to tell his wife I was the one who bit him?" My gut twisted, and suddenly I had a whole lot of self-loathing to deal with.

"He won't. He's glamoured. He'll do whatever you tell him to do."

"Anything?" I arched my brow.

"Yeah, anything."

"So, I could tell him to bark like a dog, and he'd do it?"

"Pretty much." Khalan turned to leave.

"Wait. We can't just leave him here. How do we know he'll get home okay? I don't think his wife is going to believe him about the blood on his neck and shirt."

"Then, fix it," Khalan said over his shoulder as he walked away from me.

"You're such an ass." I hissed.

"Back at you," Khalan said.

"Where are you going? You can't just make me drink some guy's blood and then leave me here alone."

"Actually, I can. I'll be away for a few days, so I needed to show you how to glamour your victims before you drink their blood." Khalan kept walking, not giving me a chance to speak.

"Where are you going?" I took a few steps and stopped. I looked over my shoulder at Cal, who still seemed dazed.

"Business. I'll be back soon. In the meantime, stay out of trouble." It was all he said before he disappeared into the night, leaving me alone with a bloody and dazed Cal.

My heart raced, and I suddenly wished I were back in my home, safe and sound, where the life I knew existed. Instead, I was out in the dark, drinking my neighbor's blood like a monster.

"Go home, Cal," I said. It was all I could say. He nodded once and then started walking in the direction of his house.

I followed behind, watching from a distance as he shuffled out of the woods and through my backyard into the street. I kept to the shadows as I followed him. I couldn't let him walk around in the dark alone, not in this state. I needed to make sure he got home before I went back to my house.

He wandered around to the fence and disappeared into his backyard. I watched from my position under the shadow of a large tree. I didn't see a light come on, but I could see him moving around in his house. I turned and headed back into my own home.

I'd taken the blood of another human.

I'd never so much as raised my hand to another person in my life. I didn't even spank my own children. I shivered, thinking about what I could have done to poor Cal. If Khalan hadn't been there, I likely would have lost control and could have really hurt him. My stomach turned.

I could have killed Cal.

I swallowed and wrapped my arms around my chest. I headed back inside my house through the back door. The house was still dark. I was sure that Miles hadn't missed me, nor had he come looking for me.

I walked to the living room window and looked out into the dark. Things appeared different now. I suddenly knew that dangerous things actually lived in the darkness. Things like Khalan. And now, things like me.

I didn't know Khalan at all, but I found myself curious about him. He'd said he was going away for a few days, but he didn't tell me where he was going.

All I knew was that I would be free of his interference, at least for a few nights.

For that, I was grateful.

CHAPTER 19

"*How* long have you been up?" Miles walked into the kitchen and grabbed a coffee cup. "I never heard you come to bed last night."

I quickly shut my laptop. I stood from the kitchen island and glanced at the time.

"I didn't go to bed. I couldn't sleep." It was the truth. After drinking Cal's blood, I'd been so energized that I couldn't even think about going to bed. Instead, I'd reorganized the pantry and dusted the entire living room. After, I'd still had hours before dawn, so I decided to do a Google search on vampires.

I'd learned that vampires were not supposed to go out in the daylight. But I knew that wasn't true. I'd been out during the day to take the girls to school, and I hadn't burst into flames.

The internet also said that vampires were repelled by garlic. Again, something that wasn't true. I'd touched the garlic when I was in the pantry, and nothing had happened.

As much as I didn't like Khalan, I knew I needed to talk to

him. He had all the answers I needed. But he was gone, and I wasn't sure when he would be back.

I reached for the creamer out of habit and stopped. I preferred my coffee black now.

"What's wrong? Is the creamer bad?" Miles looked at me over his cup of coffee.

"No, I just don't feel like creamer and sugar this morning." I put the creamer into the fridge and the sugar back in its place in the cabinet.

Miles didn't give me a second look, just picked up the newspaper he'd grabbed from the driveway and started reading.

It rubbed me the wrong way that he could go about his daily routine without a problem. He seemed to have forgotten how he had wronged us. Did he even have a conscience?

"What are you doing today?" I poured the black coffee into my cup and lifted it to my lips. I took a sip, letting the bitter brew settle on my tongue. I sighed softly, very much liking the way it tasted.

"One surgery this morning and the office this afternoon." He spoke without looking up from his paper.

I set down my coffee cup and slid my hands down the legs of my yoga pants. Unease raced through my veins, and I wasn't sure if I believed what he was telling me. I studied his face until he finally looked up.

"What?" His brows drew together, and he held my gaze.

"Just one surgery?" I asked.

"Yeah. It's going to be a long one, though. It should run about six hours if everything goes well. Eight, if I run into trouble." He went back to his paper.

I curled my fingers into my palms. I wanted to snatch that damn paper out of Miles' hands and force him to look at me. I narrowed my eyes, wondering if I could glamour him into telling the truth. The glamour had seemed to work on Cal. He'd let me have his blood without a peep. I would bet I could get Miles to tell me the truth so I would know if he'd really meant that he wasn't going to see Nikki anymore.

"Miles." I stepped closer to him. My heart was pounding like a rabbit thumping its foot. Whatever he said, I would have to accept.

"Yes?" He looked up and gave me his full attention.

I opened my mouth to ask the question I knew I didn't want the answer to.

Do you love Nikki?

"Don't forget, the girls have a soccer game on Saturday. It would be great if you could make it." I looked away. Despite needing to know, I couldn't bring myself to ask. Once the question was out and answered, I knew there would be no going back. If I was honest, I was afraid of what Miles would say.

"I'm going to do my best to make it," he said as his gaze dropped once again to the newspaper.

"Good." It was all I could say. He hadn't made a single soccer game this year. He always had to work, or was on call.

Now, I doubted everything. Maybe Miles had actually been with Nikki all those weekends he was supposed to be working. My anger flared, and I knew if I stayed in the kitchen with him, I'd likely do something unforgivable. Like drain him. So, instead of homicide, I grabbed my coffee and headed to the bedroom.

I glared at the unmade bed. Miles never lifted a finger. He'd been like that since we got married. Maybe even before. I'd never really given it a second thought before, but now it bothered me. I glanced at the clock on the nightstand. I still had plenty of time to grab a shower and dress before the girls got up. I turned on the water and stripped off my clothes. I stood in front of the mirror and examined my reflection.

My stomach was flatter than ever, and I even had a six-pack. I'd never had a six-pack, even in my twenties. My legs were lean and toned, and all my cellulite was completely gone. My ass looked better than ever, and my skin practically glowed.

I stepped closer to study my face. The tiny lines around my eyes were gone, as were the lines in my forehead. My lips looked fuller, and my eyes were shining despite the sadness in their depths.

The sorrow that had settled in my soul now reflected in my eyes.

I shook off the morose feelings and stepped into the shower. The splash of hot water shocked me, and I turned the temperature down. Usually, I loved hot showers—the hotter, the better—but today it seemed too much.

When I stepped out, I wrapped the extra towel around my wet hair and let the warmth of the terrycloth robe soak up the excess water.

I dressed quickly in some jeans and a long-sleeve, white T-shirt. I slipped on my ballet flats and quickly dried my hair. I didn't bother with makeup but curled my hair until waves hung down my back. I slicked on some lip gloss and walked out of the bedroom.

"Wow, you look…great." Miles' gaze roamed up and down my body before coming to rest on my face.

"Thanks." I'd never been particularly vain, nor did I fish for compliments. I had taught my girls that beauty was on the inside and it didn't matter what you looked like on the outside. But, with everything that had happened, I needed to hear my husband tell me I was pretty, to tell me I mattered.

"How much weight have you lost?" He cocked his head, his gaze still on me.

"I don't know. I haven't weighed myself."

"Just be careful. You could gain it all back and then some."

He set his coffee cup in the sink and walked toward the bedroom to get ready for work.

And just like that, my anger was back.

* * *

THE ALARM on my phone jolted me awake. I'd taken the kids to school, but by the time I got home, I couldn't stop yawning. After being up all night, what did I expect?

I laid down, hoping to catch a thirty-minute nap. I made sure to set my alarm so I wouldn't oversleep. I still had a ton of things to do before I had to pick up the girls.

"Rachel, where are you?" Stephanie Miller's voice spilled over the phone.

"I'm at home." I turned and glanced at the clock on the bedside table.

"You're late for coffee club," Stephanie said. "Are you feeling okay?"

Stephanie was one of my neighbors and a friend. She wasn't in our book club because she didn't particularly like the kinds of books we read. She said there was too much sex and violence. And she didn't drink, either. She was a good Southern Baptist girl through and through.

Stephanie had started coffee club about six months ago. She was a stay-at-home mom with one daughter, Mary Beth, who was in the same grade as Arianna. They used to be friends when they were little but had grown apart.. We were friends, but we weren't what you would call close. She was nice enough and would give you the shirt off her back, but she always managed, without trying, to make me feel guilty that I wasn't a good Christian.

"I'm fine, I just got busy," I lied.

"You know, some of the neighbors say they haven't seen you much. Is everything okay…?"

Her unsure tone ruffled my nerves. I didn't need to draw any attention to myself or my situation. I was hoping that no one knew about Nikki and Miles. I hoped they'd been discreet and hadn't flaunted their affair.

"I'm on my way. Be there in a little bit." I ended the call and jumped out of bed.

I cringed at the sunlight spilling in around the curtains.

I ran to the bathroom, brushed my hair, and put on some lip gloss. I decided to change into black heels instead of wearing my ballet flats. If I had to go out of the house, I needed to try and look like everything was okay in my life.

I grabbed my purse and keys off the kitchen island and headed for the garage.

As I backed out and headed down the hill, I noticed the overcast sky. I squinted and slid my shades over my eyes as I pulled out onto the street. Within a few minutes, I was pulling into a parking spot at the city's quaint coffee shop, Caffeine and Cookies coffee shop.

I slid out of the car and winced at the brightness. Though the sun was hidden behind dark clouds, the light still made me cringe.

My heels snapped smartly across the parking lot as I made my way into the coffee shop.

The scent of coffee beans and freshly baked pastries hit me as I stepped inside. I let out a sigh.

"Rachel." Stephanie stood from her table and waved.

I smiled and held up a finger, indicating I would be right there after I got my order.

It was only a little after nine, and I'd already had coffee, but I knew I needed to get something to drink while I was here. I had to appear normal.

"Small coffee, please," I said to Max the barista. I gazed longingly at the chocolate chip scones behind the glass counter and pressed my lips together.

"Hello, Mrs. Jones." Max Rainer was a college student who worked the morning shift at Caffeine and Cookies before classes. His parents owned the local hardware store and went to my church.

"Hi, Max." I gave him a friendly smile. My gaze drifted to his neck. I swallowed, wondering what his blood would taste like in my mouth.

He handed me the coffee, and I took a drink, trying to get my mind off Max's neck.

I choked on the sweet coffee and started coughing.

"Mrs. Jones, are you okay? Was it too hot?" Max's brows knit together in worry.

When I recovered, I shook my head. "No. It's too sweet."

"But I made it like you always ask. Cream and sugar." He insisted.

"It's not your fault, Max." My gaze drifted back to his neck. "I've started taking my coffee black."

"Oh. Here, let me make you another." He took away the cup and started making me a new coffee.

"Thanks, Max. Sorry for the change." I dug into my purse for my wallet and handed him my debit card. "And can I get a couple of those chocolate scones?"

"Sure thing." His smile was back, and he looked relieved that I wasn't mad about the coffee. Max was one of those people who seemed to want to please at all costs. I wanted to tell him that was a dangerous attitude to have, but it wasn't my place, and I wasn't his mother. Besides, I had to figure out how to get through this coffee club meeting without falling asleep.

I paid my bill and grabbed my plate of scones and coffee. As I made my way over to Stephanie, I stifled a yawn.

I stopped short when I reached the table. I frowned at the table near the large window, bathed in morning sun. I couldn't make myself sit down.

"What's wrong, Rachel?" Stephanie frowned.

"Why don't we sit somewhere away from the window?" I felt another yawn coming on but managed to swallow it.

Stephanie frowned but stood.

I didn't wait for her to pick a seat, just quickly sat down at a small corner table with only two chairs. It was near the bathroom but dark.

Stephanie sat and looped her purse on the back of her chair. She took a sip of her coffee and settled her gaze on me, assessing.

"Is it just us today?" I took a sip of my own coffee, hoping the caffeine would keep my yawning at bay. But I wasn't sure anything could do that. I made a mental note to ask Khalan if there was anything I could do to stay awake and function in the daylight. I needed to figure out something before Saturday's soccer game. Otherwise, I would be screwed.

"Yes, the other girls are still on spring break. I think they went on a cruise," Stephanie said over the rim of her coffee cup. "I kind of figured that you and Miles would have taken the girls on vacation."

I felt my face heat.

Stephanie was very involved with the church and her family. If you needed something, she was the first one there to help and never expected anything in return. But I couldn't help but always feel like she was judging me. Like I wasn't giving enough to the church or attending the right Bible studies. It was probably just my paranoia.

"We thought about it, but Gabby didn't want to miss her soccer game. Plus, Miles is working so much, his schedule didn't allow for it. We'll probably make up for it with a couple of summer vacations." I stuffed a big bite of scone into my mouth. It melted like ash on my tongue. Apparently I had lost my taste for sweet treats.

"That good, huh?" Stephanie chuckled.

I smiled. "You should get one."

"Oh, no." She shook her head. She wrapped her hands around her coffee cup and gave me a serious look. "I'm doing a junk food fast. I've not had anything with sugar in over two weeks." She smiled at me with bright, shining eyes. "I can't tell you how wonderful I feel not to have all that junk in my system."

I put down the tasteless scone.

"Wow, that's great." I picked up my black coffee and took a drink.

"You know sugar is the most abused drug there is."

"Drug?" I arched my brow.

"They've done studies that show that sugar is as addictive as cocaine. Yet people shove it down their throats without a care. Our body is God's temple, and we shouldn't abuse it." She nodded thoughtfully and took another sip of her coffee.

"Really?"

"Oh, yes," she said. "Science has backed it up."

I was suddenly very tired. I tried to listen to Stephanie as she continued to spout volumes of information at me, but frankly, I didn't care.

I always prided myself on having wonderful manners and being polite. Being born in the South, hospitality was steeped into our blood at birth. It was a badge we carried with pride.

But now, I couldn't care less about science, sugar, and statistics.

I looked at Stephanie as she spoke. She was an attractive woman in her early thirties. She refused to do Botox like the rest of the housewives. Instead, she insisted that women were supposed to age gracefully and that altering one's looks went against the Bible.

Her stylish black hair was always perfectly done in waves around her face. Her clear, and brown eyes were warm and inviting, but I couldn't help but feel like she was looking deep down into my soul where I kept my most private secrets.

She waved her hands as she spoke, clearly excited about the topic of detoxing from sugar and all its benefits.

My gaze lit on her neck and, all of a sudden, my mouth watered for a different reason.

The vein in her throat jumped with each beat of her heart. The more excited she got, the faster her pulse thumped against the soft flesh.

"Rachel, are you okay? You look kind of dazed." Stephanie leaned forward.

I swallowed and sat back in my chair. "Yeah, I'm fine. Just tired."

"That's what I heard." She nodded her head and looked down at her coffee.

My gut twisted, and the breath left my lungs.

"Heard what?" I placed my hands on the table and looked at her.

"I ran into Veronica in the grocery store." Stephanie shrugged and took another sip of her coffee before looking at me.

"What did Veronica say?" I narrowed my eyes. I didn't care if it was polite or not, I needed to know what kind of garbage Veronica was spewing.

"That she saw you in the car and you were so sick that you had to bundle up in a blanket to keep warm. She said that you were not looking like yourself." Stephanie's gaze slid across my face and then back up to my eyes.

"I see you have lost some weight, and you're paler than usual."

"I had a stomach bug." I shrugged and relaxed back in my seat. "I lost some weight from that. As far as Veronica seeing me bundled up in a blanket, that was not a blanket, it was a fur that Miles gave me years ago. And it was right after the snowstorm and still cold outside."

Stephanie's brow creased, and she looked at me. "But Veronica made it sound like you were on your deathbed. Like something was really wrong. Like you had cancer or something."

"Are you freaking kidding me?" Anger flashed through my veins.

Her eyes grew wide at my outburst.

"Sorry, Stephanie. But Veronica is a ruthless gossip. She will take the truth and twist it. She talks about everyone. She's vicious. If I were you, I would stay away from her."

"But she always brings donuts for Sunday school. And she's the first one to volunteer for the church bake sale." She shook her head, disbelieving. I knew that Veronica had her fooled.

"I'm sure she has an ulterior motive. She's not a good person. Trust me."

"I don't know. She seems very genuine to me." Stephanie shook her head.

I knew this was an argument I wouldn't win.

"I don't think she was gossiping about you. I think she was concerned." Stephanie nodded as if she had made up her mind about Veronica's character.

"Well, will you do me a favor?"

"Of course." Her face brightened.

"Don't bring up my name to that woman."

"You know our conversations are always confidential. I hope you know that I would never speak ill of you, Rachel." Her brow creased, and she looked like she was worried.

"I know." I nodded. "You are one of the best people I know."

A smile graced her lips, and she nodded.

And Veronica was one of the worst.

CHAPTER 20

I went straight home after having coffee with Stephanie. I barely made it into the house before my cell phone rang.

"Hello?" I stumbled towards the guest bedroom, praying it wasn't an urgent call. All I wanted to do was go to sleep.

"Rachel."

I stopped at the sound of Nikki's voice. My stomach dropped, and I couldn't breathe. I stumbled and grabbed the wall for balance.

"Rachel, I really need to talk to you." Her voice was soft and pleading.

"I just wanted to tell you I'm sorry. I never meant to hurt you. You're my best friend…"

It dawned on me that I had never really known her at all.

"You bitch." The words slid out of my mouth like acid, hurting and burning and inflicting pain.

"You don't get to clear your conscience with one fucking phone call." I fisted my hands at my sides, wishing Nikki were in front of me so I could hit her until she begged for mercy.

"I never intended to hurt you. Neither did Miles."

"Miles is my husband. What part of fucking my husband was not a deliberate attack on me?" Red flashed before my eyes, coloring my surroundings.

"It started out as a friendship. He understood me on a level that Brad never has." She blew out a breath. "I'm sorry. I just want you to see my side of the situation."

I gripped the cell phone so hard in my hand that it squeaked under the pressure. "Let me tell you something, Nikki. If I ever fucking see you out in public, I will rain down all manner of hell on you. You don't go to the same events. You don't go to the same church. And you sure as fuck don't breathe the same air that I breathe."

"Rachel…"

"Let me make myself perfectly clear." Fueled by the rapid growth of my anger, my heart was beating so fast, I feared it would burst out of my chest. "I don't ever want to see you again. Under any circumstance."

"But we live in the same town. We're bound to run into each other," she protested.

"If you ever see me in the grocery store, your ass better run the fuck out. If you see me, that's your cue to run in the other direction. And, if I ever discover you calling, contacting, or texting my husband again, I will fucking kill you. Are we clear? Do you understand, bitch?"

The line went quiet, and I thought she'd hung up.

"I understand," she said quietly.

"Good, then there's no reason for you to ever contact me again. I was a good friend to you, a best friend to you for a lot of years. And you fucked my husband to repay me. You are now dead to me." I ended the call before she could say another word.

I had never hated someone as much as I hated Nikki. Betrayal was something I didn't get over quickly, and I knew that I had a long road with Miles. Friendships were sacred. Nikki had taken ours and abused my trust and faith as if they meant nothing.

My best friend was dead to me.

* * *

I SLEPT the rest of the day in the guest bedroom. I wanted to stay awake and be angry at Nikki for having the balls to call me, but I was too tired. By the time I pulled back the comforter, I fell face-first into the bed and slept like the dead.

I wouldn't have heard the alarm on my phone if I hadn't stuck it under my cheek.

I forced my eyes open and dug out the cell. I cracked one eye open and sighed. My alarm blared on.

I swung my legs over the side of the mattress and stood, looking longingly at the unmade bed, wishing I could just crawl back under the covers where it was dark, safe, and peaceful.

But I didn't have that luxury.

I hurried to the bathroom where I brushed my teeth and ran a brush through my hair. My shirt was wrinkled from sleeping in it, but I didn't care. I was just going to wait in the carpool line to pick up the girls. No one would see what I had on or what I looked like.

I shoved my feet into my fuzzy house shoes and grabbed my purse. I stuck my large sunglasses on my face and headed out the door.

I made it to the school just as the kids started pouring out of the building like ants. I crossed my arms and watched for my girls. I usually liked them to linger so I could have my daily call with Nikki. Now, I wondered if she'd *ever* been my friend or if she had just used me to get closer to Miles.

"Fuck." I slammed my hand on the steering wheel as the sting of betrayal clawed across my heart.

"Rachel, you okay?" Liz tapped on my window.

I felt the blood rise in my face, and I quickly pasted on a fake smile. I rolled down my window.

"Liz, hey girl. I didn't see you." I was careful to keep my arms and face out of the sunlight.

"Everything okay? Thought I saw you hit your steering wheel." Liz's brow creased as she attempted to study my expression behind my sunglasses.

"I saw a spider," I said quickly and gave a fake shiver for emphasis.

"Yuck. I would have freaked out." Liz shivered. "Just wanted to let you know that a certain someone just stopped by my car with some interesting information."

"Let me guess, Veronica." I gritted my teeth.

"Yep. And guess what she said to me." Liz narrowed her eyes and leaned in close.

"No idea. For someone with so much time on her hands, she really needs to get a job."

"She needs to stay the hell out of everyone's business. Do you know she had the audacity to tell me to my face that she'd heard through the grapevine that Michael was being unfaithful?" Liz tightened her grip on the door of my car, and her eyes flashed with anger.

"She what?" Holy shit. To tell Liz that her husband was cheating on her was bold, even for Veronica.

"Yep. She patted my hand and told me she was my friend and felt that I needed to know." Liz's fingers were turning white where she gripped my door. I could feel the anger pouring off her in waves.

"When I questioned why the hell she would say such a thing, she said she saw him at the coffee shop talking to a woman. She said it was way too early for him to be going to the office." Liz pressed her lips into a thin, white line. "I told her Michael was headed out of town for a business trip and stopped by the coffee shop on his way to the airport."

"That woman is pure evil." I patted Liz's hand and shook my head. "Look, I wouldn't believe a word out of her mouth."

"I don't, Rachel. But you know how she is. She'll go share her theory with everyone she knows. Look how she talks about her best friend. She tells everyone she meets that her best friend, Helen Warren is bipolar and cuts herself. I mean, Jesus, the woman doesn't have an ounce of loyalty in her body."

"That's why I stay away from her. I'm surprised you didn't tell her to fuck off." My hatred for Veronica was growing by the second.

"I told her that if she really *was* my friend, she never would have said anything in the first place," Liz growled. "Rachel, I know it's wrong to hate someone, but so help me, I hate that woman. I mean, if she were trapped in a fire, I'm not so sure I would save her."

"Yeah, you would. You have too good a heart." I shrugged. "Me, on the other hand, I just might let her burn."

Liz let out a laugh.

"Thanks for listening, Rachel." Her gaze darted up the car line. "How many people do you think she's told?"

The concern in her voice tugged at my heart.

Ignoring the heat of the sun on my flesh, I put my hand on Liz's and squeezed.

"Let me tell you something, it doesn't matter who she's told. People that know you and Michael know how much you love each other. And people that know her know she is nothing but a vicious gossip." I shoved my sunglasses to the top of my head and looked Liz square in the eyes. "Don't let her into your thoughts. She's the devil. Once she has a hold, she won't let go. She cares about no one but herself. That woman is literally crazy. We should feel sorry for her that she doesn't understand what a good friend is."

Liz smiled. "I appreciate you, Rachel. I really do. And you tell Nikki that she better watch out. I might be gunning for her position as your best friend." Liz smiled and walked back to her car.

My chest squeezed at the mention of my former best friend. I rolled up my window, still fuming about what Veronica had said. Veronica was a shark and could smell the scent of blood miles away. She liked to see other people miserable and didn't care who got hurt by her lies and gossip. She prided herself on knowing things and being superior to everyone else. At least in her mind.

I spotted Gabby and waved to her as she headed toward the car. Arianna came out of the building next, surrounded by her usual group of close friends. I was relieved to see that Veronica's daughter wasn't among them.

A brisk knock on my driver's side window had me tearing my attention away from my girls.

"Hi, Rachel." Veronica stood on the other side of the glass with a fake smile. I knew then that she was dying to tell me the rumor about Liz and Michael.

"Hi, Mommy." Gabby climbed in the front seat and slide her seatbelt on before Arianna could claim the spot.

"Hi, honey," I said cheerfully, even though I didn't tear my gaze away from Veronica. "Where's your sister at?"

"Almost to the car. You're not going to make me change seats with her, are you?"

"No, honey. You were here first."

"Rachel, roll down your window." Veronica made a cranking motion with her hand as she spoke to me through the glass.

"Ugh." Arianna climbed into the backseat and groaned. "Not that woman again," she said under her breath.

I looked in the rearview mirror and gave my daughter a grin. I knew exactly how she felt.

I looked back at Veronica and shook my head. "I can't talk, Veronica. I've got to go." I didn't wait for her to respond and I didn't wait for her to move out of my way. I just cut out of the line, barely missing her. I glanced in my rearview mirror at her horrified expression. She seemed outraged that someone could dismiss her so easily. I pulled onto the street and headed home.

Unease settled in my gut. Veronica wouldn't take kindly to my snub. She'd been so used to people putting up with her behavior for so long that what I'd done had likely come as a surprise.

I knew that I would probably be her next target. And I knew that I would be ready.

CHAPTER 21

That night after everyone had gone to bed, I stayed up. I tucked my feet under me on the couch and tried to focus on the book I was reading. It was from an author I dearly loved, but no matter how hard I tried to concentrate, I couldn't make my brain focus. Sighing, I tossed the paperback onto the coffee table and stood. I walked over to the front door and peered out into the night.

The neighborhood was quiet. I assumed all the occupants were asleep in their comfy beds with their normal lives.

All but me.

I no longer had a normal existence, and I sure as hell hadn't slept in my own bed. Everyone assumed I had a perfect life, but I knew in my heart that I was a fraud. I sighed and started to turn when something caught my eye.

A few houses down, a figure stepped out of a front door and walked down the driveway onto the street.

It was Cal.

I glanced at the time on my phone. After midnight.

"What the hell is he doing out this late?"

I kept my gaze on him as he headed down the street toward my house. I held my breath as he walked up my driveway.

"Shit." What if he remembered what I'd done to him? What if he was coming over here to tell me that he was reporting me to the police? What if he was coming over to hurt me?

I shivered and checked the lock on my door before hiding. I watched from the dark as Cal pressed his face against my door window, trying to see inside.

I stayed still and waited. Chills ran up my spine. I'd never thought that Cal was creepy before and I'd never been afraid of him…until now.

What the hell was he doing? He didn't ring the doorbell or knock on the door. He just stayed there, his face pressed to the glass, peering inside. His breath fogged up the pane, and I was pretty sure he wouldn't be able to see inside much longer.

"I'm going to kill Khalan for this. It's all his damn fault," I whispered to myself.

"Who are you talking to, Mom? And who is Khalan?" Gabby asked.

I jumped and stifled a scream. I spun around and grabbed her and ran to the kitchen. I didn't bother to turn on the light.

"Mom, what are we doing? Why was that man standing at the door? Is he a serial killer?" Her matter-of-fact tone caught me off guard.

"Serial killer? What do you know about serial killers?" I narrowed my eyes at her.

"You do realize I have contact with the outside world." She gave me a droll look.

I said nothing.

"Mrs. Sanders talked about it during history class. She had to go over some of the most brutal serial killers in the past thirty years." She shrugged.

"Oh my God, Gabby, that's not something school should be teaching. Especially not to kids your age."

"Then homeschool me." She gave me a bright smile.

She had me on that one.

"Gabby."

"Fine. Mrs. Sanders wasn't teaching us about serial killers. She was telling us she spent her weekend watching documentaries on serial killers."

I nodded.

"Who was that man at the door? And why was he just standing there?"

"I think it was one of the neighbors. And, to be honest, I'm not sure why he was standing there. It creeped me out."

"Hmmm." She nodded and then cocked her head. "Maybe he was sleepwalking."

"Yeah, he could be sleepwalking." I nodded. "They say not to wake up a sleepwalker. That it's too dangerous. I bet if we leave him alone, he'll go on home." I gave her a reassuring look, hoping she bought what I said.

She nodded.

"What are you doing up anyway?" I whispered.

"I was thirsty. I came in here to get something to drink. What are *you* doing up? You always go to bed right after we do." She cocked her head.

"Just couldn't sleep, I suppose." I shrugged. "Come on, and I'll get you some milk." I walked her over to the kitchen island. She scooted up onto the stool and watched as I skirted the counter and opened the refrigerator. I strained my ears, trying to listen for Cal and praying he wasn't going to ring the doorbell and wake the rest of the house.

I grabbed a glass out of the cupboard and filled it half full of ice-cold milk. I set it in front of Gabby. I leaned against the counter and crossed my arms. She took her time drinking her milk and when she was done, she had a white mustache above her lip.

She grinned and wiped it off with the back of her hand.

"Mom, I had a weird dream the other night." Her grin faded, and she stared at me with serious eyes.

"You did? What was it?" I grabbed her glass and rinsed it out before sticking it in the dishwasher.

"I dreamed that I woke up and walked over to my window. It was still night. I looked out into the backyard, and that's when I saw you. With a large bear."

"A bear?" I laughed.

"And then I realized it wasn't a bear but a large man who had a dirty-looking coat on." She narrowed her eyes.

"Really?" My heart thudded in my chest, and I tried to keep my voice light. She had seen me with Khalan.

"What else happened in your dream?" I grabbed the dish-towel and pretended to wipe a spot off my already immaculate counter.

"Well, you and the man walked through the backyard and out the gate into the woods." She shook her head. "I wanted to wait to see you come out."

"You did? Why did you want to wait?"

"Because I knew the man was going to take you away from me. I needed to see you come back."

My heart hurt for my girl. In a way, what she said was the truth.

"Oh, honey, you know I would never leave you." I went around the kitchen island and wrapped her up in my arms. Her hold tightened around my waist, and she buried her face into my neck.

"I know, Mommy." When she pulled back, she had a frown on her face. "I knew when that happened that it must be a dream and not real at all. I decided to go back to bed. And when I woke up the next morning, you were here. That's how I knew it was a nightmare."

I smiled and hugged her tight.

"It's late, and you've had your milk. You need to get back up in bed."

"I know." She slid off the stool and padded toward her bedroom. She stopped at the doorway and looked at me over her shoulder.

"What is it?" I asked.

"The weird part about that dream is that I saw Mr. Cal walking out of the woods. It's weird that I dreamed about him and now he's on the front porch looking in." Her frown deepened. "Do you think Mr. Cal is some kind of monster?"

My stomach clenched.

"No, honey. I'm sure Mr. Cal isn't a monster. You just had a bad dream. That's all. And you have an overactive imagination," I stated.

"Yeah. Maybe." She gave me a grin. "Goodnight, Mommy. Love you."

"Love you too, sweetie," I said as she made her way back to her room.

When her footsteps faded, and I was sure she was in bed, I eased back into the living room and glanced at the door.

Cal turned and began making his way back to his home. I peeked through the window, careful to keep my body out of view in case he turned around.

Shit. Gabby had seen me go into the woods with Khalan.

When Khalan got back from whatever business he was on, we were going to have a serious discussion. He could not come over here anymore.

He wasn't going to like my ultimatum, but he would have to get over it.

* * *

FOR THE NEXT TWO WEEKS, I barely functioned during the day. I canceled any appointments I had and was grateful when the soccer games and practices had been canceled due to rain. It was hard enough staying awake to drive and pick up my girls from school without falling asleep at the wheel. As soon as I got home from dropping them off, I went straight to bed.

I didn't hear a peep from Veronica in the carpool line. Maybe she had a new victim in her crosshairs and had forgotten about me.

Miles and I were a different story. While we functioned as a couple for the most part, I didn't go to bed with him once the kids were asleep. I was honest and told him I couldn't sleep. He gave me a look that screamed that he didn't believe me. I didn't care. I couldn't very well tell him that I was now a vampire and that I slept during the day and was wide awake at night. Or that I still couldn't bring myself to sleep in our bed. The new gray comforter had been delivered, but it didn't make a difference. That bed was forever ruined for me.

I ran a brush through my hair as I stared at my reflection in the bathroom mirror. I had a few minutes before going to pick up the girls. The door slammed shut, and I froze. I had made sure the door was locked while I was sleeping. Miles was at work. No one else should be in the house. I crept around to Miles' side of the bed and grabbed the gun out of the nightstand.

My hand shook as I gripped the steel in my hand. I'd never shot a gun in my life. Miles had always tried to get me to go shoot with him when we first got married. But I never did. I hated firearms. I figured if someone broke into my home I'd just call the cops and they could handle it. Now, I regretted not going to the range with him.

I crept out of the bedroom with both hands on the weapon like I'd seen them do in the movies. I turned the corner, gripping the gun in my trembling hands.

"Rachel?" Miles' voice made me jump. "What the hell are you doing with the gun?" He narrowed his eyes at me, and I lowered the gun.

"What the hell are you doing home? You're supposed to be in surgery today." I glared.

"I had to cancel it. The patient ate breakfast." He held out his hand, and I reluctantly gave him back his gun.

"I've never seen you pick up a gun before. You hate them." He shook his head.

"Well, I hate being murdered in my own house even more." I pressed a hand to my racing heart and sucked in some deep breaths.

"We need to talk." Miles gave me a look and then walked toward the bedroom.

I followed.

"Sorry about the gun." *And almost shooting you*, I almost said. "I really didn't expect you to get home early."

"It's not about the gun, Rachel." He opened the nightstand and slid the weapon in before closing the drawer. He turned and looked at me.

My guard went up, and my instincts were on high-alert.

"Sit." He waved over to the sitting area by the window. When we first moved into our home, I spent every morning in our sitting area, gazing out into the backyard and thinking how lucky I was to have such a wonderful husband and home. Once the girls came along, I didn't have time to sit and reflect on my life. Maybe if I had been more grateful, then Miles wouldn't have cheated.

I sat in my favorite blue chair. Miles sat in the matching one opposite of me.

"You've got to stop this, Rachel."

I jerked my head to him. "Excuse me? Stop what?"

"You've got to stop acting like someone died. All you do is sleep during the day and wake up in time to pick up the girls from school. Hell, you won't even sleep in the bed with me at night." He shoved his fingers through his hair.

His words had knocked the breath out of me. "You think this is about you?"

"You've got to stop punishing me for what happened. It's in the past. You're stuck in the past." He shook his head.

The tremble was back in my hands, but this time, it wasn't because of fear. I was furious.

"What's done is done. You just need to get over it."

It was a good thing he'd taken the gun from me. Because in that moment, all my hurt, anger, and rage boiled up. If I still had that gun, there was no doubt in my mind that I would have shot him right where his heart should be.

"What did you just say?" I measured my words, and I didn't take my gaze off his face while I awaited his answer.

"You need to get over this. It is irrational for you to continue to pout like this. It's only hurting our family."

I took a deep breath and blew it out.

"No. What hurt our family was you fucking around in my bed with my former best friend. What is stalling our recovery is that you never once apologized for what you did. You have never once shown any remorse or regret for cheating on me and our family. Yet, you expect me to suck it up and move the fuck on?"

He sighed like I didn't understand what the hell I was talking about.

It pissed me off even more.

189

"I've said I was sorry, what else do you want from me? Blood?" He gave me a droll look.

That's exactly what I wanted from him. I wanted him to bleed. Like I had done. Nothing ever inconvenienced Miles. I needed confirmation that he would never cheat on me again.

"There's a dinner party Saturday night at the country club. The Roarks are hosting. Everyone is bringing their wives."

The Roarks were the elite family in our town. Mitch Roark was the CEO of the hospital Miles worked for, and his wife Jilly was the queen bee of high society in the South. If you were fortunate enough to get an invite to one of their parties, you had better not miss it. Once you were out with the Roarks, you were out for good with everyone else in their circle.

"Are you asking me to go, or telling me, Miles?" I cocked my head.

"I'm asking, Rachel. But before you give me your answer, I need to know that you're going to really try."

"What do you mean, *really try?*" I narrowed my eyes.

"Don't go if you're just going to glare at me all night. Everyone will know something is off between us. I don't want to give them a reason to start snooping into our family business." He looked at me from his seated position. "I need to know that when we go, we look like we are a united front." Sadness flashed through his eyes. "I need to know that you'll still want to stay together."

I really hadn't tried with Miles. I'd been caught up in my own pain, and I wanted him to feel the same way. Maybe I could try a little harder. All I had to do was focus on my girls. Keeping the family together was the most important thing to me.

"Okay. I'll go." I uncrossed my arms and looked him right in the eyes. "And I'll try to make this work."

A slight smile crossed his lips. He sat forward in the chair and took my hand.

"I love you. You know that, right?" His finger made small circles on the back of my hand.

My heart tugged in my chest at the thought of the man I'd married. In that moment, hope surged in my chest. Maybe we would be all right, after all.

CHAPTER 22

I felt eyes on me.

"What?" I looked up from my plate where I had been busy pushing my food around.

"You never eat anything." Arianna sat her fork down and crossed her arms.

I glanced down at the plate of baked chicken, wild rice, and asparagus. I'd managed to cut everything up into bite-size pieces, but never ate any of it.

"I do eat." I frowned and speared a piece of chicken with my fork and popped it into my mouth.

I chewed and then stopped. "It tastes like cardboard." I frowned and spit it out into my napkin.

"Are you kidding?" Miles shook his head. "This is probably the best chicken you've ever cooked. He took another bite to prove his point.

"Really?" I looked from him to both girls.

"Dad's right. The chicken is great." Arianna cocked her head to the side. "You don't have an eating disorder, do you?"

My mouth fell open. "Absolutely not." I couldn't believe what I was hearing. I was supposed to be a role model for both my girls. And one of them was accusing me of being anorexic.

"I eat." I speared some asparagus on my fork and looked to make sure both girls were watching. "I eat all the time." I took a big bite of the vegetable. It, like the chicken, had very little taste. I forced myself to chew before swallowing it down.

"She's just saying that because you lost all that weight." Gabby shrugged. "I don't think you have an eating disorder, Mommy.

"Good. Because I don't." I stuck another bite of chicken into my mouth and chewed. I wasn't hungry. I was tired. More exhausted than I had been in a while. I'd had a lot of energy after Khalan made me drink Cal's blood. But that had been days ago. Now, I felt like I was fading.

Blood, just the thought of it made my mouth water.

I looked at Miles' neck. The large vein on the side seemed to throb as he chewed his food. I licked my lips, wondering what his blood would taste like on my tongue.

"Mom, can we pick up Shelby on our way to the game on Saturday?" Arianna had forgotten the topic about eating disorders and had moved on to something more interesting.

"Sure. What time is the game?"

"Game starts at ten, but Coach says be prepared to stay until after noon."

Shit. That would be a lot of time out in the sun without a break. Could I even make it that long? The way I was feeling right now, I wasn't sure I could make it through the night.

I'd caught a break with the last two soccer games getting rained out. I'd been keeping an eye on the forecast and knew there was no way this game would be canceled, as well. Unless something catastrophic happened.

It was a struggle just to sit through dinner and pretend like everything was okay. I knew if I were going to have to show up at the soccer game, then I needed to get more blood. One way or another.

* * *

THAT NIGHT after everyone had gone to bed, I stayed up. I couldn't sleep, even as tired as I was. I knew what I needed. I needed blood.

I stood at the front door, looking out through the glass panes. My gaze zeroed in on Cal's house. I only had a few days before the soccer game. I had to get blood in order to, hopefully, sustain me through the girls' game and being out in the sun for half the day.

I was getting concerned that Khalan had not contacted me. He was my Maker. He was supposed to help me in times like these. As much as the vampire irritated me, I wished he were back in town.

I couldn't wait around for him to show up with blood. I needed to do something.

As much as I hated to hurt Cal again, I knew I needed blood. I eased open the door and headed outside. The weather had warmed up, and the temps were now in the sixties at night. Everyone's grass was starting to turn a pretty shade of green. I stepped out onto the street and glanced down at my yoga pants and running shoes. If someone asked what I was doing out this late, I could just say I was going for a run. Hopefully, they'd believe me.

I wrapped my arms around myself as I made my way down the street toward Cal and Carla's house. I kept glancing at the homes I passed, making sure no one was outside or watching me through their window. So far, all the houses I passed were dark inside.

I took a deep breath and made my way up to Cal's front door. I bit my lip, and my hands trembled as I reached up to knock. I froze mid-way. I'd never wanted something as badly as I wanted blood. I needed to leave. I needed to go home. I turned and took two steps before the door creaked opened.

"Rachel?"

I froze at Carla's voice. Cal's wife.

My mind raced, and my heart thudded like a rabbit running in my chest. I turned and plastered a smile on my face.

"Hi, Carla," I said.

"Rachel, is everything okay?" Carla cocked her head and locked her assessing gaze on mine.

"Yes. Everything's great."

"It's almost midnight." She blinked.

"Oh, wow. I hadn't realized it was that late. I thought I saw something moving by your front door, so I came to check it out." I looked back at the street.

"What are you doing out so late?"

"I couldn't sleep and thought I would try to go for a run," I lied.

She frowned.

"I can't run during the day anymore because of Scooby." I shook my head. "The last time I went running, he tried to bite my leg."

"Oh my gosh. I had no idea." Her eyes widened. "I thought Scooby was such a nice little dog."

"I'm sure he is," I said quickly. "I think I must have startled him when I ran by the driveway. He didn't leave a mark on my leg or anything. Please don't say anything. I don't want to cause any trouble with the Macy's," I implored.

"I won't say a word." She gave me an understanding smile.

My gaze dipped to her neck. She was wearing flannel pajamas with the collar pulled up around her throat. I couldn't see her veins, but I could still smell her blood.

My mouth watered.

"There's something I've been meaning to ask you." She stepped closer and lowered her voice.

"What is it?" I didn't lift my gaze from her neck.

"It's about Cal."

"What about Cal?" I jerked my gaze to hers and tried to keep my voice calm.

Had she seen how bloody his shirt was? Worse, had she seen me following him?

"The other night, he came in late." She looked back over her shoulder and then back at me.

"Yeah? Maybe he was working in the garage," I said a little too quickly.

"See, that's the thing. He didn't come in from the garage." She stepped closer. "He came in from the back door."

"And?" I frowned.

"And Cal never uses the back door. He rarely goes out to the backyard at all unless he's cutting the grass." She cocked her head. "I was in the kitchen when he walked in. Nearly scared me to death."

"Maybe he heard something and was checking it out."

"I saw you, Rachel," she said quietly.

"What?" My mouth tasted like ash, and I felt the blood drain from my face.

"I saw you outside. You were watching him."

"I …" I couldn't think of anything to say.

"Rachel, I need to know the truth." Sadness stretched from her face into her eyes. "Are you and Cal having an affair?"

"What?" I screeched. I felt my expression stretch into a look of horror and insult. "Of course, not. I would never do that. Ever." I pressed my lips into a thin line and glared.

She smiled and relaxed. "I can tell by your reaction that you're telling the truth."

"Of course, I'm telling the truth," I shot back.

"I'm sorry, but I had to ask."

"You probably saw me because I saw him stumbling around outside. I was just watching to make sure he got home."

"Thank you." She gave me a sheepish look. "He must have gotten drunk over at the neighbors' house." She cut her eyes to the neighbors to the right. "You know Malcolm Jenner is a bad drunk when his wife, Alice, goes out of town. I don't like Cal hanging out with him. He turns into a different person." She rubbed her neck, and the collar of her shirt dipped, revealing her throat.

"Well, men will do what they do." My gaze landed on her neck. In the dim light of the moon, I could see her vein pulsating with every beat of her heart.

"Carla, where is Cal?" I cocked my head.

"Asleep," Carla said.

I tried to step inside, but it was like hitting an invisible wall. I tried again but was once again met by a barrier.

I bet I have to be invited in.

"Carla, invite me into your house," I said.

Her eyes glazed over, and she stared at me. "Rachel, please come inside my house," she said in a monotone voice. She was glamoured.

I took a step across the threshold and smiled when I successfully moved inside. I would have to remember this trick. I turned and looked at Carla. She didn't move away from the door but turned to look at me.

"Shut the door," I said.

She obeyed.

I stepped into the living room and glanced around. It was decorated in traditional décor with monkey paintings and bronze accessories. Cal and Carla were older than me by about fifteen years. They'd been married since forever and only had one child that had graduated college years ago.

They were empty-nesters with a large RV that they took out for six weeks in the summers to go out West.

Carla had never worked outside the home, and Cal was up for early retirement in a few years from his engineering job. They drove older-model cars and never tried to impress anyone. Miles had told me once that Cal was actually very wealthy and probably had close to three million in the bank. That didn't even count all the money he would likely get from retirement and his investments.

They were also heavily involved with the church, leading Sunday school and going on mission trips every couple of years.

I turned and looked back at Carla. My gaze landed on her neck.

"Come here," I said quietly.

Once again, she obeyed and walked over to me, stopping only a foot away.

"Sit down on the couch." I licked my lips and stared at her neck some more.

She walked over to the couch and sat down. I sat on the other side of her.

"Give me your neck."

She pulled her flannel pajama top away from her flesh and leaned her head to the side.

I could literally taste her blood in my mouth, and I hadn't even bitten her yet.

In the moment, alone in the dark living room of my neighbors, I didn't hesitate. My thirst for Carla's blood was too much. I grabbed her neck and ran my tongue across my teeth. They had changed. They were now razor-sharp, and I could taste my own blood where my tooth—fang—had cut my tongue. It only fueled my lust for Carla's blood.

I let out a soft growl as I buried my face in the crook of Carla's neck and bit down, hard. She moaned but didn't fight or try to get away. The coppery taste of her blood spilled onto my tongue, and I sucked hard, pulling more into my mouth. I groaned at the flavor as it reminded me of Valentine's Day chocolate.

I tightened my hold on her and sucked harder, pulling the sweet nectar into my mouth as it spurted out like a spring. I felt her pulse grow weaker, and the blood began to slow.

I was killing her.

I pulled away and stood. Carla slumped to the couch, eyes squeezed shut and mouth slightly open.

"Carla?" My own heartbeat echoed in my ears, and I prayed she would answer me.

Silence.

I leaned down and pressed my fingers to the wound on her neck to stop the gentle flow of blood.

"Carla, open your eyes," I said a little louder this time.

She struggled to hold her lids open. Shit. Maybe I had taken too much blood. I might have killed my neighbor.

"Shit. Shit. Shit." I wished Khalan were here. He'd know what to do.

"Rachel, what are you doing here?" Cal's sleepy voice made me jump about a foot in the air.

I spun around and looked at him.

He rubbed his eyes and looked at the couch. When he spotted Carla, his eyes widened.

"Oh my God. What's wrong with Carla? Why is she bleeding?"

I looked at Carla. Her bleeding had stopped, but there were blood stains on the collar of her white flannel pajamas.

"What did you do?" Cal's eyes hardened on me. He pushed past me and knelt beside his wife. He took her head between his hands and assessed her situation.

"Cal, I didn't do anything," I said quietly. It was a lie.

"Rachel, tell me what happened?" He glared up at me from his position on the floor.

I was scared shitless. Scared that Cal would call the cops. Scared that Carla would die. Scared that I was a monster. I had to protect my family. At all costs.

I placed my shaking hands on Cal and forced him to look up at me. He glared and tried to shake me off. I had to make him understand that I hadn't meant to harm Carla.

What do people need when they get blood taken from them at the blood bank? I took a deep breath and met his gaze.

"Cal, look at me," I commanded.

He looked at me, and I held his gaze. "You found Carla in the kitchen where she'd fallen and hit her neck on the counter. The blood on her pajamas is from where she cut herself. She's fine. She just needs some orange juice and cookies. She'll be fine. I was never here. Just you and Carla in the house. Just a small, little accident where she hit her neck. But there's no damage. You'll stay up with her for the rest of the night and make sure she's okay. You'll take care of her. If she loses consciousness, you'll call the ambulance. Understand?"

"I understand," Cal answered in a monotone voice. His expression was relaxed and neutral. Gone was any animosity towards me. He was back in his zombie state.

I sighed with relief. I'd managed to glamour him.

I looked down at Carla. Her eyes were barely open, yet she was still breathing.

"Carla, look at me."

She obeyed. Her weak gaze landed on me.

"Carla, you got up in the middle of the night. You slipped on something wet on the kitchen floor and hit your neck on the edge of the counter. You bled a little, but the bleeding has stopped. Cal is going to make you eat something to make you feel better. If you start to feel worse, tell him, and he'll call an ambulance or take you to the hospital. Understand?"

"Yes. I understand," Carla whispered.

"I was never here. Understand?" I stared hard at her.

"I understand," she said.

"Cal, take care of Carla," I demanded.

He took his gaze off me and wrapped his arms around his wife. "Let's go get something for you to eat. It will help build your strength," he said to her.

I took a few steps toward the door, blending in to the darkness as I watched Cal assist Carla to her feet. He carefully helped her into the kitchen and then sat her down in a chair. He grabbed a glass out of the cabinet and filled it with orange juice. He handed it to her while he gathered up some shortbread cookies and placed some on a platter for her.

Once I was satisfied that he would do what I'd said, I eased out the front door and moved out onto the street. I glanced at my house but decided that I wasn't ready to head home just yet. If I went home, I wouldn't go to bed. I glanced down the street in the other direction.

Instead, I decided to actually go for a run. I started out in a slow jog, my feet pounding the pavement with each step. With the new blood in my system, and my cravings satisfied, I couldn't go slowly. I needed to go fast. I ran faster until the wind was blowing in my hair. Tonight, I felt free as the crisp air hit my face and skipped across my bare arms.

I heard the growl of the beast before I spotted him. Scooby. The neighborhood nuisance.

I glanced over my shoulder and saw the dog coming up behind me. Usually, he was a fast runner and always caught up to me. But tonight, I was the faster of us. He generally growled and nipped at my leg when he got close enough. But this time, he made an odd sound.

I glanced over my shoulder and saw him barreling toward

me. Before I could turn around, my foot landed on an uneven spot on the asphalt. I lost my balance and landed on the ground with a thud.

"Shit," I muttered as pain raced across my shoulder where I had hit it. It would hurt like a bitch in the morning.

A loud howl had me scrabbling to my feet. I didn't want to be an easy target for Scooby. Before I could gather my legs under me, the dog launched himself in the air right at me. I opened my mouth to scream but was pushed to the ground and pinned.

I braced myself for the feel of his teeth sinking into my flesh.

He bent his head, and I squeezed my eyes shut.

A long, wet tongue licked me from my chin to my forehead. I cringed and opened my eyes. Scooby stared back at me with his tongue hanging out of his mouth in a goofy grin. Slobber dripped from the tip of his enormous tongue and soaked into my shirt.

"Gross." I lifted my arm and wiped the saliva away from my face with my elbow.

"Get off me," I muttered.

Scooby complied and jumped off my chest to sit by my side, his eyes trained on me the entire time. When I was confident that he wasn't going to bite me, I slowly stood.

"What's wrong with you? Why are you licking me? You've always tried to bite me." I narrowed my eyes and glanced down at my shirt. I lifted the material to my face and sniffed the drool spot and cringed. "Your breath could kill a horse." I narrowed my eyes.

He cocked his head and gave me a look like he understood what I was saying. He laid down and belly-crawled toward me. He stopped and laid his head on my running shoe.

"What? Is this your idea of an apology?" I asked.

He let out a pitiful whimper and tried to crawl closer.

"Get off my shoe, please," I said.

He obeyed and scrambled to his feet, his eyes still on me like he was waiting for another order. I walked to the side of the street and found a stick. I picked it up and waved it at him. He didn't budge.I threw it into the neighbor's yard. Scooby sat there, still looking at me.

"What are you waiting for? Go fetch it." I shook my head.

He took off at a run and grabbed the stick in his mouth. He trotted over to me and laid the stick at my feet. I shook my head and turned back to the dark street ahead. It was late, but I knew if I went home now, I wouldn't sleep. I needed to run, I needed the distraction to get out of my own head.

I launched back into a jog that quickly turned into a fast run. I heard a howl behind me. I glanced over my shoulder and saw Scooby running after me. And he wasn't alone.

He'd picked up the Walkers' shih-Tzu, a couple of white cats, and a Doberman. I stopped and turned to face the parade of animals. When I stopped, they did, as well. They all looked up at me with expectant faces. I couple of black birds and an owl flapped through the air and then landed near my feet.

"Okay. This is weird."

I took a step backward. The animals took a step towards me.

"What the hell is going on? Don't you all have homes to go to?" My gaze landed on the owl and birds. "Or nests to…sleep in?"

They all stared back at me with glazed looks in their animal eyes.

"Look, I don't know what's going on here…" My voice trailed off. And then the idea hit me that they were acting a lot like Cal and Carla.

Shit. Could I also glamour animals? I swallowed the lump in my throat and looked at the Doberman.

"You, Doberman." I looked in his direction. "Go get me..." I racked my brain, trying to think of something the dog could get me this late at night.

"Doberman, go get me a door wreath." I crossed my arms and looked at the dog. I figured if I were going to order the dog around, I needed to see exactly what he would do. Door wreaths in our neighborhood were a source of competition among the wives. And they changed just about every month. No wife wanted their door to look unadorned.

The Doberman took off at a trot toward the nearest house. He ran right up to the iron glass door and placed his paws on either side of the large wreath.

The house belonged to the Jeffreys. They were a young couple with two children. Dana was Jack's second wife, and rumor had it that Dana had broken up his first marriage. She'd gotten pregnant and forced Jack to leave his first wife and baby. Rumor also said that Dana was very jealous of Jack's first wife and that she discouraged any attempt by Jack to see his firstborn.

I never listened to rumors or gossip, so I tried not to judge on hearsay. But after my recent experience, I was beginning to see Dana in a different light. A light that made her perfect life and her friendly smile seem more like a façade.

The Doberman tugged at the wreath of lilies and yellow bows on the door until it came off the hook. Grasping it firmly in his jaws, he trotted the prize back to me and laid it at my feet.

I bent and picked it up. A couple of the Easter lilies had fallen off, and the yellow bow had teeth marks.

"Ah, thanks." I looked at the Doberman and then glanced at the owl.

"Owl, can you please go hang this back on the door?" I held out the wreath.

The owl picked up the wreath with its claws. The weight of the decoration caused the owl to dip a bit in the air.

"Scooby, go help her," I said.

I watched as Scooby ducked under the wreath until it was resting on his head. Together, Scooby and the owl went back to the Jeffreys' front door and placed the wreath back where it belonged. When they were done, they came back to me.

"Okay, so apparently, I can glamour animals." I shrugged. I spun on my heel and began to run. When I heard small footsteps behind me, I stopped and turned.

They were all still following me.

"Go home. All of you."

I shot them all one last glare over my shoulder before I continued on my run. I was too wired to try and figure this shit out. Right now, I needed to run hard and fast to release the emotions threatening to break through my skin like exploding fireworks into the night sky.

My feet barely touched the street as I ran as hard as I could. Even now, giving it all I had, I still wasn't out of breath. The fast pace was easy for me. I could run all night.

And that's what I did. I lost count of how many times I ran through the neighborhood. When I saw the little red truck that belonged to the newspaperman, I knew dawn was approaching, and it was time to go home.

I headed down the street toward my house. I had about an hour before I had to get the kids ready for school. A little less time before the sun would be up. Sadness hit me. The thought of the sun made me wish it could be night forever.

God, I was pathetic. I had a good life with two beautiful girls, and I was acting like a depressed woman. I slowed my run as I approached my house, my heart heavy. Maybe I would never walk in the light again.

$\mathcal{I}$t was only a few more days until the dinner party. I had to go and make this work for my girls. Even if it meant swallowing my pride. I glanced over at the clock on the microwave. It read six o'clock. Miles wasn't home yet. Today was his late day at the office.

I quickly put together a cilantro and lime shrimp salad with a strawberry salsa dressing for dinner. It was one of the girls' favorite things to eat. I was fortunate that my daughters usually liked real food instead of just junk food. As a mother, it was one less thing to worry about.

Another sharp pain zinged across my stomach. I'd had these stomach cramps all day. So bad they even had me unable to sleep. I was exhausted and in pain. I'd tried to tell myself that it was stress. But I knew better.

It had been more than three days since I'd had Carla's blood. I was running on empty and needed more.

"Is it ready?" Gabby hurried into the kitchen and sat at the kitchen island. We usually ate in the dining room, but on nights when Miles worked late, the girls and I gathered around the kitchen island and ate there.

"Yes." I turned, and the scent of Gabby's blood washed over me. My stomach pains increased. I doubled over in pain and gripped the island to keep from dropping to the floor.

"Mommy, you okay?" Gabby eased off the barstool.

"I'm fine." I forced my body to straighten despite the pain. I slapped a tight smile on my face. "Is your sister coming down for dinner?" My cramps eased, but the scent of my daughter's blood made my mouth water. I'd never craved something as much as I wanted her blood in that moment. My own blood ran cold, and I fisted my hands at my sides. How could I even entertain the idea of drinking my child's blood? The very thought terrified me.

"Arianna is on the phone with a friend." Gabby shrugged.

"Go ahead and fix a salad for you and your sister." My voice wavered. I needed to get out of that room before something bad happened. Something I didn't have any control over.

"Where are you going?" Gabby's brow creased with worry.

"I've got to check on something outside. Just start eating without me, okay?" I gave her my best reassuring smile and headed toward the living room and out the back door.

I'd made it five steps before the pain stretched across my stomach again. I doubled over. I would have screamed if the pain hadn't stolen my breath. After a few seconds of white-hot pain, the cramps lessened again. I managed to stand erect and forced my feet to move to the woods behind our house.

The sun was hanging low, and I'd forgotten to grab a hat or any kind of protection against it. My strength was ebbing, draining out of my body with each step. I needed blood, and I needed it now.

I planned to slip over to the neighbors' house through the backyard. I had no idea if they were even home or how many people were there. It was a shitty plan, but I needed blood, and I needed it now. If they did have a house full of people, maybe I could glamour them all so they wouldn't remember the heinous act I was about to commit.

The distinct sound of a twig snapping had me freezing in my tracks. My heart thudded in my chest, and I slowly turned to see who was following me. A raccoon popped its head out from behind a tree.

"You scared me, you know. You should be ashamed." If I'd had the energy, I would have narrowed my eyes at the furry creature.

He blinked and stepped out from behind the tree. He walked up to me and stood on his back legs with his paws at his chest.

"I don't have time for this." Pain launched itself across my stomach again, and I cried out. My knees buckled, and I fell. I tried to breathe through the pain as I knelt, but it was too difficult.

A tiny paw with sharp claws patted my back. Great. The raccoon probably had rabies and was preparing to chew my face off since I was in a vulnerable position. Just what I needed.

I lifted my head and looked the raccoon right in the eye.

"I need blood," I spat out between gasps of breath. The pain wasn't lessening. Instead, it was growing in intensity. The raccoon looked at me and cocked his head.

"Don't you understand? I need blood," I said again.

The raccoon cocked his head farther and leaned toward me.

"What are you...?"

He did understand. He was offering his neck...he was offering *his* blood.

"Look, little guy, I appreciate the offer, but I've never had...you know...that kind of blood before."

I caught the scent of the raccoon's blood. My mouth

watered, and my stomach cramps increased. I had no choice. If I didn't get blood, any blood, I would likely end up hurting someone.

"Fine. But don't let me take too much. I don't want to drain you." That was the last thing I needed on my conscience.

I reached out and cradled his furry little head. He didn't blink his bandit eyes and let me draw him closer. The scent of dirt and urine made me wrinkle my nose. It reminded me of Khalan. He'd probably been drinking raccoon blood too and didn't tell me. Hypocrite.

I closed my eyes and leaned down. Fur brushed across my lips as I opened my mouth. I found his neck and bit down. Blood spurted into my mouth. This blood was different, I wasn't expecting the bitter taste that lingered on my tongue. But I didn't care. Blood was blood, and I swallowed down the warm, coppery fluid like a woman dying of thirst.

A sharp claw swatted across my forearm. I pulled back and hissed in pain as I looked down at the scratch across my bare flesh.

"You little…" My words dropped. "I told you to stop me from draining you, didn't I? I guess you were doing what you were told."

The raccoon sat back on the ground and stared up at me. His black eyes seemed weak, and I reached out to stroke his fur. He leaned into my hand, and I smiled.

"You go on back to your home now and rest." I stood and looked down at him. "Thanks for the blood. Maybe, one day, I can pay you back." I smiled and turned back to the house.

I didn't hear any footsteps following me as I hurried home.

The sun was gone, and dusk was stretching across the backyard. Already, the blood had made me feel stronger, and I didn't have any more cramps. My cells seemed to pulse with energy, and I bounded up the back steps and entered the house. I walked into the kitchen to see Gabby and Arianna eating their salads. They looked up at me and frowned.

"What happened? Did you hurt yourself?" Arianna frowned, her gaze on my shirt.

I scowled and looked at my hands and shirt. There were a few drops of blood on my fingers from where I'd stroked the raccoon. I looked at the spots on the front of my shirt.

"I cut my finger moving a flower pot." I shrugged. "I must have wiped it on my shirt. I'll be right back."

I headed into the laundry room and tugged off the shirt. I squirted some stain remover on the blood spots, setting the garment in the sink to soak. I washed my hands and then headed into my bedroom to change clothes.

I slipped on a navy shirt and glanced at my reflection in the mirror to make sure there was no more blood. I grabbed my toothbrush and quickly brushed my teeth. For some reason, the raccoon's blood had lingered on my tongue with a not-so-fresh feeling. Satisfied with my clothes and my breath, I headed back into the kitchen.

My girls looked up when I walked in.

I turned and grabbed a plate out of the cabinet and served myself some shrimp salad.

"You look different," Arianna commented. She waved her fork in the air as her astute gaze studied my face.

"Oh, yeah? Better, I hope." I averted my eyes and eased onto a barstool next to Gabby.

"You look brighter. Like you just had Botox or something," Arianna said.

"Well, thanks. I think." I gave her a grin. "So, how was school?" I hoped to change the subject.

"Fine." Arianna dropped her eyes to her plate and began pushing her food around.

Gabby narrowed her eyes at her older sister and pursed her lips.

"What's going on, guys? Everything okay?"

"Tell her, Arianna," Gabby hissed.

"Shut up, Gabby." Arianna glared.

"Tell me what? Did something happen at school?" Worry gnawed at my stomach, and I dropped my fork onto my plate.

When Arianna didn't say another word, Gabby sighed and turned to me. "Elizabeth Grace is being mean to Arianna."

"Mean? Like how?" A spark of anger flared in my gut. I hated the thought of someone being mean to my Arianna, especially Veronica's daughter.

"She told Arianna that she was ugly and fat and that she'd never have a boyfriend." Gabby scowled.

"What?" I felt my mouth drop open, and I suddenly wanted to rip out Veronica's daughter's tongue and feed it to the birds. Maybe give it to that owl.

"Gabby." Arianna glared at her sister.

"Is that true? Did that vile creature say that to you?" My anger was palpable, and Arianna's eyes bulged.

"Did you just call her a vile creature?" Arianna asked.

"Yes." I stood up from my stool and walked over to my eldest. I took her precious cheeks between my palms.

"I've never heard you say anything bad about anyone. Even if they deserved it." Arianna looked at me with incredulity.

"Yeah. You always tell us to be nice. Ignore what others say. You always say that…" Gabby had cocked her head and was clearly trying to tick off the many lessons I'd instilled in them over the years.

"Listen to me, Arianna. You don't need someone like that

in your life. If they treat you like shi…err, crap, then you are better off without them."

"Who are you and what have you done with my mother?" Arianna raised her brow.

I released my hold and took a step back. Did they know?

"What do you mean?"

"I mean, you never rock the boat or make a scene. You always make excuses for other people's bad behavior." Arianna frowned and cocked her head.

"I do not." I crossed my arms over my chest. "I can't believe you girls think I wouldn't take up for you or protect you. You mean everything to me."

"Ugh, Mom." Arianna rolled her eyes and went back to her food.

"If someone were being mean to you and doing mean things to you, would you still be their friend? Would you still want to hang out with them?" Gabby asked.

"Of course, not. That's a toxic relationship," I stated.

Arianna said nothing but gave me a heavy side-eye over her salad. She set down her fork and looked at me. "Come on, Mom. Be real. You would just suck it up. Like you do with Elizabeth Grace's mom. You wouldn't say anything, because you know she'd start making trouble for you, like starting a rumor or talking to other people about you behind your back."

Damn. Arianna's words hit home. How in the hell was I going to tell my girls one thing while I did another? Was I staying in my marriage because I was sucking it up and not wanting to rock the boat? Was I a hypocrite?

"You're right, Arianna. I haven't always been true to myself." I swallowed and took my daughter's hand in mine. "Starting now, I'm going to stand up to Veronica. And I think you should stand up to her daughter. It may cost me, but I think it will be worth it in the end."

Arianna's expression twisted. I knew that look. She was torn over what to do.

"Listen, honey, are you and Elizabeth Grace good friends? Or do you tolerate her because you are afraid of her?" I asked.

Arianna looked away. I already had my answer.

"What if she makes up stuff and tells my friends?" Arianna looked up at me with glassy eyes.

"If they are your friends, then they will know the truth. Besides, I'm sure everyone at school knows your character and knows what kind of person Elizabeth Grace is." I cocked my head. "If they're your friends," I repeated, "they'll still be your friends in the end."

"Mommy's right," Gabby said. "Besides, if Elizabeth Grace gives you any trouble, I'll punch her in the nose." She balled up her little fist and scowled.

I bit my lip to keep from laughing. "No, you won't, Gabby. No violence. That's not the answer. If you want to battle, then do it with your words."

"Ugh. That's no fun." Gabby sighed and laid her head on the kitchen counter in a dramatic display.

That elicited a tiny smile from Arianna. "I actually like Gabby's idea better."

My eldest looked at me, and we all broke out into laughter.

When dinner was over, Miles came through the door in a rush. He stopped when he saw me rinsing off the dishes and putting them in the dishwasher.

"Sorry I'm late. The office ran later than I expected." He threw his briefcase on the island and scrubbed his hand down his face.

"I figured. We had shrimp salad for dinner. I saved you some in the refrigerator." I finished loading the dishwasher then added the soap and turned it on.

"Sounds great." He gave me a tired smile. "I think I'll have some wine with that. Would you like a glass?" He pulled a bottle out of the wine refrigerator and poked around in the drawer for the corkscrew. I always loved a glass of wine after dinner, but lately, I had lost my taste for it. Or maybe it was because I was still bitter about what Miles had done to me.

I had to make this work. I had to try for my daughters. I wasn't going to tear their family apart just because their father was a selfish asshole.

"I'd love a glass," I said as I finished wiping down the counters and setting everything to rights. I loved a clean house. It gave me a sense of peace and comfort.

Arianna said it was because I was a neat freak. Lately, I'd not felt like that. I'd felt like everything was spinning out of control. Maybe that's why cleaning always made me feel better. It was something I could control.

Miles pulled down two long-stemmed wine glasses. Those were my favorite, and I usually only used them on special occasions. Miles knew that. Maybe he was making an effort. Perhaps he really was sorry for what he had done. Maybe he now realized what he stood to lose. He poured me a liberal amount of the ruby-colored liquid into the glass and handed it to me.

I took it. "Thanks."

"Long day?" he asked. He used to ask me about my day all the time, but as the years passed, he stopped.

I smiled. "Yes." The small gesture touched me.

"How about you? Any interesting cases?" I took a sip of the cabernet and sighed as the wine slid down my throat.

"Same old, same old." He chuckled and took a drink.

I went to the fridge and pulled out the Tupperware container of shrimp salad I had put up for him. I grabbed a plate and poured the meal onto it. It was weird how I fell right back into making him dinner. As if nothing had happened between us. It gave me a sense of comfort and stability.

He eased onto the barstool and set his wine to the side.

I slid the plate in front of him and took another sip of my wine. I really didn't want it, but Miles was making an effort, so I decided that I could make an effort, as well. I walked around the kitchen counter and eased onto the seat next to him.

"This is really good, Rachel," he said before forking another bite into his mouth. He reached over and grabbed my hand.

I froze. It had been so long since he'd touched me in such a simple yet profound way. In our early years of marriage, we'd made an effort to touch each other often. Keeping our hands off each other had been hard. But as the years went by, and responsibilities and children and stresses crept in, we hadn't touched as much. I squeezed his hand. He looked at me over his glass of wine. An expression of something easy and familiar filled his gaze. It was a look I hadn't seen in a while.

For the first time in ages, I felt hope.

"Are you ready for the party Friday night?" he asked.

"I guess. I'm not sure what to wear. It's been a while since I went to one." Miles hadn't gone the last few years due to his work schedule. He'd always been on call when they held the party. But this year, he was off.

"You'll probably have to get a new dress since you've lost so much weight." He smiled.

"I'd forgotten about that." I'd been too busy trying to make sure I was staying out of the sun and getting a supply of blood to worry about clothing choices.

He gave me an odd look. I pulled my hand away from his and took another sip of wine.

"Who will be at the party?"

215

"The people I work with. All the doctors and their wives."

My stomach knotted. I usually liked going to parties where I got a chance to dress up. But just thinking about this party made my head hurt.

"I'll go shopping tomorrow and see what I can find to wear. Black tie, right?"

"Yep. My tux is ready to go."

"Good, then all I have to worry about is what I'm wearing," I said.

I got up from my seat. Miles grabbed my wrist. I looked down at him.

"Rachel, I miss you in our bed," he said softly.

His voice made my chest ache.

"I know." It was the only thing I could think to say.

He stood and slid his hands up my arms to my face. He gently rubbed his thumb against my cheek and stared down into my eyes. He looked at me the way he always looked at me, with love. I swallowed hard, a little afraid of the kiss that I knew was coming. He bent his head and placed his lips on mine. The embrace was gentle and caressing and warm. It was comforting.

I opened my mouth, and he deepened the kiss. I wrapped my arms around his neck and leaned toward him. He kissed me long and deep, and it felt like old times, like when we'd first gotten married. His hand slid down my back and rested on my hip. I tensed but didn't pull away.

When he broke the kiss, he looked into my eyes. "I love you, Rachel."

"I love you, too." I did. He was the father of my children. He was my husband. He'd hurt me deeply, but God help me, I still loved him.

"Mom, can you sign this? It's for a field trip next month." Gabby ran into the kitchen waving a piece of paper. "Hi, Daddy."

216

Miles let go of me and stepped back. "Hey, Pumpkin."

I signed the paper then watched the interaction between my husband and my child. Something warmed in my chest. Home. This was our home. And we were a family.

I wouldn't sleep that night. I couldn't. But I did get into the bed with Miles. We didn't have sex and after he'd fallen asleep, I slipped out of our room and made my way into the living room.

I opened my computer and pulled up the designer boutiques in town that specialized in black-tie events. I clicked through the dresses until I found one that caught my eye and, fortunately for me, it was in my size. Or what I hoped was my size. The plan was to get there when they opened and get the dress. Hopefully, it wouldn't need any alterations. But with my weight loss, there was no way to know for sure. I closed my laptop and tucked my feet under me on the couch. Everything would be okay. And this party was going to be the first step back into my old life.

CHAPTER 24

*A*fter I had dropped the girls off at school, I hurried over to Tara's Boutique to try and find a dress for the party. Tara's was the best shop in town for little black dresses and gowns.

It was an unusually bright day, and I made sure to wear long sleeves and skinny jeans, despite the temperature being in the seventies. I adjusted my oversized sunglasses and pulled my long hair forward to help shield my face from the sun.

I slid out of the car and hurried to the front door of the boutique. My short boots clacked on the sidewalk with every step.

I stepped inside, and the bell over the door rang. Mrs. Jenkins, the owner of Tara's, came out from behind a rack of gowns.

"Mrs. Jones." She smiled broadly. Her salt-and-pepper hair was pulled up into a tight bun, and she had an apron over her black dress that held all her alteration supplies. "I'm so glad to see you. It's been too long." She took my hand between hers and squeezed.

"Yes, it has, Mrs. Jenkins." I gave her a warm smile. "I'm hoping you still have a dress that I saw on your website. I'm kind of in a bind and need it today, and I don't have time to get it altered." I bit my lip.

"Of course. Anything for you, dear." She released my hand and ran her assessing gaze down my body. "My dear, you've lost some weight."

"I have."

"Well, you look wonderful. Although you have always been beautiful." She tapped her finger to the corner of her brown eyes. "And do I detect some Botox?"

I swallowed and forced a laugh. "Well, I've always had that done."

"Yes, but you look radiant. And there's not a line in sight. You must tell me who you are using."

"Oh, just getting Miles to shoot my face up." I shrugged. "I think it's having a cumulative effect and finally kicking in," I lied and looked around the store.

"I see. Well, let's go find that dress, shall we? What color was it?"

"It was a deep blue. Almost sapphire."

"Ah, yes. I know just the dress." Her smile widened. "Come with me."

I followed her over to the section of blue gowns. I loved coming to Tara's. The dresses were always displayed by color and not size. The entire room looked like a rainbow.

After a quick second or two, Mrs. Jenkins pulled out a stunning blue dress and held it up.

"Is this it, dear?" she asked.

I could feel my eyes lighting up. My chest expanded with excitement.

"Yes." I reached out. The silky material slid between my fingers like melted butter.

"Let's get you a dressing room." Mrs. Jenkins marched

over to one of the private cubicles and unlocked the door. "I'll go pick out some other dresses in case this one doesn't work."

"Oh, no need." My gaze was glued to the dress. "I won't be trying any others on. This is the dress for me."

"That confident, are you? I love it." She clasped her hands together and shut the door behind her, leaving me alone.

I quickly undressed and stood in the middle of the small room in nothing but my panties and bra. I looked at my reflection. Even under the harsh lights, I still looked good. Maybe being a vampire had its perks.

I slid the dress off the hanger and unzipped it. I pulled the material over my hips and up my body. I zipped the dress up as far as I could reach. I opened the door and stepped out.

"Oh my." Mrs. Jenkins' face lit up. "You look like a dream come to life." She pressed her hand to her lips and stared at me with unshed tears.

"Thank you." I gave her my back. "If you could just zip me up..."

"Of course."

Once zipped, I walked into the next room where there was a platform in the middle of the room and mirrors on all four walls.

I carefully stepped onto the platform and lifted my gaze to the mirror in front of me.

The dress clung to my curves, accentuating my now-slimmer figure. The color looked great against my skin and brought out the blue of my eyes.

Mrs. Jenkins was right. I looked like a dream.

"Well, well, well." Veronica's cackling voice scraped across me like sand blasting across my flesh.

My stomach dropped. Veronica was the last person I wanted to see, and the only one who could ruin my good mood.

"I'm surprised to see you here, Rachel," Veronica quipped.

I turned to the doorway and kept my expression neutral.

"Hello, Veronica." I decided to ignore her last comment. Veronica was just trying to bait me. She was probably still pissed that I had almost run her over.

"What are you doing here?" Veronica asked and took a few steps into the room. I glanced around the space for Mrs. Jenkins, only to see her horrified expression when she spotted Veronica. The older woman made a quick escape out of the room.

I didn't blame her. Veronica had that effect on people.

"Since I'm obviously trying on a dress, it would appear I'm shopping." I gave her my profile and continued to admire my reflection.

She was always making digs about my appearance, like how I looked tired. Not to be mean, but Veronica had no room to talk. She was overweight, average-looking, and had horrendous breath. I never understood why someone so unattractive could find fault with others.

"What are *you* doing here?" I asked. Usually, I tried to avoid conversation with Veronica. She was a snake and a gossip with nothing better to do than stick her nose into other people's private matters.

"I followed you here to talk." Veronica smirked.

A shiver ran down my spine. "You followed me here?" I knew she was crazy, but I had no idea she was batshit crazy.

"I can't seem to find you out during the day anymore." She curled her lips into a smirk. "You left me no choice but to follow you."

"Stalk much?" I arched my eyebrow.

Her smirk slid off her face. "I needed to talk to you. Besides, I don't think you want the whole town to find out about this."

My stomach turned. Shit. Veronica knew what I was.

Somehow, she knew that I was a vampire. Or a soon-to-be vampire. I wasn't sure how long the transition took. Khalan never said.

How the hell had she found out? I bet the old bat had some kind of satellite pointed at my house and had been filming me twenty-four-seven.

"What do you want, Veronica?" I narrowed my eyes.

"I wanted to let you know that Arianna has been sexting a boy at school. Elizabeth Grace saw her phone and can verify." She tossed her hair over her shoulder. "When there are problems at home, it always trickles down to the children."

My mouth dropped open.

Veronica's cruel lips curled up to a smirk again.

"I think you are mistaken," I said tightly. It was best to say nothing until I got home. I bit my lip to keep from lashing out at the old bat. I knew that she could make life unbearable for me. It was best to shut up and get out of the store as fast as possible.

"My daughter doesn't lie," she snarked.

Anger flared in my gut. I spun around on my heel. "Arianna doesn't lie either," I countered. I could feel the blood pulse in my veins, and my head began to swim. If I didn't get out of that store, I was going to hurt Veronica.

"Mrs. Jones, would you like me to hem that dress for you?" Mrs. Jenkins peeked out from behind a mannequin dressed in a white ball gown. Her eyes flickered over to Veronica, and I knew the older woman didn't want to be in her crosshairs, but she didn't want to lose a sale either.

I held my arms out to my sides and glanced down the front of the dress.

"Actually, I think it fits perfectly." I looked up at her and smiled. "It may drag on the floor a little, but I can hold it when I walk and wear taller heels." I smiled at her.

"Oh, good." She let out an audible sigh and headed to the

back of the store. "I can put it on your account if you wish," she called over her shoulder.

"Yes, thank you," I said. I didn't blame the seamstress for not hanging around. I turned back and faced Veronica.

"Rachel, don't worry. I haven't told anyone else about this. And I made Elizabeth Grace promise not to say anything either." She tilted her chin upward. "As long as Arianna and Elizabeth Grace remain friends, then I'm sure this will all just go away."

I was being fucked, and I didn't like it. I knew that Veronica was a vicious bitch, but to blackmail my child was beyond vile. Veronica was pure evil. But I wasn't about to question my child's character over some stupid rumor.

I didn't say anything as Veronica turned on her heel and walked her chubby ass out the front door. Anger blazed behind my eyes.

I slammed my fist into the wall. Pain raced through my hand, and I cradled it to my chest. Mrs. Jenkins came running around the corner and stopped when she saw me. Her gaze landed on the wall, and her eyes widened.

"What happened here?" she asked.

I followed her gaze to the wall and froze. I'd knocked a hole in it.

I started to blame it on Veronica, I really and truly did, but in the end, I told the truth.

"I'm so sorry, Mrs. Jenkins. I did that." I looked at the door and narrowed my gaze. "Veronica just makes me so mad."

"She scares me," Mrs. Jenkins admitted and looked at me. "I wish I were as brave as you, but I'm afraid to be in the same room with her." She shook her head. "She takes my words and twists them into lies. And if you go against her, she spreads vicious rumors that are more lie than truth."

"I know." And now I was Veronica's next victim. "Just put

the repairs on my bill, as well. And again, I'm so sorry." I headed into the dressing room and slipped out of the beautiful, blue dress. I took my time and hung up the gown before placing it back into its protective bag.

Only Veronica could ruin my perfect day.

CHAPTER 25

By the time I arrived home, I was exhausted. Between the run-in with Veronica and the exposure to the sun, I was physically and emotionally drained.

I hung up my new dress and slid into bed. I pulled the covers over my head and quickly fell asleep.

"What were you thinking?"

I was jolted awake by a dark, thunderous voice. I forced my leaden eyes open. Khalan stood over me with a glare on his face.

"What time is it?" I could tell it was still light outside from the sunlight trying to creep under and around the closed curtains. "What are you doing here? I thought you were away on business or vacation or something." I forced myself up into a seated position.

"How could you?" His eyes were dark and angry. I'd never seen him look so dangerous and deadly.

"What are you talking about?" I leaned back.

"You took animal blood."

I blinked. "I took some blood from a raccoon, yes. He offered it. Plus, it wasn't like I drained him."

He was deadly silent.

I narrowed my eyes at him. "Why didn't you tell me that I could drink animal blood? I could have been doing that all along."

"Because it's wrong. You are taking blood from an animal that hasn't done anything to you." His eyes blazed.

I flung the covers back and stood.

"Yet you would rather I take human blood? How wrong is that?"

"You are such a snob to place human life over that of an animal. An animal has never hurt you."

"And a human has never hurt you," I countered.

"That's where you are wrong. The most savage animals of all are humans." Pain slashed through his dark eyes.

I wrapped my arms around myself and studied the floor. Immense guilt hit me in the gut.

"You're asking me to choose between animal blood and human blood. It's not like I'm taking their life."

"But you are," he said softly.

I jerked my head up. "What? What do you mean?"

"Animal blood is weaker than human. It won't strengthen you like a human's, and you'll have to consume it more often. You can only take blood from an animal once. More than that, and they will die. Animals are incapable of replenishing their blood like humans."

"The raccoon? Is he okay?" I searched Khalan's face for an answer.

"He was trying to cross the road and wasn't moving fast enough. He was hit by a car and killed." His accusing eyes landed on me.

"Oh, God." My knees buckled, and I sat on the bed. "I'm so sorry."

"If you had come with me when I told you to, I would have taught you everything you needed to know about being a vampire. You would have known that you can't weaken an animal and leave them helpless. But, in your selfishness, you refused to leave your life of comfort, fancy clothes, and fake friendships. You're so afraid of what people think that you would rather pretend to be human instead of the monster you really are," he spat out.

His words hit their mark and made my chest ache.

"Khalan, I…"

He turned and headed out of the bedroom and into the hallway. "Why are you sleeping in that bed anyway?" He tossed the question over his shoulder as he stormed away.

"It's my bedroom."

"It's the bedroom where your cheating husband sleeps." He turned and smirked. "Let me guess. You decided to stay with him despite his inability to be faithful because you refuse to give up your lifestyle."

"I have two children who love their father…"

"You have two children that need someone to protect them from the evil that is so rampant in the world. You have children that need an example." He turned and shoved open the French doors leading into the backyard.

"Wait." I grabbed his shoulder. I caught a familiar scent. It was the raccoon who'd given me his blood. Khalan must have found him on the road.

If I hadn't felt like dirt before, I definitely felt like a worm now.

"What?" he growled.

"How are you able to walk around in the sun at this time of day?" I squinted and stepped out of the beam of sun shining on the hardwood floor. "I go out for a few hours, and I'm exhausted.

"I'm older than you. By a lot of years. And, I had a snack before coming over here."

"Anyone I know?" A chill ran down my back.

"You know what they say, an eye for an eye." He gave me a sinister grin and strode out into the backyard. I watched him as he disappeared into the woods before I shut and locked the door.

Shit. Had he hurt someone I knew? Someone I was close to?

I stumbled into the kitchen and sent a quick text to both of my girls to ask if they were okay. Arianna texted right back with a one-word confirmation. I swear that girl could spend paragraphs texting her friends, but all I ever got was one word. Sometimes, I only got a letter.

I strummed my fingers on the countertop, waiting. My cell dinged. It was Gabby's phone, but it was her teacher texting me a reply back. Apparently, she'd forgotten to turn her cell phone off in class, and the teacher had confiscated it. I was thankful that she took the time to send me a reply.

I was really tired. More exhausted than I'd been in my entire life. I looked at the time. Only ten a.m. I needed to sleep so I could pick the girls up after school. I stumbled back to the master bedroom and crawled into bed.

* * *

I BARELY MADE it to the carpool line before the bell rang. I'd overslept and didn't have time for a shower. I'd slipped on a long-sleeve shirt and jeans, along with my oversized sunglasses—now my go to eyewear—before heading out to get the girls.

I saw Veronica standing by Stephanie's car window, chatting her up. Veronica cast a glance at me and then strode over to her own car with a smirk. My stomach tightened. She hadn't tried to come over and gossip. But after our run-in this morning, I was sure she would try to chat me up.

Knowing her and her MO, it felt like she had all the dirt

on my family and me and was just waiting to use it against me any time she chose. Veronica was in charge, and she knew it.

Why couldn't Khalan have drained that bitch dry? Maybe I should give him the heads-up next time and slip her address into his pocket. I still felt plenty guilty about that poor little raccoon. The little guy had given me his blood, and now he was dead.

I finally saw Gabby skipping over to the car. She had something that looked like a sword made out of paper in her hand, and she was wielding it like a knight.

I searched the crowd of kids until my gaze landed on Arianna. She was walking with her head down like she was studying the ground. She held her books tightly to her chest as she hurried toward the car.

Elizabeth Grace was walking past her. She shoved Arianna, causing her to fall to the ground. Elizabeth Grace stood over Arianna with her hands on her hips. The girls around them stopped to help Arianna up, but Elizabeth Grace shook her head, forbidding them from helping. Arianna scrambled to pick up her books and loose papers that had slipped out of her hand. Elizabeth Grace put her foot on a piece of paper and wouldn't let Arianna pick it up.

"Say the magic words, Arianna," Elizabeth Grace taunted.

Apparently, my hearing had improved, too, because I could clearly hear the vile girl's taunts to my daughter from inside my car.

I wanted to hurt that little bitch. I'd never felt the intense anger I felt in that moment.

I snatched open my door and barreled out toward my daughter. Every step I took, I felt my strength leaving me as the sun bore down on me.

I didn't care.

"What's going on, Elizabeth Grace?" I narrowed my eyes at the girl and tried to keep my anger on a leash.

The other girls, friends of Arianna, all got wide-eyed when they saw me. I made sure to meet each of their gazes.

"Hi, Mrs. Jones." Elizabeth Grace gave me a bright, innocent smile. "You look lovely today," she cooed.

By this time, Arianna had gathered up her books and papers. She stood and gave me a horrified look.

"Let's go," Arianna mumbled.

"No, wait a minute. I want to talk to Elizabeth Grace." I didn't take my eyes off the girl.

All the other girls around her had slowly backed up and were drifting to their cars and getting on buses to head home. It was perfect. I wanted Elizabeth Grace alone.

I grimaced as more strength seemed to leave my body.

"Mom, let's go." Arianna tugged on my arm.

"I want to know what's going on, Elizabeth Grace. I saw you shove Arianna." I glared at the girl.

"You must be mistaken, Mrs. Jones. I would never shove Arianna. She's one of my closest friends." She gave me a syrupy smile.

It turned my stomach.

"Rachel." Veronica had slunk her way over to us and was standing beside her daughter. She wrapped her arm around her daughter's shoulder and lifted her chin.

"Is there a problem here?" Veronica asked.

"Yes. Elizabeth Grace shoved Arianna."

Veronica shook her head and laughed. "I'm sure it was an accident. Friends wouldn't do that to each other."

"You are exactly right. Friends wouldn't." I gritted my teeth.

Arianna let go of my sleeve and hurried to the car. I turned and frowned at her quick retreat.

"You know, Rachel. I would be very careful about

accusing someone. Who knows what retribution you might bring on yourself and Arianna." Veronica's voice was low.

In that moment, I saw who the woman truly was. She was a vile monster without a conscience or a heart. She was willing to hurt a young girl just because she could. And she enjoyed it. Veronica didn't give me a chance to retort. She turned and hurried to her car with her daughter.

I wanted to go after them. To hurt them both for what they'd done to my daughter. But the sun and my anger were draining me in a way I'd never experienced before. Instead, I headed to my car.

I got in and slammed the door, turning around instantly to look at Arianna in the backseat.

"I can't believe you did that!" Arianna screeched. Tears streamed down her cheeks, and she buried her face in her hands.

"Did what? I was just trying to help."

"You just made everything worse. I stood up to her today, and now she's never going to stop."

Gabby reached over and patted her sister on the shoulder. "If I had a real sword, I would chop her head right off her body for you, Arianna." She scowled.

"Gabby. No, you would not. That's murder." I gave her a stern look.

"So? It's not like anyone would miss her," Gabby retorted. She crossed her arms over her chest and pouted. "Maybe her mom. But she's just as nasty. So, I'd chop her head off, too." She made a slash with her paper sword.

"Arianna, let me help…"

"You can't help. You're just making things worse. I've gone from being talked about behind my back to her now threatening to tell everyone at school that my dad has a girlfriend."

"What?" My mouth had turned to ash. I barely got the question out of my mouth.

"She says her mom knows that Dad has a girlfriend. She said if I stop being her friend and doing what she says, then she's going to tell everyone," Arianna sobbed.

Gabby looked at me. "It's not true, is it, Mom?"

"Of course, not." I clenched my teeth so hard I thought they would crack.

"Arianna, I have to tell you something else," I said.

"Well, can we just please leave? I just want to go home." Arianna sobbed uncontrollably.

"Of course." I turned around and started the car. I sped out of the car line and merged onto the street. I needed to get home where it was safe for my babies and me.

How the hell had Veronica found out about Miles and Nikki? And why the fuck was that batshit crazy woman so interested in my life?

As soon as I pulled into the garage, Arianna ran into the house.

Gabby climbed out of the car and looked up at me. "Bet you're now wishing I had that sword."

I watched as she entered the house

"You have no idea."

CHAPTER 26

I waited for about fifteen minutes before heading into Arianna's room. I wanted to give her some space, and I needed to gather my thoughts as well as tighten my control over my anger. I knocked on her door.

"Go away," she said.

"You know I can't do that, sweetie." I opened the door and peered inside. She was lying on her side in the middle of her bed, curled up and clutching her pillow. Her cheeks were wet with tears. My heart broke into a million shards and scraped down my chest wall. I shut the door behind me and sat on her bed.

"You told me if I stood up to Elizabeth Grace then she would leave me alone. But all it did was get worse."

I swallowed. I would have to tread carefully with my next words.

"How long has this been going on?"

Arianna looked at me and shook her head.

"Honey, please talk to me." I brushed her long hair from her forehead.

"I don't know? Forever it seems."

"So why do the other girls go along with what Elizabeth Grace does?"

"Because they know what she'll do to them if they don't." Arianna sniffled and sat up in bed. She clutched the pillow under her chin and looked down. "Monica said something to her last month about her being a bit—er, I mean brat. Now, she's been shunned by the rest of our friend group and eats by herself at lunchtime."

"I bet Elizabeth Grace threatens you with horrible things," I said quietly.

"You have no idea," Arianna replied softly.

"Oh, I do."

She looked up at me.

"I ran into Veronica today at Tara's. I was there to get a gown for Daddy's party this weekend. She had the nerve to tell me that you were caught…" I bit my lip. I couldn't bear to say the words to my sweet, innocent little girl.

"Let me guess. She said that I was sexting a boy." Arianna's eyes widened.

"Yes. I told her it wasn't true." I looked at my eldest and held my breath. "I mean, you don't even have a boyfriend yet."

She looked away.

"Arianna. You don't have a boyfriend, do you?"

"Not a boyfriend. There is someone I like."

"What's his name?" My stomach twisted. I wasn't ready for this to be happening.

"Brice Carlson. He just moved here from North Carolina. But it's nothing like what Veronica said." She narrowed her eyes. "And it doesn't matter anyway. After what Elizabeth Grace did, I'm sure he wants nothing to do with me."

"What did she do?" I glossed over the fact that my daughter had just admitted liking a boy. I had bigger fish to fry.

"She took a picture of herself naked and sent it from my phone to him. I had no idea she'd taken my cell until I found it missing from my backpack. When I got it back, I tried to text him and tell him it wasn't me. That it was Elizabeth Grace. He didn't respond."

"So, Elizabeth Grace was sexting. I knew Veronica was a liar."

"Mom." Arianna cocked her head "She said Dad has a girl-friend. That he's cheating on you. She said she's going to make sure it gets all over town."

I swallowed hard.

"I told her it was a lie. And that my daddy would never do that. And if he did do that, then you would throw him out of the house." Arianna looked at me.

My heart broke for her.

"I want to change schools. Or do homeschool. I don't ever want to go to that school again. Please, Mom, can I be home-schooled?" she pleaded.

"How about this. Since tomorrow is Thursday, why don't you take a personal day? And if you still feel bad, then take Friday off, too. But Monday morning, no matter what happens, you go back to school. Okay?"

"A personal day? Really?" Hope shone in her eyes.

"Yeah." I shrugged. "We all need personal days."

"Thank you, Mom." She threw her arms around me and hugged me tightly.

When she pulled back, she looked at me, and sadness settled in her eyes.

"You know taking two days off won't solve anything. Elizabeth Grace will still be at school on Monday, and she'll be meaner than ever."

"Who knows? Maybe she'll have a change of heart." I caressed Arianna's cheek and then stood. "Everything will be okay, I promise."

She gave me a look like she didn't really believe me.

"Mom, you didn't say anything about what she said about Dad. In fact, you're being pretty calm about it." She cocked her head.

"I guess I'm just too damn old to care what other people say about me."

"Since when?" She snorted.

I let the comment slide as the reality of her words settled in. I needed to make some decisions and make them quickly. For some odd reason, I wished Khalan was there to talk to. But he was probably still mad at me.

I was in this whole thing alone now. I had to figure out a solution.

* * *

FRIDAY NIGHT ARRIVED. It was the night of the black-tie party. I had been dreading what to do about blood, but I'd finally come up with a solution. Wednesday night, after the family had gone to bed, I'd driven to the twenty-four-hour grocery store. I needed blood, and I was scared to take it from someone I knew. I had a sinking feeling that Veronica was spying on me to gather some dirt. And I still felt too guilty to take it from an animal again.

I decided to get a bunch of steaks at the grocery and then suck the blood out of them. I got home and settled down at the kitchen island. I went through thirteen steaks, and the blood was watered down and cold. After I'd managed to drain them all, I got brain freeze.

In the end, it did its job and gave me the energy I needed. I went back the next night, and when the butcher gave me a weird look, I told him I had family coming in and needed steaks for the weekend.

He shrugged and wrapped up my order.

It was now Friday, and I had already snuck out to the garage to finish off the steaks while Miles got ready. Afterwards, I headed into the bathroom to get ready for the party.

"Rachel, are you ready?" Miles called out from the bedroom.

"Almost. I need you to zip me up." I slipped my feet into my favorite silver Louboutin's and put on my diamond earrings. The plunging neckline of the gown drew attention to my diamond necklace and my cleavage.

I took a final look at my hair and studied my makeup. I looked amazing.

I stepped into the bedroom and gave Miles my back before he could see the front of the dress. He zipped me up, and I slowly turned around.

"Wow. Rachel, you look beautiful." His gaze drifted down my body as he took in my dress.

"Thank you. You look very handsome yourself." I smiled and patted the front of his tux.

"Thanks." He grinned.

"I'm ready to go," I said.

"Great." He took my hand in his and looked into my eyes. "Let's make this night one to remember. Just you and me."

His eyes seemed to plead with me, and something twanged in my stomach. But I shoved aside the weird feeling and nodded.

"Just you and me," I said quietly.

"This event is very important to me, and I don't want you to…rock the boat."

"Miles, I…"

"Look, I know you were hurt. And I said I'm sorry. I want to move on. Just forget the rest."

"I know." I licked my lips. I felt guilty that I wasn't as good at forgetting and moving on as Miles apparently was.

He smiled and stuck out his elbow. "Shall we?"

I hooked my elbow in his and walked out of the house and into the garage. He went around the passenger's side of his Tesla and opened the door for me.

I smiled and eased into the car. I placed my black satin clutch in my lap and watched him, dressed in his tuxedo, skirt around to his door.

Usually, whenever Miles wore a tuxedo, it made my heart beat a bit faster. I rested my palm over my heart, feeling the slow thud of my heartbeat.

"Everything okay?" Miles slammed the door behind him and started the car.

"Yes," I lied. I kept my gaze on Miles as he backed out of the garage and lowered the door.

I fought a shiver that sprinted up my spine. I needed to relax. I'd made sure to drink the blood out of ten steaks. I knew that it should get me through the night without a hitch. Now, all I had to do was relax and enjoy the party.

Tonight would be an official starting point. A new journey for our marriage.

CHAPTER 27

*T*he valet greeted us at the country club. A young man assisted me out of the car while Miles handed over the keys and a tip.

We stepped inside and headed toward the large banquet room.

"Miles! Rachel! Oh my, aren't you two the Ken and Barbie of the night!" Jilly Roark gave Miles a quick kiss on the cheek and then brought me in for a hug. She was wearing a white evening gown that flared out at the waist and ended in a train that pooled at the back.

"Thank you for inviting us, Jilly." I smiled and looked at her gown. "You look stunning."

"Why, thank you, dear," Jilly leaned in and whispered loudly. "But I have to say, you are going to be the one that everyone has their eye on tonight."

My smile slid off my face, and my lungs clenched. "Me? Why?"

"Rachel, don't be so modest. You look like you've lost weight and had a little something done." She motioned to her own face and winked. "Not that I'm jealous. You must give me the name of the plastic surgeon you are using."

Miles let out a laugh. "She's not had any work done, Jilly."

Jilly gave him a droll look. "Whatever you say, Miles." She laughed. "Why don't you two head on over to the bar. They are serving a special cocktail tonight, just for my party."

"Sounds yummy." I smiled and gave her hand a squeeze.

We made our way over to the bar. I looked around the room and saw many couples I knew and a few that I didn't.

"What can I get you, sir?" the young bartender asked. His gaze wandered over to me and dipped to my cleavage.

"I'll have a gin and tonic and …" Miles turned to me.

"I'll have the specialty cocktail."

The bartender smiled. "Very good." He turned and quickly made the gin and tonic. He slid the drink over to Miles and then began work on mine.

When he was done, he sat a pretty blue cocktail in front of me.

"What's it called?" I picked up the fluted drink and took a sip. "It's good."

"It's called Tiffany Blue."

"Perfect name. Jilly does like her diamonds." I said and turned back to Miles. He turned his gaze back to me and smiled.

"Oh, I see Gina and Liz." I waved to my friends in the corner. They smiled and waved me over.

"Go on. I'll go find the men." Miles chuckled.

I made my way over to my friends.

"Oh my God, Rachel, that dress is to die for," Gina said, wide-eyed.

"Thank you. I love your dress, too. That red looks great on you." I smiled and admired her short, red dress with crystals adorning the sweetheart neckline. Gina had a great, slim figure and she pulled the look off flawlessly.

"Did you get that dress at Tara's?" Liz frowned.

"I did."

"I don't remember seeing it. I know I went through every dress in that store, trying to find something that would fit me." Liz cocked her head.

"Well, I love your dress. Looks like you found the perfect gown for you." Liz had on a floor-length, white dress covered in sequins.

"Thank you." Liz leaned closer. "We're friends, right?"

I frowned. "Of course, we are. Why would you say that?"

"Because I want to know the truth, Rachel."

I could feel the heat rising in my face. Did she hear something? Did she suspect something?

"Who is doing your Botox?" Liz crossed her arms over her chest. "You have to tell me. I feel like my forehead is gaining more lines with each passing day." She waved her hand at me. "And you, well, you seem to keep getting younger by the day."

I relaxed and let out a laugh. "I actually haven't had anything done. Just vitamins. Oh, and I did have that stomach bug. That's how I lost the weight."

"I wish I could catch a stomach bug," Gina snarked.

"No, you don't," I murmured and looked around the room. Everyone looked beautiful in their black-tie attire and cocktail dresses. A sense of comfort settled over me. I'd seen this a dozen times, but I was grateful to be here now. I was among friends, and in some ways, family.

My gaze landed on Miles, and he lifted his glass to me and winked. I smiled. And just like that, we were falling back into our old lives.

"So, has anyone picked a date for our annual girls' trip?" I asked and looked at Gina.

She blinked and looked away. "No one has said anything to me about it. I'm assuming it's going to be in July again.

Aruba, maybe? I really don't know." She took a sip of her cocktail and waved at someone across the room.

"Well, I am looking forward to it. It seems like ages since I've gotten together with my best girlfriends." Liz smiled and gave me a side hug.

"You just saw us at book club." Gina snorted.

"Yeah, but a girls' getaway is totally different."

"Yeah, it's extended wine club." Gina laughed. "I have to detox every time I get back from a girls' getaway."

The time seemed to pass quickly. I was having a good time and enjoying myself. Miles had even pulled me onto the dance floor for a slow dance. I felt like a princess in his arms. When the dance was over, he walked me back over to my friends, and he went back to talk to the men standing around the bar.

"Oh, no. Look who it is," Gina groaned.

I followed her gaze to the doorway just as a voice screeched out across the room.

"I'm here. The party can begin." Veronica threw her hands up into the air, trying to look like Marilyn Monroe but failing miserably.

"Damn. Just when I was having a fabulous time." I looked back at Liz. "Why in the hell did Jilly invite Veronica?"

Liz shrugged. "The same reason everyone tolerates her I suppose. She probably has some dirt on Jilly so she was invited."

"Yeah, you do not want Veronica as an enemy." Gina turned her back to the door.

"Well, I think it's bullshit. We are a bunch of grown-ass women, but we still let Veronica bully us."

"The day you stand up to her, we will be right behind you," Liz said and averted her gaze from the woman.

"May I have everyone's attention, please?" Jilly clanged her spoon against the side of her champagne flute.

The entire room quieted down, and the band stopped playing. Everyone turned their attention to the hostess at the front of the room.

"I have a surprise for everyone! Tonight, we are having a contest for the best-dressed." Jilly's eyes sparkled with delight. "Now, what you didn't know, is as you entered the party tonight, our judges were picking out their favorite couples of the evening."

A round of applause went up in the room.

Liz elbowed me. "You and Miles are sure to be one of the couples."

"Oh, I don't know. Everyone looks so lovely," I lied. I knew from looking at everyone that, for the first time in years, I looked amazing. And Miles looked handsome as always in his tuxedo. I had a really good feeling that we were going to win. Another step in our start at a second chance.

"If the following couples will please come to the front of the room." Jilly unfolded a piece of paper. "Harvey and Gina Randle."

"See! I knew you'd be one of the couples!" I gave Gina a hug before Harvey came over and escorted her to the front of the room. Everyone clapped.

"James and Sondra McNeil," Jilly announced.

I clapped along with the crowd and pretended that I wasn't holding my breath.

"And our last couple is…Miles and Rachel Jones."

Miles ambled over to me all smiles and held out his arm. I took it and let him escort me to the front of the room.

"Now, I need everyone's help," Jilly announced. "In order to pick our winner, I need crowd participation. Here we go!"

"How many think Harvey and Gina are the best-dressed couple tonight?" Jilly waved her hand in the couple's direction, and a chorus of whistles and shouts rang out across the large room.

"What about our next couple? James and Shonda McNeil?" Jilly once again waved her hand at the couple like Vanna White showing off a prize. People applauded and cheered.

"And last but certainly not least is Miles and Rachel Jones!" she shouted.

The whole room lit up with shouts and whistles and loud applause. I didn't need Jilly to announce who had won the contest.

Jilly walked over to a table where a small trophy sat. She picked it up, and her gaze met mine.

"Congratulations to Miles and Rachel Jones! Our best-dressed couple of the night." She held out the trophy, and Miles grinned and took it. He pulled me close and gave me a full kiss on the lips. Just like when we were younger. He pulled back and looked across the room. Something flickered behind his eyes, and his smile dropped. I followed his gaze but didn't see anything out of the ordinary.

"Everything okay?" I asked.

"Yes." He kissed the back of my hand. "I'm going to put this thing out in the car." He held up the trophy.

"Okay. I'm going to the powder room." We parted ways. I took the last sip of my cocktail and placed the empty glass back on the counter of the bar.

I headed down the hallway and into the bathroom. It was empty, and I walked around the corner to the private seating area. I sat at the stool and pulled my lipstick out of my purse. I swiped my lips with a fresh wash of color and pressed my lips together. I leaned forward and studied my makeup in the mirror.

"Did you hear? They found that missing college student. Dead." A female entered the bathroom. From where I was sitting, they couldn't see me.

"I know! And I still can't believe who the murderer is," the other female said.

"I know. Cal Dennery."

I froze, unable to move. My neighbor, Cal? That was impossible. He wouldn't hurt a fly.

"I know. They found her in a plastic bin in his storage unit."

"Which is stupid on his part." The other female snorted. "He had to know that the body would start to decompose and smell."

"He claims he doesn't remember anything about the night of the snowstorm, which is the night she disappeared. But it's hard to ignore the evidence. Her body was found in his storage unit, and he has the only key. His poor wife didn't even know he rented the thing."

A shiver ran down my spine. Cal couldn't remember the night of the snowstorm. Because of me. I'd glamoured him into forgetting about it so he wouldn't tell anyone that he'd seen me naked.

"I can't believe Miles brought his wife." The voice made me freeze.

"Especially after he brought his mistress to the doctors' conference in Biloxi," another woman chimed in.

All the blood in my face dropped to my stomach. The doctors' conference had been six months ago. I'd asked Miles about going, but he'd said that nobody was bringing their wives. Like a fool, I'd believed him.

Nausea rolled through my stomach, and my vision blurred. My heart sped up, and I forced myself to stand. I walked around the corner and faced the two women. They both gasped when they saw me. I recognized them from the hospital. They both worked there. But I didn't know their names.

"Who did Miles bring to the conference?" I looked at the petite brunette in a short, black dress.

"Mrs. Jones, I-I really don't want to get involved," she stuttered, and her face went red.

"You got involved when you opened your mouth." I glared at her. I fisted my hands at my sides to keep from strangling her.

"We really should go…" The other woman with the red hair tried to step to the door.

"Stop." I turned my gaze on her.

She stopped in her tracks. She got that dazed look in her eyes.

"What's your name?" I asked.

"Jessie," she said, her eyes glazed, and her tone monotonous.

"And you?" I turned to the brunette. "What's your name?"

"Elle," she said, her eyes glazing over, as well.

A tremor of tiny cramps raced inside my stomach. I ignored the pain and looked at both women.

"How do you know my husband?"

"We work in surgery," they both answered in unison.

"How did you know about the doctors' conference in Biloxi?" I cocked my head and tried to keep my anger and pain under control.

"I am engaged to a doctor, and he brought me," Jessie said.

"I didn't go. Jessie told me," Elle stated.

So, Jessie was there.

I turned and looked at the brunette. "How do you know Miles had a mistress?"

"Because they stayed in the same room, and they went out together with the rest of the doctors and their wives."

My stomach turned, and I wanted to vomit all over my Louboutin's.

"What did the wives say about this?"

"They didn't say anything. The doctors told the wives to stay out of it and not say a word," Jessie said.

Humiliation and betrayal struck me in the heart. The other wives had known, and no one had bothered to tell me. The whole fucking hospital knew.

"What's the mistress's name?" I demanded.

"Nikki Stollings," Jessie and Elle spoke at the same time.

My vision blurred, and my knees buckled. Miles had lied. He'd said he'd only slept with her the one time. Not only had he been fucking around with Nikki for over a year but he also hadn't tried to hide it. He'd paraded her out in front of his colleagues.

I shoved past the two women and stumbled out into the hallway. Hurt, humiliation, and anger raced through every nerve ending in my body. I could feel retribution pumping through my veins and filling the shattered pieces of my heart.

He'd lied.

I had been a fucking fool to believe him. I pressed my hand to my heart and tried to ease the pain that was slowly filling my chest. My mind raced. Miles had been having an affair for over a year. And I had been too stupid to realize it. I barely heard the drone of voices as I stepped into the party. I scanned the space and found Miles talking to Jilly at the front of the room.

My stomach cramped and, suddenly, I was reminded of how much I needed blood. Miles met my gaze and smiled.

It's a funny thing. When you are married as long as I have been, you can almost read a person's mind with just a look. Miles must have read my mind because in the matter of three short seconds, his smiled faded, his eyes widened, and the blood drained from his face.

I stopped in front of Jilly and Miles.

"Why don't we go get some fresh air," Miles suggested, taking me by the arm.

I snatched my arm out of his hold and glared at him.

"Don't touch me," I spat out.

Jilly's eyes widened, but she didn't step away. Instead, she studied us both, intently.

"Rachel, let's talk about this…"

"Here. We are going to talk about this here." I glared at him. I wished I had superpowers so I could fry his ass with just one look.

"Rachel, this is a public place…"

"You've been having an affair for over a year." I noticed the music had stopped, and the room grew silent. But I was beyond caring.

"Rachel," he warned and looked around at everyone.

"You took your mistress to the doctors' conference. The conference that we always go to. You said that spouses weren't invited this last time. You lied to me." Something wet rolled down my cheek. Despite my tears, my voice was calm and lethal.

"You think you can fuck around on me and stay married? You are dead wrong." I turned on my heel and straightened my back. I could feel everyone's eyes on me, but I kept looking straight ahead at the exit sign.

"I hope that pussy was worth losing everything." I threw the last comment over my shoulder. Whispers rose up around the room and, suddenly, I felt like I was in enemy territory. They knew. They all fucking knew and didn't tell me. They were not my friends. None of them.

I made my way out the door just as pain lanced across my stomach. It almost matched the agony in my heart.

Almost.

CHAPTER 28

I stepped outside and looked at the valet. "I need my car."

"Yes, ma'am." He ran over to the parking lot to retrieve Miles' Tesla.

"Rachel, how could you do that?" Miles stepped through the door.

"Don't come near me."

I turned and saw two very large swans come barreling toward the front door. The country club kept the two swans, affectionately named Prissy and Hissy, on their pond on the golf course. They were gentle birds and usually came up to golfers to get a snack of crackers or bread.

Not tonight. They both hissed and tried to bite Miles every time he attempted to take a step towards me.

"Get away!" he yelled at the birds.

Everyone from the party was now gathered at the door to watch the scene unfold.

The valet pulled up in front of me. He hopped out of the car and handed me the keys. I pulled Miles' wallet out of my clutch and grabbed all the cash out. I handed it to the valet and threw the wallet in the shrubs.

"Before you give that to Mr. Jones, I expect you to take all the cash as a tip."

His eyes got wide. "Why, thank you, Mrs. Jones."

"That's my wallet," Miles yelled as he tried to kick one of the swans. Hissy stretched out his long neck and bit Miles right on the crotch. My bastard husband let out a yell and doubled over in pain.

"Good bird," I said and walked to the driver's side. I slid in and shut the door. I peeled out of the country club's lot and headed home.

By the time I pulled into my garage, my cell phone had thirty missed calls. The majority of them were from Miles, but some were from Gina and Liz. I knew by tomorrow, everyone in our little town of Charming, Mississippi would have found out about tonight, and I would have triple the amount of calls.

I forced myself to get out of the car and go inside. I made it three feet into the house before the pain in my stomach increased. I doubled over and cried out.

I went to my knees and tried to catch my breath that the pain had stolen away. Thank God, the girls were spending the night at Maggie's house. I wasn't sure what I would have done if they had seen me like this. The pain itself was too much to bear. It felt like it might kill me; there was no way I could survive this. I had to get out. I had to try to find some blood.

I kicked off my heels and crawled to the living room, my dress scratching my legs as I went. I was probably ruining the gown, but I didn't care. I made it to the living room couch before another hard wave of pain hit me. I collapsed on my side and clutched my stomach, screaming and praying that the pain would go away. White stars danced in front of my eyes, and I knew I would likely pass out from the pain.

"You're an idiot," Khalan's voice drifted over in the dark.

I didn't even jump when I heard his voice. His breaking and entering seemed normal to me now.

"I know. I trusted him. I believed his lies. You're right. I'm an idiot and a fool." Khalan was somewhere in the house, but I couldn't see him. He was probably waiting for me to die so he could be rid of me. It seemed to be a running theme with the men in my life.

He snorted. "That's not what I'm talking about. You glamoured two humans and the two swans tonight. Not to mention the guilt you feel about that dead body that your neighbor was glamoured into forgetting about. Doing that kind of thing when you haven't had blood in days is deadly to your system."

I swallowed. My mouth was like sand. "But I drank…"

"Sucking the cold blood from steaks is not a meal replacement." I could tell by the tone in his voice that he was upset with me.

"You're right. Make it stop. Just make the pain stop." Tears streamed down my face, and my voice cracked. I was as vulnerable now as the night he'd met me. This time, he really might kill me.

A heavy sigh followed by footsteps echoed in the silent house. His face came into focus as he knelt beside me.

He slid his arm under my head and held me in a seated position.

"I don't care who the donor is. Just give me something and make the pain stop."

He cocked his head. "You'll start listening to me?"

I couldn't lie. "Probably not."

A ghost of a smile crossed his full lips. His eyes locked on mine.

3

"Please."

His smiled disappeared. "Don't beg. You and I don't ever beg. Not anymore."

I nodded. He held up his arm, and I realized he wasn't wearing his long, ratty-looking coat. He bent his head to his arm and tugged up the sleeve of his black, long sleeve T-shirt. After he'd worked the sleeve up to his forearm, he looked at me and opened his mouth. Two sharp fangs extended down. He held his wrist to his mouth and bit down. When he pulled his mouth away, I saw two punctured wounds on his wrist and two resulting streams of blood. He held his wrist to my mouth. "Drink."

The scent of his blood shot through my body. I latched on to his wrist and sucked hard. The sweet taste of roses and chocolate spilled onto my tongue, and I moaned. I closed my eyes and held his arm against my mouth as I feasted. His blood was better than anything I had ever tasted. The more I drank, the more I craved. His blood had chased away my pain with the first mouthful. Strengthened me as I sat up and continued to drink.

A craving of a different kind warmed my stomach. This one sexual. My body hummed and warmed and, suddenly, all I could think about was sex. Khalan rested his back against the sofa while I drank his blood. I looked up at him from under my lashes to find him watching me. A deep groan erupted from the back of his throat. The sound made my nipples hard. I swiped my tongue across the puncture wounds on his wrists as I sucked.

He cupped my face with his free hand and looked at me, hard.

"If you don't want to do something that you will likely regret in the morning, then you should really stop licking me like that." His gaze hardened—not with hatred but with lust.

An image of us naked and having sex on the living room

floor filled my head. It shocked me. I hardly knew him, and I was married. It was completely unlike me to entertain such an idea. I forced myself to pull his wrist away from my mouth.

I sat back on my heels. "The pain in my stomach is gone. But the pain in my heart is still there," I said.

"I know."

"Do you know that Miles has been fucking around on me for a year?" I dropped my gaze to my lap. The moonlight splattered its light on my blue gown.

"Do you know that I was stupid enough to believe him when he told me he'd only cheated on me one time?"

"You will survive this. You are stronger than you believe." His deep voice echoed and washed over me.

I looked up at him. I placed my hands on either side of his hips and leaned closer until I was only inches away from his face. I finally realized that he didn't stink anymore. He actually smelled like green grass and pine cones. He frowned when I leaned closer but didn't move.

"Why do men cheat?"

"Not all men cheat." He cocked his head. "But that's not the question you really wanted to ask. What you really want to know is why your husband cheated on you."

He was right. I couldn't speak, but I could feel the tears welling up in my eyes again. I simply nodded.

"Your husband cheated on you, not because of who you are, but because of who *he* is. He's a selfish asshole who puts his own needs above anything else. He thinks he can do anything he wants because he deserves it." He grinned. "And, deep down inside, you know that's who he is. Who he always was. You know it here,"—he placed his finger on my temple and then moved it to my chest—"and here."

My heart sped up. Khalan was right.

I took a deep breath and let Khalan help me to my feet.

"I looked like a fool tonight." I spread my hands and looked down at my gown. "I walked in there like the perfect wife, blissfully unaware of the extent of my husband's deceit."

"And you walked out the perfect vampire," Khalan countered. "Stronger than ever and ready to handle your shit." I looked up at him and blinked.

Khalan had saved me.

"Khalan, thank you for giving me your blood."

He didn't say anything but strolled to the dining room and pulled his coat off the back of my dining room chair.

"You actually don't smell like skunk anymore." Had he cleaned up for me?

"I don't normally do. I was caring for a liter of baby skunks who were orphaned when I met you that night."

"You did?"

"Yes. They would have died if left out alone. They are not used to sudden snow storms."

"Neither am I." For such a big guy he sure did have a heart for animals.

He walked over to the back door that led out to the backyard. I joined him and grabbed the doorknob.

"Wait. I have something for you." I ran to the closet and pulled out the freshly dry cleaned quilt. I handed it to him wrapped in plastic. "I had it cleaned."

He took the quilt and his expression softened for a fraction of a second.

I reached for the door., Khalan cradled my cheek. My heart jumped in my chest, and longing swept over me.

He leaned in, and my lips parted. "In case someone didn't tell you, you look beautiful tonight."

I swallowed and held my breath, waiting for him to kiss me.

"Oh, and you really should wipe your mouth after you

eat." His words were teasing, but the look in his eyes was anything but.

He bent his head and gently licked the outer corner of my mouth. When he was done, my body was on fire.

I stepped back and reached for the door. "When will I see you again?"

"Soon." He let his eyes drift over my body before he stepped out into the night.

I stood at the door, watching him disappear into the night.

My pain was great but something inside me was ready to fight and not lie down.

Maybe I would never figure men out. Perhaps I was meant to be alone. Maybe the world had other plans for me. All I knew was that in order to survive, I would have to accept what I was and be the best mother, friend, and vampire I could be.

After tonight, there was no turning back.

The End...for now

ALSO BY JODI VAUGHN

The Vampire Housewife Series
LIPSTICK AND LIES AND DEADLY GOODBYES (Book 1)
MERLOT AND DIVORCE AND DEADLY REMORSE (Book 2)
BULLETS AND BOOZE AND DEAD SUEDE SHOES (Book 3)

BY THE LIGHT OF THE MOON (Book 1)
BENEATH A BLOOD LUST MOON (Book 2)
DESIRES OF A FULL MOON (Book 3)
DARKSIDE OF THE MOON (Book 4)
SHADOWS OF A WOLF MOON (Book 5)
SECRETS OF A WOLF MOON (Book 6)
FALL OF A BLOOD MOON (Book 7)
RISE OF AN ALPHA MOON Volume 1 (Book 8)
RISE OF AN ALPHA MOON Volume 2 (Book 9)
RISE OF AN ALPHA MOON Volume 3 (Book 10)

VEILED (RISE OF THE FAE) Series
VEILED SECRETS (Book 1)
VEILED ENCHANTMENT (Book 2)

Contemporary Romance Series